# Adva

"Clever, mind-bending and darkly original, *The Truth About Thea* had me hooked from page one. In Thea Brown, Amy Impellizzeri has created a brilliant, complicated, flawed character that gets under your skin and stays there. Fast-paced and twisty, the unexpected ending will have you gasping for air."

**Heather Gudenkauf**
*New York Times* bestselling author of *The Weight of Silence* and *Not A Sound*

"A man's past and a woman's present collide in Amy Impellizzeri's latest up-all-night thriller where nothing is as it seems. Filled with questionable characters, long-held secrets, and a tangled web of twists and turns, *The Truth About Thea* will keep readers guessing who—if anyone—can be trusted. A perfectly compelling read all the way to the shocking end."

**Kimberly Belle**
Bestselling author of *The Marriage Lie*

"Filled with tension and twists you don't see coming. Amy Impellizzeri's dialogue crackles and her characters scheme and surprise. I was invested and thrilled—what a ride!"

**Kelly Simmons**
International selling author of *One More Day* and *The Fifth of July*

"Just try to keep your eye on the ball in this intricate thriller. No matter how carefully you follow all the moving pieces, nothing will prepare you for where Impellizzeri takes you. A twisting story where everyone has secrets, and no one can be trusted."

**Rena Olsen**
Author, *The Girl Before*

# The
# Truth
# About
# Thea

# The Truth About Thea

## AMY IMPELLIZZERI

Award-winning author of LEMONGRASS HOPE and SECRETS OF WORRY DOLLS

*Wyatt-MacKenzie Publishing*
DEADWOOD, OREGON

ALSO BY AMY IMPELLIZZERI

*Lemongrass Hope* (Wyatt-MacKenzie, 2014)
*Lawyer Interrupted* (American Bar Association, 2015)
*Secrets of Worry Dolls* (Wyatt-MacKenzie, 2016)

*The Truth About Thea*
Amy Impellizzeri

ISBN: 978-1-942545-80-4
Library of Congress Control Number: 2017949851

The characters and events in this book are fictitious. Any similarity to real
persons, living or dead, is coincidental and not intended by the author.

Wyatt-MacKenzie Publishing
DEADWOOD, OREGON

Wyatt-MacKenzie Publishing, Inc.
www.WyattMacKenzie.com
Contact us: info@wyattmackenzie.com

# Dedication

*To my sisters, Megan and Katie, for all of the reasons ...*

Three things cannot be long hidden:

the sun, the moon, and the truth ...

Buddha

# Prologue

*October 17, 2017*

If Audrey Brown had survived, she probably would have wanted to take back a great many life decisions including, but not limited to, her insistence on driving that enormous gas-guzzling imported SUV, with more blind spots than the mice in her stepdaughter's fairytales, all the way down to an empty gas tank every time, until she had to literally roll into a gas station—any nearby gas station at all—to refill it.

Audrey might have—had she survived—spent an agonizing and yet healing (maybe?) time drawing a line backward connecting moments that were overlooked with those that were life-threatening and life-changing even at the time they occurred, let alone with the benefit of hindsight.

If Audrey had survived *and* if she had been privy to all the true facts (who knows if she would have?), then she would surely have traced and retraced all the lines in her journey back to one definitive day.

And it would not have been the day she helped John die, or even the day of his funeral. Not the day her daughter was born, or the day that Audrey stood up to John's drug dealer before she left town. No—not any of those days. But rather another day altogether when Audrey clicked "accept" on a seemingly innocuous Facebook request. That might have been the day Audrey would have wanted to take back above all others, if she had the chance.

But she was never given the chance.

Instead, Audrey found herself standing at a gas pump with a missing purse. She was distracted from all that she had recently found out, and was just about to fill up her SUV with gas when she realized she couldn't pay. She remembered leaving her purse inside the gas station's market where she had popped in a few minutes earlier for a ginger ale and a pack of mints to settle her nervous stomach.

And when Audrey with her distracted brain sprinted away from the useless pump and across the parking lot, in an effort to retrieve her purse in a panic, she did not see that red pickup truck come out of nowhere. She only felt a powerful sucking of air from her lungs like the worst case of getting the wind knocked out of her that she had ever had.

In that last moment, all of her prior thoughts dissolved like sugar in a science beaker. They rearranged their molecular structure, regrouping and simplifying themselves into one solitary and all-consuming final thought. The few witnesses on the scene would later tell the police they heard her say one thing only before she lost consciousness. A word. A name, maybe.

*Thea.*

# Part I

# Chapter 1

The television news channel was droning loudly in the background with promises of bad weather, a terrible electrical fire of unknown causes, and the rampant breakout of shoplifting in the local area "just ahead."

Will tried to ignore all the bad news, as he stared down and thought only:

*The desk is too small.*

Not: *I can't believe it.*

Or even: *What are the odds, truly?*

His current stack of client files housed in yellowed folders with errant pen marks and worn sides sat on the desk where he had spread the intake files of hundreds of recovering addict inpatients every day for the last nearly 20 years. He reviewed new files almost weekly, just before he tried (and sometimes succeeded, he would like to hope), changing lives or helping transform a few lives at least. But now, as he listened to the news, he stared down at the dark, dated, and scratched up veneer of the desk that he had worked at for two decades—and he questioned the size of his desk for the very first time.

Her arrest was the lead story on the night's news. What little they knew about her was indeed little. But still. Will couldn't ignore what they knew. What they said.

*Her name was Thea.*

She was still a local story, not quite gaining enough momentum to become a more prominent national story—what with all the chaos in the world, he wondered if this bit of chaos in his small rural Pennsylvania town might just go unheeded by anyone else *but* him.

For the first time, Will wished his airless office had a window to open. He had always liked the protection and the anonymity a windowless office provided. He felt safe here. Since he had come here as a patient 23 years ago, stumbling and sick, already in forced withdrawal, he had viewed this place as a haven.

He had come in as a patient, and stayed on as one of the most revered counselors at Juniper Lane Rehab Facility, a small treatment center in a quiet farming county about an hour outside of Philadelphia. Will kept to himself. He devoted much of his free time to his patients. He didn't bother himself with outside news or politics. But tonight's lead story didn't feel like "outside news."

Will listened without looking at the screen, and kept his focus downward on his desk.

*And it's too small*, he lamented as he gathered up the latest files of addicts whose stories he had become such a big part of, whose healing and struggles gave meaning to his own.

As Will stood up from his desk, he felt the familiar temptation—the recognizable physical pull—as he shut off the television and heard in its place the loud call of his demons who wanted to drown the news story with remedies they were still offering him twenty plus years into his sobriety.

*Some nights were easier to ignore the demons. This was not going to be one of those nights.*

"I don't remember much about the night I died."

Will had left the windowless office and his too-small desk, and headed for an AA meeting 45 minutes away from the rehab facility where he worked, the movie theatre he frequented, the gym he sometimes used, and the grocery store where he shopped.

Even with the promise of confidentiality and the empathy he found at these meetings, Will generally sought out meetings far enough away from the people who usually crossed his paths. Grocery clerks, coffee baristas, and gas station attendants. Ordinary people who could become patients, even. Those who would need privacy. These meetings were not the settings in which he'd want to meet up with or see any of the ordinary people in his life.

And that night, Will was feeling particularly vulnerable. He needed to tell his story out loud. He needed to share his secret with strangers and get it off his chest every so often. He had found that if he didn't purge himself of his secret regularly, it clung to his chest, squeezing the sides tight in its grip until he was certain he was dying—or at least having a heart attack. Over the years, Will had refused various anxiety medicines and anti-depressants, fearing their effects on a recovering drug addict much more strongly than he feared the way his heart closed shut during his panic attacks.

This was his medicine. Sharing his past in a musty church basement in a town where no one knew Will Cann? It helped.

Will waited patiently through tales of drug deals gone awry, eating out of dumpsters, and pornographic acts done in the name of need. He chewed on his nails, missing the days when smoking was allowed indoors. In those days, the time it took for the others to speak and for him to listen seemed much shorter than it did these days. After each addict spoke, Will shook his head kindly, meaning it when he replied softly to each one, in a whisper no one could hear but him, "You can be forgiven. What you've done is nothing compared to what I've done."

When Will's turn came, he thought about getting up and leaving, but his hand went up involuntarily to his chest, and he thought about how much pain he'd be in and how useless he'd be when the new week's patients arrived, if he didn't get this all off his chest right now.

"I don't remember much about the night I died," he blurted out when his turn came, before he collected himself and remembered protocol.

"I'm sorry. Let me start over. I'm Will."

"Hi Will," the chorus replied, without shock or alarm at Will's prologue.

"Well, I didn't really die, of course. I was coming down from a heavy night, and was already thinking about how to get high again. That much I remember. I had no remorse. I remember that, too. Watching my wife, Audrey, stand there in our bedroom with her very pregnant belly jutting out from her hospital scrubs didn't make me regret the night or make any sad promises. In fact, I was angry at her for asking me stupid questions like 'What are you doing?' 'How can you keep doing this to us again and again?'

"I remember thinking that she looked ugly. That her pregnancy and anger and judgment was making her ugly. And this—of all the things I should regret—is the one I actually *do.*"

Will heard—or rather saw—from his peripheral vision some head nods and sympathetic gestures from his comrades which propelled his story forward at the critical point.

"It wasn't remorse or sadness or suicidal ideation that prompted what came next, even though those feelings were no strangers to me. It wasn't any of that. It was an epiphany. It was a realization that there was no other logical end *but* death.

"Audrey said, 'I can't do this anymore.'

"And I replied, 'You're not doing it. I am.' I was bored with the conversation, frankly.

"She reminded me then—as if I needed reminding, 'We're having a baby. You're never going to grow up. You're never going to stop this.'

"And I said simply, "No I'm not. Who told you I was stopping?"

"And it was then that she gave me my out. She said, 'There's a John Doe at the hospital, I'm on my way in to deal with him right now. He came in last night. A dead heroin addict that was picked up next to a dumpster at the shopping center in town. I have to go in and supervise his autopsy now. I actually had a fleeting thought that it could be you until you stumbled in here just now.'

"I didn't understand what she was saying at first, so I just said, 'So what? That's your job, isn't it? Congratulations.'

"And Audrey looked cold. And cold was even worse than ugly. I might have shivered. Of course, I might also be adding that part in for dramatic effect."

There were a few chuckles in the room. It occurred to Will that they might think he was making up this entire story. He even hoped so. That would make it easier to finish.

"Audrey said, 'He *could* have been you.'

"So I said, 'But he's not. Too bad.' I laughed—at what I couldn't tell you—and reached over to the table next to our bed to grab a half empty pack of cigarettes, and I lit one. 'But lucky you,' I told her. 'My dealer, Bruce, says he will indeed make me a John Doe before year's end. So you just might get your wish after all. I owe him a lot of money, Audrey. A *lot* of money.' I described my relationship with my homicidal heroin dealer with a tone that may have even sounded like pride.

"Audrey asked me, 'Does it bother you to think of me raising this baby with you dead in the ground? Not knowing her? Her not knowing you? Not knowing any of the reasons I first fell in love with you? Before you did this to yourself?'

"And I told her the truth: 'No.'

"Audrey leaned forward and looked at me closely. *What was she staring at*, I wondered? She was making me feel self-conscious and I scratched at my cheeks wondering if there was something there that I could scratch away. Audrey was a forensic pathologist in case you haven't figured that out by now. It was her job to tear things apart to figure out what went wrong with them. And back then, I resented being one of her specimens.

"While she was staring at me, I said, 'Audrey. I can't be anyone else. I'm trapped in this life. Even if I got clean. Even if one of my little field trips to rehab actually worked? Bruce and his boys would find me. They'd kill me. Let's face it, eventually, I will be going out … in style.'" I swirled my hands theatrically in the air as I said it. I wanted to make Audrey laugh. But she didn't. I wish she had, though. I wish my last memory of Audrey was of her laughing. I really do.

"She asked me then: 'Do you think if you could erase this life, maybe then you could start over?'" Audrey was standing next to the bed still looking at me with her you-are-my-specimen look, so I started scratching my cheeks some more before I replied, 'Maybe.'

"I turned away from her and her belly and blew out a smoke ring so she couldn't see that my eyes were welling up.

"'It's too late in this lifetime. I need another one.' I laughed as I said it but then I started to sob with the realization that the words were giving me. *Nothing could change until I was dead. I had no choice anymore.*

"Audrey reached over to the nightstand and I lunged at her thinking she was going to take my cigarettes. I grabbed at the squashed pack and tobacco flakes sprinkled the nightstand, as Audrey grabbed instead for my wallet. She fished my license out of it and held it up like a trophy, and said, 'There.'

"'You're dead,' she announced.

"And I said, 'Great. How did you make that happen?'

"She was all business then with her instructions. 'I'm giving the John Doe an identity. Yours. Don't be here when I get back. You have nothing to do with me or this baby and we'll have nothing to do with you. I'll make this work on my end, but only if you leave us alone. Completely alone. This baby can never know what you were. What I did. Use this one last chance. Get your second lifetime.'

"I watched her dangle my license, my name and identity above me as I lay on the bed, and the last words I said to her were, 'Why are you doing this?' Because it occurred to me that this was a shitty thing for someone to do and I should probably be mad at her. But I didn't feel mad. I felt free.

"And her last words to me? 'Because I love you.'

"And that, if you must know, *did* make me mad."

The room was silent. Will was used to this part. When he first started purging this story, he used to be afraid that police would come in and handcuff him at this point. But 20 years of telling this story occasionally in anonymous groups of strangers had taught him that everyone carries their own heavy baggage around, and no one wanted to stop or prevent him from telling his story.

In fact, what he had come to realize was that his story seemed to make others more comfortable in the room. Shoulders relaxed, legs recrossed more lightly. Coffee cups were refilled. It's not so much that misery likes company, Will had discovered over the years. It's that misery likes more miserable. People liked Will's story because it made them feel better about their own.

"Did you do it? Did you stay away? Did you ever go back?" The woman to his left prodded Will.

He didn't answer. Instead, he just went on.

"I stumbled out of the room after Audrey left. I called my dealer and asked him to meet me at the diner for breakfast. 'It's on me,' I smiled as he met me in the back of the restaurant and pushed a small plastic bag into my palm. I was inviting him for breakfast. Like we were old pals or business comrades. He said, 'No thanks. And that is *not* on me. Where's your cash?'

"I pulled some wrinkled bills I had taken from Audrey's tampon box above the bathroom sink. She was getting more and more clever about hiding money at that point—never keeping any in her underwear drawer or wallet anymore—

but I was still able to find some loose 20s when I needed them. After she left that day, I tore the bathroom apart, and the tampon box stuck out like a sore thumb, since she was, you know, pregnant. The handful of money I pressed into Bruce's hand was hardly enough to pay my outstanding debt. I don't even know how much I owed him at that last meeting, to tell you the truth. I wasn't exactly keeping a reliable spreadsheet of expenses in those days. In the back of the diner, Bruce took the money, left me with the fresh plastic bag, and called me a few names. Most of them were true.

"I think maybe I stayed to eat a little bit—maybe not—the next part is a blur and I think it lasted a few days ... but apparently it took me getting good and high to follow through on Audrey's instructions. I ended up on the front steps of some posh rehab not too far from our home—one I'd tried a few times. They didn't seem to recognize me— maybe my appearance had changed so dramatically—maybe the volume of addicts was simply too much for this small tony rehab. They were known to cater to celebrities and pro- fessional athletes. They took me in as a charity mission— funded by some altruistic benefactors who allowed them to take a few non-famous and very poor people every month. I had hit the jackpot. Literally. When I got out of detox, they asked me to fill out some paperwork. And as the memory of Audrey and her ugly face and protruding belly and our deal came back to me, I formulated a story that I would stick to for the next two decades. I said, 'I don't remember. I don't remember anything about where I came from or where I was before this.'

"'Is anyone reporting me missing?' I asked almost hope- fully, but with resignation, too.

"They ran some info. They checked with local police. No. I wasn't a missing person. I wasn't a wanted person. 'We'll call you John,' they said. 'For John Doe.' I shuddered. My name before had *been* John, actually. I shared that fact also with the John Doe that Audrey buried in my place. So I said, 'No I hate that name. I don't want to be John or John Doe.' 'So what do you want us to call you?' they asked.

"I looked up at the sign on the wall and saw a litany of affirmations.

"My eyes landed on the first two: I will be a better me. I can and I will.

The circle nodded in shared recognition.

"So I said, 'Will. Just call me Will.' And with that I started my first real period of sobriety. And I became Will Cann. I have never been that other man—John—again. Nor will I ever be."

Will's coffee cup was empty by that point, so he tore at the Styrofoam, just to have something to do with his nervous hands.

"I have someone new in my life now. Her name is Margot. Margot is a really, really bright light in my life." Will didn't add: *She doesn't know all that I've told you strangers tonight.*

The group simply smiled and nodded around Will.

And while Will didn't regret purging his story, he regretted telling them about Margot as he watched their confused smiles. *Yes*, he thought. *Finally. After all this time, I've found someone to love me. But of course it isn't the real me she loves.*

*The real me is a hopeless drunk. A user. A John Doe. Someone who would give up his identity and his family just to stay alive.*

# Chapter 2

"I was seven when I found out my father had died of a drug overdose and not from cancer as the previous story had gone." I swirled a cup of jailhouse coffee in its paper cup as I remembered.

"Honestly, I'm not even sure where the cancer story came from in my head. Probably from something I'd seen on TV, and I guess my mother just never bothered correcting me in those early years after she realized that was the story I was clinging to.

"My friend Lizzie's father had just been diagnosed with cancer—lung I believe. And Lizzie made the announcement in sharing time in school—in the second grade. Sharing time was supposed to be some version of show and tell—a time to bring in a new book or stuffed animal or some such possession and show it proudly and boastfully to the room of other envious second graders. But instead a number of kids insisted all year long in leaving their prized possessions at home and bringing into the sharing circle such private and intrusive information as: 'Mom and Dad were up all night fighting about their checkbook last night' or 'Dad is very grumpy when his baseball team doesn't make it to the play-offs and he threw an empty beer can across the room at the TV when they lost' or in Lizzie's case: 'My dad has cancer.'

"It's not that the feelings were encouraged or discouraged. It was just that the teachers didn't really know what to do with them because to address them in any real way might lead to the students going back home and telling their parents that 'My teacher doesn't want us to talk about your checkbook or your fights or your cancer' and then the teachers would have to be included in the circle of embarrassment that they were all trying very hard to stay out of, thank you very much.

"And so in some unspoken, understood way, we were permitted—subconsciously encouraged in fact—to share our most secret information in those circles with absolutely no consequences. Pure truth and authenticity ran rampant in those circles. It was really heady stuff for a seven year old, if you ask me. Which you didn't, I get that. But still—"

"I'm dying to know what this has to do with anything, Thea," Roy interrupted me, which was kind, because I had actually forgotten he was there. I'd also forgotten that he was the one I was supposed to be telling this story to in the first place.

Roy was my very slick-looking public defender, assigned to my case by some well-meaning judge who thought this sweaty man in a cheap suit with a boldly patterned tie would somehow be a step up from me representing myself in the trial the judge had promised me was "a real possibility that I needed to be prepared for, young lady."

*Young lady?* I had thought. *Do 20-somethings actually qualify as young ladies? Do I?*

"Oh—right you are, Roy—look at me with my own little version of a sharing circle—or square—or whatever this is." I pushed my finger back and forth in the space between us and drew a square that included each of us at two vertices apiece.

Roy rolled his eyes. And so I kept on.

"So Lizzie said it—right there at sharing time. Lizzie who used to be my very best friend up until that point," I responded in a way that sounded unnecessarily wistful—

even to my own ears.

"'My dad has cancer,' she said.

"And so I said, 'Like mine.'

"And then Kevin Murphy turned his sorry ass around in his seat to face me, and said, 'Your dad didn't have cancer. Your dad was a druggie. And he was a loser. And he ran off.'

"I wasn't even clever enough to cut the conversation off. I had no idea—literally no idea what he was talking about—so I just said 'A what?' again and again.

"Freaking Kevin Murphy." I leaned back into my chair across from bored-looking Roy.

"He started laughing so hard at me. He actually laughed into his shirt sleeve and a little snot came out his nose, as I looked at the teacher whose sad eyes were pointed at me. She was stuck between the truth and her usual paralysis caused by the over-sharing in her classroom. I saved her; I nodded quickly, so quickly, I must have looked like one of those bobbleheads that people win if they are number 1 through 3,234 at the home baseball game. And I just ended it all with, 'Oh I know THAT.'

"Even though I didn't. I didn't know what a druggie was— or what it meant that my dad *was* one. I just knew it was bad and shameful, from the way everyone was looking at me, including the teacher and Lizzie, who was never again my friend after that day. And I knew enough to know it was something I *should* know. I just didn't. I went home from school that day and nearly pushed my mom over with my anger as I came in the door screaming.

"'Yes, it's true,' she said. 'Drugs killed your father and not cancer. No need to discuss all of this terribleness any-more. Now wash your hands for dinner.'

"And that was it. That was my mom's grand apology for letting me go right on thinking it was cancer and not drugs that killed my dad, so that I ended up looking like an idiot in front of freaking Kevin Murphy, Lizzie, and the rest of my second-grade class."

"And you are still—to this day—mad at your mom about this? And that's why you don't want to call her and let her know where you are? And that's why you're going to stick with me instead of getting a real lawyer?" Roy put the air quotes in between us with his fingers as he repeated the words I had said upon meeting him. Funny enough, the words sounded meaner to my ears now that he was saying them instead of me.

I grew defensive. I'm not a sociopath for heaven's sakes. "Oh Roy." I mockingly pushed the space between us with my finger again as I nodded, "I know you're a real lawyer. I was just kidding about that. How are we going to work together if we don't have a little light-hearted humor between us, right?"

Roy shrugged like I had a point, even though I knew he didn't think I did, and I stopped tracing the air and finished my muddy jailhouse coffee instead.

Roy had showed up to our first official client meeting with his tie strewn around his neck untied and with his top buttons undone, like someone had told him I was some kind of emergency and he needed to get to the courthouse right away. As we were talking, decorum suddenly became important, and he started tying his tie, while I tried not to laugh.

At subsequent meetings, he showed up with his tie already tied, and for that I was grateful. He smelled of hair product and kitty litter, and wore no wedding ring. I created a narrative within the initial moments of our first meeting in which Roy had a girlfriend with a cat, as he really didn't seem too cuddly or like a cat person at all. I decided not to ask him if I was right about the cat being someone else's. I didn't want to be wrong.

Roy asked me a series of personal questions that I had more trouble answering than he probably expected me to, and then he asked for like the third time, if I was going to let Audrey come visit me in prison.

"Come on, Roy. I really don't want any visitors, right

now, least of all, *her*."

"Is she very judgmental, your mother?"

I cringed at all the layers and implications of that question, and settled for answering simply, "After all that Audrey has done, I'm not sure how judgmental of a leg she gets to stand on. I'm not worried about Audrey's judgment, Roy. I'm not worried about Audrey, at all."

Roy followed my lead, and said, "Well, Audrey wants to come see you, and she keeps contacting me directly. I will tell her that you are not seeing any visitors right now, and that we are working steadily on building your defense. Hopefully she will be satisfied for now."

I nodded, "Fine. Good strategy. I approve. Now let's go back to talking about *me*, Roy."

"Ok, Thea," Roy sighed. "We need to talk more about this business of yours. You need to tell me everything."

I laughed because it was sort of a stupid thing for him to say, but then again, I *had* been trying to tell Roy everything—even letting him in on the story of my dad and Kevin Murphy, and Lizzie and the second-grade sharing time. It didn't seem to be making too big an impression on him.

So I decided to stick with telling him everything I wanted him to know, which is all anyone ever tells anyone, if you think about it.

When a new client used to come to me at my business, called Alibis, I always opened the conversation with one question:

*Tell me the story you want me to know.*

I told Roy about my signature tagline and I didn't get nearly enough excitement from him. So I tried going at it from another angle.

"So here's the thing, Roy. Alibis is my own brainchild. I started it a year and a half ago—right after I dropped out of college. Without an actual degree or any letters of recommendation, I was left to pursue something a little more entrepreneurial. Something a little less, shall we say 'traditional.' I met this techie college kid at a frat party once who was so good at computer hacks but not so good on big picture stuff. I watched every one of his amateur YouTube videos and figured out how to develop this program on my own—I mean others keep calling it a hack—but it's a program—a legit program and it sort of scrambles the GPS and the time feature of social media apps, like Facebook, so you can post things from a different place. And even a different time. I mean, not like actual *time travel*, but you know, you can post things time-stamped in the past."

"Hold up, hold up. Let me catch up." Roy scribbled notes, but apparently couldn't keep up with me. He must have been writing down every single word I was saying. Instead of actually listening to me.

"I never interrupt clients when they're speaking, Roy. I just try to jot down a few notes, while listening to the story they want me to know. Yes, I do still write. Mostly, in life, I text and type but when a new client wants a face-to-face meeting, I know they feel more comfortable seeing me write stuff down on a yellow writing pad. Writing stuff down these days apparently seems more confidential—less permanent and viral—than communicating electronically. But I have to be honest. I would never interrupt a client to tell them to 'hold up.' My notetaking is usually just an exercise in humoring my potential clients. I write with absolutely no intention of ever later transcribing the notes—but just with the intention of putting on a show."

"Well, we're different, you and I," Roy said while still scribbling, and without any sense of irony.

*A show.*

Indeed that's what my life had become by the time I met Roy. Ever since a wave of not-so-tech-savvy clients started hiring Alibis to create fake social media profiles and fake social media lives, my life had become a façade—no clear line where reality started and ended. I had come to like the blurriness—there was a comfort in it—one that prevented me from clearly remembering where I started and ended, too.

As I explained to him the founding of Alibis and the basic premise of altering time and place through my program—like he was a client—Roy's expression transformed into a scowl that was hard to interpret—but also hard to ignore.

"So, if not Lizzie, who's your best friend now?"

I stared at Roy intently while he paused the note-taking. I kept debating, before taking the easy way out. "Well, no one I'm going to offer up to you, Roy. You'll just call them up to the witness stand, start some weird sharing circle, and muck everything up, like that second-grade teacher of mine."

"Thea. Do you have *any* friends?" Roy asked as if I wasn't actually holding out on him, but rather didn't have any friends to offer up in the first place. "Do you know anyone who might be able to vouch for your character? Your truthfulness, your integrity? Anything along those lines?"

I realized that what Roy was really asking me was: "Do you have any friends that are not made up on one of your social media accounts?"

So I told him about the day Renata arrived at Alibis with a healing bruise on her cheek and a messy ponytail. He sat up straighter in his chair like maybe we were getting somewhere after all. After a very long after all.

*Tell me the story you want me to know.*

"I was married for a long time," Renata started while she was still standing in front of me and my desk. My desk wasn't mahogany or glamorous or even pretty. It was just … utilitarian.

The whole Alibis office was in a word—serviceable.

There wasn't anything in that space that didn't need to be there. A steel-framed desk and matching file cabinet. An alarm clock and a one-cup coffee maker. I didn't even have sugar packets sitting next to the sparse coffee station for clients. Because I didn't use sugar, I didn't indulge in the luxury of thinking that maybe someone would.

I had one chair that I worked in, and when potential clients came in, I gave them the chair, and moved my seat onto the front of the metal desk in front of them.

When I first opened the office and decorated it—using the term loosely, of course—I determined that I really didn't need to have two chairs when there was only one of me. All those clients later—by the time Renata arrived—I was starting to question that philosophy, as I really just wanted to sit in my own seat for once and let Renata tell me her story.

"I was married for a long time," she repeated again, once I had pulled the lightweight chair around to her side of the desk and offered it to her, as though in the time it took that transaction, I might have forgotten why she was here.

"He brought me here from Russia 18 years ago. I have not seen my family since. I was grateful to come here to America. I told him that all the time. But I did not understand how hard my life would be here in America either. My husband was much older than me." She fingered her purple-green cheek.

I stared long and hard at her mottled bruise and wondered if she had killed the bastard husband of hers. And if so, how? Had she fed him rat poison over a matter of days or weeks? Had she cut off his balls when he was sleeping? Had she waited to call 911 while he was having a heart attack after too arduous and too forced sex with his much younger Russian mail- order bride?

I didn't ask any of those questions. I simply asked, "Have you filed any police reports?"

Renata looked at me carefully. "No, not yet."

"You are entitled to protection, you understand that? In this country, even if he is your husband, he's not allowed to do these things to you."

Renata's eyes went wide and her fingers grazed the colorful bruise on her cheek: "No. Not my Carlos. He was a good man. He is dead. But he was a good man. Carlos never hurt me."

I shook my head a bit as if shaking off some sleep. I wasn't sure what we were talking about anymore. Why was she even here?

"I'm sorry—Renata—what do you mean your husband's dead? Did you kill him?"

"No! Of course not. He was my husband." She hissed the word *husband* at me, making it sound less romantic than she was letting on, I feared.

"Well, people have killed men for less compelling reasons than that." I laughed a little at my own joke while Renata plowed ahead unknowing and unknowable.

"My Carlos—he died of cancer last year. A long, good fight the doctors say. A terrible thing to watch him waste away from such a terrible disease. Remind me of the terrors I see in Russia—the reasons I want to leave so badly. I start—how do you say?—dating men for company while Carlos was sick and dying. We need the money and I don't want for Carlos to worry so I don't tell him. I just carry on with the guilt and shame of doing something that would kill Carlos if he knew."

*Ah.* I thought. *So my Russian mail-order bride is actually a call girl with a cause. Charming.*

I began to trust my usually strong instincts again.

"Right. Would kill him. If he wasn't already dying?" Admittedly I was just entertaining myself at this point, because Renata went on without understanding any of my sarcasm, simply nodding violently, "Yes, yes. He was dying. He did die."

"Last year Carlos died and our hospital bills go away and I don't want to work this way anymore, but Roger, he make me. He say I have a 'client list.' That I cannot just walk away from him. I say why not? Lots of people just walk away. Look at Carlos. Look at my parents. Look at me. I walk away from bad life in Russia. I can walk away from bad life in America too."

Somewhere in the middle of that litany, I realized that Renata is not the only one who believes she can walk away from her bad life in America. I'm a convert as well.

And before Renata left my office, we filed a restraining order against that pimp of hers, got her a new identity online, found her a temporary relocation at a women's shelter nearby, and shook hands on a new receptionist job at Alibis.

I made a mental note to pick up a new chair. Because there were going to be two of us.

◆

Roy looked a little disappointed by my story of Renata. Like she wasn't enough of a friend to count. Maybe she wasn't, but rather than telling Roy that, I tried to make her sound so interesting he'd be satisfied just by knowing about her.

When that didn't work, I turned inward on my own thoughts, forgetting about Roy for a moment.

*I'm in prison.* I played the words over and over again, wondering if the sting would ever diminish.

I felt hysteria come over me. I dug my fingers into my palms to try to control my breathing—but my breathing only became more erratic as a result of the inflicted pain. When I looked down I saw that I was scratching the side of my wrist with too much frequency and too much force to be an accident. I closed my eyes and willed myself to inhale.

*Stop it, stop it, stop it.* I told myself.

*You are not this person. You are not. This person.*

The red splotched marks from my imposed scratches crawled up the side of my wrists to my forearms. I kept my arms under the table that Roy and I were sitting at, and tried to keep them out of his view, while he wrote and wrote on that damn legal pad.

I leaned back a little, and I could see my arms under that table. Pink and puckered skin peeked out between white scratch marks not yet sure whether or not to bleed, and I counted to myself.

*One. Two. Three. Four. One. Two. Three. Four.*

I kept counting until that rhythm felt too short for me and I had to inhale more deeply and pace my counting to seven. And then eight. And then nine.

Roy kept writing. What he was writing, I couldn't imagine. I became dizzy waiting for him to catch up. I tried to remember some of those mumbo jumbo new wave meditation techniques Renata was always telling me to try.

Renata is like the zen master of zen. She had one of those rock gardens with sand on her desk, and she forced the tiny ridiculous rake through the sand alongside the marbly rocks every morning as she oriented herself to her desk and her energy. She would actually say those words: "orient myself to my desk and my energy." Her English is still broken, so I know she read these words from some kind of a meditation manual, and I respected her earnestness, even though I always rolled my eyes when she oriented herself.

Renata even bought me one once—a sand garden—but of course I spilled my coffee in it—and I declared it very useful for sopping up wet coffee which felt like a compliment when I said it, but Renata was not amused. She just brought the trashcan over to my desk and swooped the whole mocha scented sand trap into it with one frustrated motion.

After I ruined her gift, I noticed Renata took even longer to orient herself each morning. And neither she nor I bothered to replace the zen garden. But sitting there with court-appointed Roy, I was feeling like I'd do a lot of bad things to remember a few of those zen tricks to get me through the next however long I was going to be trapped in prison.

I am a successful businesswoman and yet I don't run a perfectly above-the-board business and never bothered to put any "my lawyer" on the payroll—an arrogant rookie mistake that became evident the moment Roy showed up. Since all the Alibis money was immediately frozen in light of the charges against me, the only money I had any access to after my arrest was my mother's.

In other words, I was stuck with Roy for the time being. Roy, who, as I was thinking, and scratching and counting, and breathing, was sitting across from me with all the obliviousness of a bad first date, still asking questions that he thought were hopelessly important here, like: "I need to understand more intimately the details of your business."

It was his use of the word "intimately" that annoyed me more than the substance of his questions about Alibis. Eventually I decided to stop playing along quite so willingly.

"I know I'm being vague here, Roy, but it's just that— well, do we really have to talk about all that?" I looked over my shoulder, like I was hiding from eavesdroppers, baiting him a bit, and he nodded hungrily.

"Ok—well, this *is* confidential, right? Because discretion is sort of the point of the whole company."

He nodded zealously again. Poor guy almost looked like he was holding his breath.

"Have you heard of Ashley Madison?"

He exhaled loudly, pornographically. "You mean, your site—it's—?"

I stopped the bleeding. "No, Roy. I am not running an online dating site for married people. That's disgusting. My company is much more dignified. It helps people pretend they are somewhere they are not. At a time they are not. It helps them pretend they *are* something they are not."

I nodded at Roy with his lawyerness oozing all over the space between us. "And yes, Roy, it sounds much worse when you say all of this out loud. Which I don't. Ever. My clients hire me to create and maintain online personas consistent with their brand.

"So they're all, like, what? Established companies? Corporations? Your clients?"

*Great. Now Roy thinks I represent Coca-Cola and Xerox. So clueless.*

"Well, no. They are people. Regular old people. Who don't have a brand, or think that they need a brand. But then I fix that. I give them a brand. I give them *everything*. That's why what I do is so *dangerous*." I leaned far in as I said this to Roy, and he either lost interest in the vagueness, or got deathly afraid, because he leaned back away from me and started asking me much more boring questions.

"So, Thea, what about alcohol? Drugs?"

"What about drugs and alcohol, Roy?" I sighed, deciding to keep playing along with all of this inane direction-less strategy, until I could come up with something more effective than Roy.

"Do them? Drink it?"

I shook my head, lazily.

"Come on, you must—sometimes—"

"No, Roy. I don't sometimes anything. Not anymore. I just think by the time a person is in her 20s like I am, she should understand her relationships with three things."

I put my fingers up and started counting out for Roy: "Herself. Alcohol. And—"

I stopped short, worried that this was going to re-open all sorts of questioning from Roy that I had just put an end to.

He looked up from his legal pad at my pause. "And what else?"

"Her mother."

After Roy left me with some vague promises about potential developments in my case involving expert witness testimony, I lay on my cot and stared at the ceiling, letting my eyes go in and out of focus until the cracks in the cement above my cot arranged themselves in soothing shapes, like hearts and puppies, and mushrooms.

Shut up. I don't know why mushrooms.

Without Roy there to entertain me, the talking to myself continued.

*I can't believe I'm in a prison cell.*

Something my mother always used to say to me as a teenager popped into my head just then and struck me as darkly funny.

"You just never have the essentials on you. When are you going to start carrying the essentials? Like tissues? And a nail file?"

*I could probably use a nail file right about now, Mom.*

"Let me guess. No tissues?" My mother had lamented the day I came home in 7th grade, mad and crying, with dark mascara staining my face like deep bruises. Marc Turner stole my history notes without asking and I had been summoned into the Principal's office where the teacher accused me of stealing from *Marc*. He wasn't brought in. No one was interested in the truth. Just the story. And there weren't two sides of the story. Just a one-sided tale, in which I was the tragic character killed off in the end. I failed the semester, and ultimately I failed history for the year, as I came to realize that doing the work was not going to be rewarded in the least, and in fact would only enable Marc Turner to *pass* history, a result I decided to do my small part in preventing. I stopped doing any work, and failed the class spectacularly. In the end, of course, Marc pulled it off. An A in history to counterbalance my F. Whether he found someone else's notes to copy, or whether the teacher simply chose to overlook his lack of brains, I wouldn't ever know for sure.

I was too young then to understand the privilege that comes not only with gender, but with socioeconomic status. The Marc Turners of the world lived on the side of town where the big refurbished-on-the-inside brick colonials looked downwind on the same-old-same-old-on-the-inside brick row homes where my single mom and I lived at the time. A row of homes that stood just inside the school district lines for the affluent suburban school district where the poor and rich of the district learned next to each other in a precarious struggle.

There were hushed whispers about the advantages of "diversity" in the school which I didn't understand because we were white and at that time, I thought "diverse" meant black. When I found out that "diverse" also meant poor, then I didn't understand why it was such an advantage for the rich kids to hang around with or learn next to us, if all they seemed to be learning was fear, which maybe they wouldn't have learned, if we weren't so *close* to all their *things*.

Close enough to rub the rich suede of their backpacks along our dirty fingertips if we happened behind them in the cafeteria line. Close enough to lean up against their shiny black Range Rovers with our decidedly unfashionable clothes and outerwear as we passed by their VIP parking spots from the corner where the public bus let us off each morning. The truth was we *were* eyeing their stuff and they were right to fear us trying to take their things.

*I mean for God's sake, look what ended up happening.*

*Fast forward 7 months, July 2017*

# Chapter 3

Nearly seven months after the musty church basement AA meeting in which he was able to purge his faked death story once again, Will Cann got word that Thea Brown was going to be his new patient at Juniper Lane. He knew from her file that she was not going to be like any other patient he had treated previously.

But he pushed all which that might mean out of his mind long enough to warn his Wednesday session co-ed mix at Juniper Lane that they'd be having a new patient join in for group therapy very soon.

"The new patient is arriving any day, but won't start group until next week."

"Boy or girl?" Zak asked.

"A woman, Zak," Will said pointedly. "But this is not supposed to be a singles group, so get that smirk off your face."

"How do you spell your name, Zak?" Cassandra sat stiffly in her usual spot on the floor, legs straight out in front of her as if someone had placed her there and told her not to move. She was leaning against the overstuffed golden couch that Ali had commandeered for herself weeks ago.

Ali always kicked her shoes off and climbed up on the velour cushions of the couch with her legs tucked under her, looking comfortable and confident, and nothing like an addict is "supposed to look." Those were Zak's words on the day he met her. Ali had laughed him off, and said, "I'm not sure what an addict is supposed to look like? Like you?" And Zak had stared through her instead of responding or laughing and a line had been drawn between them in that moment—a line that would make group sessions uncomfortable, impossible even, if not for Cassandra arriving a few weeks later, taking up her place on the floor, and surprising everyone with her odd moments of engagement, including the day's question: "How do you spell your name, Zak?"

"Z-A-K. Why?"

"Ah, interesting. I had a marriage counselor named Zack—Z-A-C-K. And he insisted we call him that—Zack—instead of by his last name, which I thought was odd. The whole experience of marriage counseling was so gruesome that I've hated the name ever since, but since you spell it without the C, I can get over it. Zak without a C." Cassandra blended the last syllables together to make Zak without a C more a name than a funny spelling lesson.

It was clear to Will and to the group that Cassandra was holding herself together very carefully. Her hands shook visibly in group, and the remnants of old bruises lined her pale cheeks, which were framed by straight brown hair with light-colored highlights that were starting to grow out and fade into the darker color of her hair, revealing just how long she'd been at Juniper Lane. Cassandra always had nice clothes on—she never wore pajamas in group like many of the others—and she always wore makeup—which actually had the effect of making her bruise remnants look even more garish. But no one ever mentioned the makeup or the bruises, as it was clear Cassandra was not interested in talking about them publicly, and was, in fact, trying very hard to keep her outside appearance under control.

Will knew things about Cassandra that the others didn't know yet, but were starting to suspect.

After her intake, Cassandra hadn't spoken much in the last three weeks, so the marriage counselor reference and the spellcheck inquiry into Zak's name were considered a breakthrough for Will. He decided to interrupt his original plan for the Wednesday group and run with it.

He had been trying to find an opening with Cassandra ever since that first day she showed up seeming to need battered woman counseling more than addiction counseling and Will worried that he was in over his head. A not too unfamiliar feeling over the years, if he was being honest. Which he always tried to be.

"Why didn't you like marriage counseling in general, Cassandra?" Will asked. He knew about some specific marriage counselor failures, but he didn't want to betray Cassandra's confidence by revealing what she had told to him outside of group.

Cassandra spoke through gritted teeth. "My husband always seems to con the female counselors and with the male counselors? He acted like a frat boy at homecoming. He's charming. And horrible. He thinks feminism is a dirty word and that women 'exaggerate their causes.' That's an actual quote of his. He forbade me from driving to Washington D.C. and joining in the Women's March on the day after the inauguration in January.

But the response Cassandra was looking for with that line was lost within this group. They were neither political nor dried out enough to understand that the world had been changing and moving without them on the outside. Cassandra seemed to have multi-tasked through her recent struggles to have formed current events opinions, something the rest of the group had no luxury to have done.

They looked at her blankly, and Cassandra's expression closed up again. She was gone, and Will was left to carry on the Wednesday session without any more input from Cassandra. After they filed out of group, he remained in his chair instead of following them out. He shook his head at the floor in front of the sofa where Cassandra had sat stoically only moments before, frustrated with how little progress he'd made with Cassandra in three long weeks.

◆

Will knew from Cassandra's file that her husband was a prominent figure in the neighboring town—a pastor with a large, affluent congregation. Cassandra had—a year ago— quit her decade-long job as a receptionist in a local pediatrician's office to, in her words, "play the role of the pastor's wife." She was—also in her words—"terrible at it." Three weeks into her treatment, Will was still trying to deter- mine if "it" was playing a role, or being a pastor's wife.

Cassandra was brought to Juniper Lane by a police offi- cer named Ben, a hulking, muscular, bald man who looked not unlike the famous Mr. Clean from the vintage television commercials. To break the ice, Will asked him, "Has anyone ever told you that you look like Mr. Clean, Officer?" He looked at Will stone-faced and, after an uncomfortable silence, asked who Mr. Clean was. Will saw Cassandra shoot him a secret glance, that seemed to say, in addition to "Help,"—"Do you see what I'm dealing with here?"

Cassandra had gotten a DUI arrest, and had pled guilty in a quick plea bargain within days of her arrest that got her a 90-day visit to Juniper Lane—even before her bruises had healed. Apparently her husband was quite anxious for Cas- sandra to dry out and clean up before the parishioners noticed her missing. According to the police report, the hus- band had reported her drinking as excessive and completely out of control. The police report had also assigned all her bruising and physical signs as injuries from the car accident. No follow-up investigation had been done as far as Will could see through a quick flip of the police records while the Offi- cer and Cassandra were still standing in his office waiting for intake paperwork to be finished.

Will had asked Officer Ben, out of earshot of Cassandra as he escorted him back out of the building, "Are all those bruises from the car accident? Are you sure about that?"

Officer Ben shrugged in a way that made Will uncomfortable; but not as uncomfortable as when he said, "Between you and me?"

Will nodded.

"Not clear. But honestly, you can't really assign too much outside blame here. She was screwing one of the parishioners. Husband has been very cooperative. He admits he got angry when he found out. But you know, come on. Who can blame him, right?"

Will would succumb to embarrassment only later when recalling that at that point he was so anxious to be rid of Officer Ben, he just nodded in agreement and punched the exit code that helped the misogynist officer leave, and then Will returned to Cassandra, hoping to provide some better counseling than Officer Clean.

Will started explaining to Cassandra the detox procedures, and the likelihood that her physical symptoms would be minimal since she had already spent 14 days in a holding cell at the county prison.

Her lack of expression changed to one of general confusion.

"What is so great about me being in county prison all this time? I don't get it."

"You're likely dried out a bit. Were you sick in prison? You've probably weathered the initial physical symptoms of detox already and now we can focus on the emotional ones. Which are no less difficult. I don't mean to mislead you. I'm all about authenticity here. From here on out, we are going to work on a lot of truth-telling from me to you and you to me and we'll hopefully create a safe working environment that will allow us to achieve some real recovery. Recovery that will last outside of these walls."

Will noticed Cassandra cringe when he said that last part.

"You're nervous about leaving. I get that. But one day at a time starts now, ok?"

"Yeah, I'm nervous about leaving." Cassandra spat out

after a long silence. "That's an understatement. But don't worry about physical detox. I'm not a drunk. My husband let the court believe that because he didn't know how else to spin this whole mess."

"What mess?"

"The mess in which he—oh forget it—the mess in which his wife almost killed herself."

She slouched back in her seat as if just the admission was too much for her.

"Cassandra, are those bruises on your face from your husband?"

Cassandra looked like she was sizing up Will. He could see her visible desperation—her hope to trust someone, anyone, after her ordeal. He feared something else won out when she answered, "No."

Will sighed. He conceded that he was making little headway with Cassandra, but then she spoke again.

"His bruises have mostly healed. He's usually more careful about those. Open slaps. Ripped out hair. Those sorts of injuries can be hidden from the eyes of the police and parishioners. He's so very careful. He rarely screws up. Rarely loses control." The expression in Cassandra's eyes was starting to convert to a glazed sadness.

"Two months ago, my husband came home from the church office midday to confront me about a love affair he had just discovered a few days earlier that I had had years before. Before we were even married. But I had nearly married the man, and now he's a parishioner. A single parishioner who helps out on Church activities and functions. We had been alone together. But never in an inappropriate way. I made sure of it. I was very protective of our reputation in the community. Of my husband's reputation.

"My husband—he found a message on my phone in which I was replying to this same man. He was asking me why I stayed married to my husband when clearly I was so unhappy—and I responded simply 'it's complicated.'

"I had quit my job to take care of my husband and our home and the congregation and to begin a family. By the time I realized what a mistake that decision was, my position at the pediatrician's office wasn't open any more. There are very few jobs in a small town for the pastor's wife—especially when the pastor has made it clear that his wife already has a job: taking care of him.

"I felt stuck. I told the man that."

Cassandra sighed quietly. She looked smaller than she had when Officer Clean dropped her off.

"And my husband had found my phone and read the messages. I hadn't thought to delete them. I hadn't known he was paying any attention to me at all. But he read the thread apparently, and saw that I did not deny the unhappiness. I did not stick up for my husband. All of these sins were repeated back to me that day my husband came home to confront me.

"I asked him if he wanted lunch. He had come home to beat me up, and without realizing that, I greeted him by ladling soup for him."

From her chair in front of Will, Cassandra mimed the action of ladling soup and he realized she had transported back to that day in her mind. He waited for what came next.

"He cornered me in the kitchen and slapped me until I broke away from him and ran out of the room where I made it only as far as the powder room. I had my cell phone in my back jeans pocket, so I locked myself in the bathroom, and started dialing 911, but my husband busted the flimsy door open while I was still dialing and yanked my hair so hard I saw stars. I begged him to stop, but he grabbed my phone from me, pushed me onto the floor, and smashed the phone repeatedly on the hardwood, next to my head, while his knee pinned me to the ground. Shards of the cell phone face shattered next to my ear, embedding themselves in my hair and scratching at my eyes. He was out of breath from exertion he wasn't used to, and I took advantage of one small moment of opportunity while he kept his knee on me, and just as my lungs felt like they were collapsing.

"'Please get off me.' I gasped. 'I'll listen to you. If you just get off me.' I begged. I saw some small window in his hesitant movement. He was probably thinking about what it would look like if he killed me. I knew he wanted to hurt me very, very badly but not go to jail for it. When he released his knee ever so slightly from my chest—I jumped up and ran for the door. He was in close pursuit, but I got out the door somehow before him. When I started screaming 'help!' into the empty air outside, he retreated—the coward that he is—allowing me a head start up the driveway.

"I kept running away from the house, screaming 'help, help!' and he walked after me, staying back, obviously worried that one of my neighbors would come to my aid. He needn't have worried, as it turned out. None did. I ran all the way up to the end of the driveway and crossed the street to the nearest neighbor's home. I banged on the door.

"What luck! A single woman who often worked remotely from home was indeed home that day. I thought she might actually help me. I yelled through the screen door, 'My husband is trying to kill me!'"

Cassandra's face flushed and she wiped away tears as she told the story. Will worried about letting her go on in such an agitated state, but he worried more about trying to stop her at that point.

Cassandra took a deep breath and resumed. "Just then, my husband reached the driveway behind me and apologized to my neighbor for his wife's hysterical episode, advising that a doctor was on his way. My husband was just ambling slowly up the drive, as if he didn't have a care in the world. My neighbor looked at me sadly and said only 'Ok, no problem, I really don't want to get involved. I'll leave her in your care, Pastor.'"

Cassandra's shoulders slumped and she looked even smaller as she finished this part of the story.

"'Leave her in your care, Pastor.' That's what she said. I had glass bits in my hair and a ripped shirt and bruised face, and she more easily believed that I was having a nervous breakdown than that Peter had done anything wrong to me.

"I realized then that I had no choice. I would have to walk back down to my house with my husband. No one was going to help me. No one.

"And when we got home, Peter said, 'We're going to have to just put this whole thing behind us. I'm going to have to forgive you. I have no choice. I'm not going to lose my congregation and everything I've worked so hard for, just because you're a whore and a nutjob.'

"I looked at him and said, 'What am I supposed to do? How am I supposed to forgive you?'

"And he laughed. He just laughed at me. He said, 'Forgive me? What the fuck are you supposed to forgive *me* for? You expect me to be happy about those texts I found? That you've been hanging out with your old boyfriend behind my back? You expect me to take it well? You're nuts. You know that? You are really *this* close to being committed to an insane asylum, which frankly, would help me forgive you a lot faster. If you actually get a diagnosis of crazy, I might truly forgive you, instead of going through the motions.'"

Cassandra was silent then. When the silence became too long, Will asked her, "When did the car accident happen?"

"Six weeks later. After Peter's midday rage episode which was not the first—but was certainly the worst episode of our marriage, I got him to agree to marriage counseling. We tried a few marriage counselors, but each one was worse than the one before. We would sit on a couch with a tissue box shoved between us—Peter painting me as Hester Prynne and denying any abuse, and then nudging the tissue box closer to me like we were living in a bad made-for-TV movie.

"The last counselor's name was Doreen. She was utterly charmed by Peter. I said to her, 'You like him too much. This isn't working.' And she said, 'No, I like you both.'

"I asked her, 'How can you like *him*? He's saying horrible things about me. He's telling you that he gets angry when the house isn't perfect, when I don't shower for days because I'm too busy with housework and congregation duties, that he can't really forgive a relationship I had before we were even married. How can you still—with all of this information—say you like *him*?'"

"What was her response?"

"Doreen said that maybe I need a psych eval. 'Just to rule things out,' she said. 'What's the harm,' she said. And he practically jumped out of his seat. 'Exactly. That's what I keep saying to her.' And I broke into tears right there on her stupid couch. 'Yes, you see that's the harm, Doreen. He has been trying to have me declared insane so that he can forgive me. For being a lousy wife and homemaker, and for a relationship I had before we were married. And so he can explain me away to the congregation.' 'And the texts! Don't forget about the texts!' Peter yelled from his seat again, bouncing up and down like an immature toddler.

"Doreen looked at him springing off his seat, and looked at me crying, and she said, 'Yes, a psych eval is what I'm recommending.' And she made it sound like she was doing me a big favor—like I was supposed to just collapse in gratitude before that wonderful woman, Doreen, who supposedly liked us *both*."

Will leaned back in his seat. Cassandra had opened up so much. And yet, this woman had been the product of so much bad counseling and abuse, it was going to be incredibly difficult to pierce her wall of cynicism in just 90 days. But that's all her DUI plea was going get her.

He couldn't exactly keep her here longer, unless ...

"And the accident, Cassandra? Can you tell me more about that? How long have you been medicating with alcohol?"

Cassandra looked at Will with icy clear eyes. "The last time I left Doreen's office, Peter and I got into separate cars like we had arrived, as always. And as I drove away I thought, 'Maybe I will go have a mammogram and learn I have advanced stage cancer and maybe I can escape this hell. Maybe the early seeds of dementia are making their way into my brain and I will soon forget this is my life. As I left her parking lot, I daydreamed that a tractor-trailer sideswiped me and killed me instantly. It was the biggest wave of relief I had felt in years really. And so I swerved off the road after our last appointment with Doreen, just as I was getting on the bypass. I let the daydream overtake me, and you know what? It really did lead to some temporary relief."

Cassandra pushed up on the arms of the chair. She was visibly exhausted by all she had confessed to Will. It was only her first day.

"I'm done now. I want to get some rest and see to those symptoms you mentioned. I'll be ready in 48 hours. I just need some sleep and I'll be ready to do the work and show up for sessions and hard labor, and whatever else you do here. I'll even submit to your psych evals and tests, and all of that. Cross my heart. After all, what's the harm?"

And with that wry statement, she was gone. The openness of her face was replaced with a hardness, and Will realized he had gotten all that he could from Cassandra that first day, and so he had called for an escort to take her to her room, and he didn't bother asking any more questions about her alcohol use.

As she walked away, Will thought about how to extend Cassandra's stay. The staff at Juniper Lane were authorized to treat addiction and depression, but without true chemical addiction, Cassandra's condition and suicidal revelations just might buy her a ticket to the psych floor she was so afraid of at the end of her 90-day sentence.

After what he had just heard and seen, Will believed Cassandra had due reason to be afraid, after all. The psych ward was where her husband would be in control of her patient care and her path from here on out, unless she could designate another. If what she was saying about her husband was true, he was not likely to cede control over Cassandra without a fight.

Will replayed Cassandra's admissions and took copious notes after she left his office. He might well have to start gearing up for that fight. For now, he wouldn't let anyone know what he suspected. He needed the full 90 days with Cassandra that the DUI plea had bought her. That's why Will hadn't asked her the question he already knew the answer to: *Cassandra, you weren't even drinking that day of the car crash, were you?*

Will blinked hard at the empty spot on the floor Cassandra had occupied in group that day, before finally leaving the long empty room where Cassandra, Ali, Zak without a C, and the others had made little progress.

*Maybe the new patient will shake things up*, Will thought in spite of himself.

*Maybe Thea will help me help Cassandra and the rest of this group.*

*One month earlier, June 2017*

# Chapter 4

I read the expert report Roy had just handed me with "Thea Brown" typed neatly across the top like I was reading a novel.

*How will it end?*

*What will come next?*

I admit it. I was riveted.

Certain phrases just wound down the page without meaning. Credentials and degrees. Published research about the effects of social media on contemporary relationships. My eyes took in the titles and volumes and page numbers without taking too much time to read them. And then I got to the real meat.

*Sociopathic.*

*Delusional.*

*Narcissistic.*

*Unattached.*

*Addiction.*

Addiction? Wait. I stopped at that one. All those other words used to describe me and it was addiction that held me up.

"I'm not addicted to anything, Roy. We went over all this. I drink decaf coffee and I never have more than one glass of wine per week.

*"Per. Week."* I repeated again for emphasis and noticed

that Roy was not blinking at me.

"How do you do that?" I asked him.

"What?" Still not blinking.

"Not blink."

His eyes fluttered then and he shook his head like he was trying to figure something out. Me, I guess.

But Roy's blinking broke the spell. And I was sent back to the document.

"I know I said I'd go along with this, but I'm just not sure this is going to work after all, Roy. Addiction? I'm not an addict."

"The expert seems to think you are. Addicted to social media."

"Come on, Roy, that's ridiculous. That's just what bored housewives say when they are looking for excuses to log in and check on their high school boyfriends.

"Oh! I'm just so addicted to facebook! I can't stop." I mimicked what I imagined a bored housewife would sound like. High pitched and shrill. I had no basis for such imitations. I had never actually met a bored housewife. They weren't exactly my target demographic at Alibis.

"Listen, Thea. This expert reached out to *us*. She studies social media and its behavioral effects for a living. I'll admit, she has something to gain here—notoriety, and probably funding for her research. But I don't care about all that. Dr. Barrett is willing to take the stand and testify as to something that has never been argued before: that your pathological addiction to social media, and to creating these false identities, is a real mental condition—a real psychiatric condition, that has prevented you from understanding the true nature of your actions. That your addiction has prevented you from intending the consequences. Therefore you cannot be culpable of the crimes you are accused of."

I snapped my fingers at Roy, hoping to get him to stop talking like that.

"Hey Roy—what the hell are you saying? Culpable of

intending the consequences?" I garbled his words and spit them back at him in the even and non-emotional tone he had originally delivered them.

Unlike the bored housewife impression, I did have a basis for *this* imitation. Roy himself.

He looked at me again with his non-blinking expression.

"Thea. What I'm saying is that this doctor—if the court accepts her testimony—has the ability to turn this entire thing around.

*No blinking.*

"Listen, Thea. The prosecution is being greedy. The charges include conspiracy, aiding and abetting, *and* first degree arson. They are looking to make an example of you. And if this doctor's testimony is accepted by the court first, and the jury second, it disproves their entire case.

*Still no blinking.*

"And then you can get out of jail. That's the goal here, right, Thea?"

I drummed my fingers on the table over the report, over the words delusional and sociopathic. They didn't bother me nearly as much as "addiction," a word that meant out of control.

That word meant, as much as I had tried to deny it all those years, that I really was my father's daughter.

Roy startled me out of my brooding over the so-called expert report. "Thea, come on. How much did you know?"

"That's a pretty broad question, Roy, don't you think?"

"Stop it, Thea. This is getting old. I need to know exactly what your last client told you. Did she send any emails? Anything at all in writing? Anything like that could very well come out in court, and I don't like surprises."

"Well that's uncomfortable at holiday time, isn't it?"

Roy glared at me with an expression that reminded me of one I myself use when I am just about to drop a problematic client.

"Ok. Ok," I said penitently. "How much did I know? She

was my client. I know as much as Carmen told me. Which wasn't much. You should know that as well as I do, Roy." I batted my eyes a little and saw Roy's expression visibly soften.

*God, Roy was so easy.*

"I'm here to help you, Thea. You get that, right? The jury could very well believe that you aided and abetted Carmen Fierro in setting her husband's factory on fire. The police tracked several phone calls to your office from her cell phone that was found at the scene of the explosion."

"Wha—that's ridiculous. How can they pin anything on me based on a few missed calls?"

Roy ignored me.

"Thea, the name of your company is Alibis. Certainly, you understand that this kind of thing could be, you know, foreseeable." Roy's use of air quotes when he said "kind of thing" was sort of charming.

"And one of the many troubling things about this case is that the trail of Carmen Fierro seems to have just disappeared. No one can find any recent pictures of her or any documents pertaining to her for like the last 5 years. It's as if she's just been scrubbed out of existence. If it wasn't for the social media accounts that Alibis set up for her, pinging her to the location, no one would even know it was her remains they found in the factory after the explosion. There wasn't enough for her husband to identify. Just some burned clothes with DNA traces. Not that he stuck around too long. Duke Fierro seems to have fled the country, what with all the unsafe and illegal practices at his factory now under scrutiny."

"Oh poor him. I gave Carmen a fake social media persona so she could spy on her cheating no good soon-to-be ex-husband who was trying to screw her out of alimony. That's all. I posted for her from times and places where she was not."

"Right. You gave her an alibi. And she used that alibi to

blow up his billion dollar factory. There could have been people inside."

"But no one else was killed or injured, were they?" I had never heard any reports of deaths from the factory explosion—other than Carmen herself—and I was curious whether anyone else had been injured; but I only asked this question from a damage-control standpoint. Roy looked stricken with a real sense of a happiness like maybe I was not the sociopath described in the report by Dr. Barrett. Although, since that would in turn hurt his case, I was concerned that Roy was so goddamned happy. I started to fear that I might have a dumb lawyer. That scared me. Also, I started to fear that I might have a freaking honest lawyer with a bit of integrity. That scared me even more.

"No. No one else was inside that factory. But there very well could have been."

"True. There very well could have been." I repeated and nodded along with Roy, trying hard to stifle a chuckle at the thought that he was interpreting this whole exchange as yet another moment of shared comradery between us.

"So, Roy, assuming the judge, and then the jury, actually believes this craziness," I passed a hand over the expert report like I was afraid to touch it, "what then? I just walk out of here a free woman? Go back to running my underground business like nothing happened?"

"Well, no." Roy grabbed the report back, and started leafing through, pointing to some paragraphs near the end that I hadn't yet gotten to.

"Dr. Barrett is recommending you enter a 90-day treatment program. A rehab facility."

"Rehab? Like for drug addicts?"

"Well, they'll be there, too. And you, if you agree to this."

"Oh for the love of—what am I going to do for 90 days trapped with a bunch of drug addicts?"

"You're going to work on yourself. Try to get a hold on this problem you have. Maybe Dr. Barrett's right, Thea.

Maybe this life of creating false identities, of living only through false social media accounts, maybe it's an actual addiction, and you need help."

I choked on my bitter jail coffee and stared at Roy, sizing him up carefully, before I treaded out, "Roy? Are you—are you starting to believe this nonsense? I waved my hand holding the coffee cup over Dr. Barrett's report and a bit splashed out. I was momentarily distracted by the watery brown stain that started over Dr. Barrett's educational history and moved quickly upward to her cell, fax, and twitter handle.

*Twitter? I really need to remember to follow Elizabeth Barrett on Twitter when I get out of here.*

"Thea!" Roy jostled me out of my daydream.

"Sorry." I blotted at the report with a balled-up napkin from the table before I realized that the napkin might have actually been there when I sat down. I got grossed out suddenly and threw the napkin on the ground. Roy pressed on his eyebrows like he was trying to push something back inside.

"Sorry," I said again. Unsure what I was apologizing for. "It's just that—Jesus, Roy, rehab? What would that mean? Nonstop therapy for 90 days?"

"Yeah, it would be some intensive therapy. It would probably *help* you, Thea. Figure out what to do *next.*"

Roy had a point. Even if I could beat these charges from the Fierro factory explosion, this trial was going to blow my business—and me—wide open. I wouldn't likely have a future helping people secretly hide their identities after a spectacular trial in which I wouldn't even be able to hide my *own* identity. Alibis would be toast. And what would be left for me? How would I even make a living after everything hit the fan?

*But, therapy?*

"Roy, I don't know about this. I tried therapy once. It was wonderful. For 59 minutes."

Roy just stared at me, so I kept going.

"Marta was her name. She was very bohemian. You know what I mean by that? Like the kind of woman who smokes pot medicinally." I borrowed Roy's air quotes for "medicinally."

"It was in high school and I was feeling a little lost. I saw a flyer outside the dean's office and I thought, what the hell? I told her about my father's dark drug history and my totally in denial mother. Marta clucked her tongue and shook her head and rolled her eyes at the exact right moments. I felt I had a friend in the room. We laughed and talked and she leaned in as she said, 'You don't have to have all the answers right now. It's ok. You realize that?' I was about to say, 'When can I see you again? When can we talk again?' I think I might even have been tempted to suggest coffee next time. 'Let's meet at the new café around the corner,' I might have offered, if she had not right then craned her neck uncomfortably to look at the clock hanging over the exit door. Then she tapped on her watch. 'Oops. It's time,' she said. 'That session was complimentary. But if you want to see me again,' she said, 'it will be $75 an hour. Here's a flyer to take home to your mother with more information.'"

I sat back in my chair and swirled the jail coffee atop Dr. Barrett's report with abandon, angered anew at the memory, and at Roy for making me remember it.

"Well, Thea, you're going to have to get over all of that." Roy said impatiently. "Dr. Barrett is being paid to testify, and Dr. Barrett was paid to come in and talk to you last week, too."

I thought back on my hour-long session with Elizabeth Barrett the week before Roy came in and delivered the report to me with its written observations and conclusions. She was dressed in dull, ill-fitting clothes with a drab mousy brown hairstyle. She looked like any other psychologist. She didn't stand out in any way. I had mentioned that to her, and she assured me that dullness was indeed a cultivated look and was what both the judge and the jury would be looking for.

I shook off Roy's words about Dr. Barrett being paid to listen to me, by remembering that Roy was *not* my friend. *He was being paid to listen to me, too.*

Sometimes I lost my focus. That was why I started Alibis. I actually thought it would help me sort through what was real and what was not. By the time I was sitting there with Roy, I was so damn tired of pinning my hopes on the possibility that people could actually be *real.*

"How about you, Roy? You just doing this all for the money, too?" I tried to keep my tone light and teasing, but staring at Roy and the coffee-stained expert report, I tried not to feel like a hooker's john. Even though it was just court-appointed wages, Roy was being paid to be there. Paid to listen to me. He wasn't a friend. He wasn't sympathetic or interested in having coffee sometime when this was all over. He was pretending.

*Just like me.*

"The defense calls Dr. Barrett to the stand for the *Daubert* hearing." Roy had remembered to actually tie his tie before coming into court for the hearing, I noticed with renewed gratitude.

Dr. Barrett headed from her seat at the table alongside me to the witness stand next to the same judge who had called me "young lady" months earlier. When Roy first mentioned this hearing to me, I had imagined the courtroom overflowing with interested spectators, but quickly realized what a complication that could be. Hell, maybe Audrey would even show up if the courtroom was open to voyeurs.

I raised that with Roy, and he said that Dr. Barrett had helped him prepare a motion to keep the hearing closed to the outside. The judge approved the motion the day before the hearing was scheduled.

As we entered and took our seats inside the courtroom, Roy explained that the hearing, which was called a "Daubert" hearing after some boring old lawsuit from the 1990s, blah, blah blah—was a preliminary something or other in which Dr. Barrett would be poked and prodded to see if she was really as clever or smart as she claimed to be.

"What exactly *is* a Daubert hearing?" I asked, only after much deliberation. It kills me to ever ask a question. I'd like to research and come up with the answer on my own rather than admit weakness, but unfortunately without access to wifi or internet, or even my freaking phone, it's a little hard these days to know all the answers. So I succumbed to the painful act of asking Roy a question—of admitting that he just might know more than I in this small little field called the law.

"It's where the court decides if her testimony will even be admissible at trial. The name comes from a seminal case called Daubert versus Merrell Dow Pharmaceuticals."

I debated whether or not to stop Roy or let him go on. Something told me, from the use of the ridiculous legal word "seminal," that Roy was gathering some self-righteous steam and that I might not have a chance to stop him very soon; so I could make a decision right then as to whether or not to let him go. I let him go. I simultaneously congratulated myself on my uncharacteristic patience.

"According to the Supreme Court's decision in Daubert, the judge is the gatekeeper for expert testimony. He gets to decide—if the other side objects—whether the jury will ever hear the expert testimony or not. And of course, the prosecution *has* objected here."

"What do you mean 'of course' they've objected?"

"Because Dr. Barrett's opinion is so unique. So novel."

I liked that. Novel. Unique. I imagined that the uniqueness of Dr. Barrett's testimony was a direct reflection on my own uniqueness—and I *loved* that. As someone who has strived every day not to be a cliché, another drunk's or addict's daughter or a drunk and addict herself, this was such a comforting thought—the thought that I might indeed be unique.

"Why does the judge get to decide whether Dr. Barrett's opinions make sense? Why not just let the jury decide?"

"Because they might be so incredibly swayed by the fact that she is a supposed 'expert' witness, they will believe anything she says. The court has to make sure that doesn't happen."

"You make this sound very official."

Roy looked at me like I had bitten the head off a mouse. "Thea, this is a trial in the Philadelphia Court of Common Pleas. This is about as official as it gets."

I shook my head, wondering how many times poor Roy had dreamed of this day. Representing a kid from the wrong side of town in a high profile case and summoning a rotund Dr. Barrett to the stand to talk about the very unique, very novel Thea Brown in the Philadelphia-Court-of-Common-Would-You-Please.

I let him go on.

"So. We will put her on the stand and let the other side try to poke holes in her credentials—which they cannot, and try to poke holes in her research—which they cannot, and try to poke holes in her conclusions."

I waited for the "which they cannot" after "her conclusions." It didn't come.

"What gives, Roy? What's wrong with her conclusions?"

"Well we are certainly going to take the position that nothing at all is wrong with them. That her 72-page detailed curriculum vitae filled with international conference abstracts and published articles, degrees, and letters after her name, allows her to reach the very interesting and very helpful conclusion that you are addicted."

"But addicted to what exactly?" While I have been thinking about whiskey more than usual behind these cell bars, I was not exactly comfortable with Roy's easy use of the word. Especially in connection with *me*.

"Addicted to social media. And creating false identities."

I shook my head like I had been doing every single time Roy got to this point.

"Addicted to social media. How is anyone going to take that seriously?"

*Maybe I'm just in denial—like any other addict?*

But no. At the hearing, I convinced myself otherwise as I listened to Roy and Dr. Barrett blather on and on largely uninterrupted about Daubert and novel scientific theories and pronged tests for evaluating expert opinions. The other side asked plenty of questions when it was their turn, but Dr. Barrett didn't look surprised or flustered by a single one.

I was feeling more and more confident as the hearing went on.

*I'm not like every other addict. I'm not a cliché. I'm special.*

*Dr. Barrett even says so.*

Two days after the Daubert hearing, Dr. Barrett and Roy both came to see me in jail. That seemed ominous, so I braced myself for bad news.

Roy didn't think it was bad news, but I was having trouble seeing it that way at first.

"Ninety days in rehab? And a hefty fine?"

"Yes, the judge has recommended the prosecution put an offer on the table. He's stalling on the decision on the Daubert hearing. He doesn't really know what to do, and he's not sure he wants to be the one to approve this fairly novel theory of Dr. Barrett's. But on the other hand, he looks like he's searching for an excuse not to put you on trial for blowing up the Fierro factory, just because Carmen Fierro isn't around to stand trial for the explosion herself." Next to Roy, Dr. Barrett looked all puffed up with excitement that she had even gotten us this far.

I sat staring at them both for a little while. I couldn't

believe that after all I had been through, my fate seemed to rest with these two characters.

Dr. Barrett broke my silence. "Basically, Thea, the judge agrees with us. He agrees that your addiction is as real as heroin, and that you need help—real help—not jail."

"Who's us?" I turned to Roy ignoring the good Dr. Barrett.

"What?"

"Who's *us*? Dr. Barrett said the judge agrees with *us*. Are you in on this little brokered deal, too, Roy? This is really going to put some money in Dr. Barrett's pocket isn't it? Some real credibility for her ridiculous theories. And I guess you're getting in on the action, too, right? I get how this works—I'm in business too, you'll recall. You need reviews. Positive feedback. No matter your business. I guess the judge sending me to rehab instead of jail kind of validates Dr. Barrett's preposterous theory here and you get to ride her enormous coattails all the way to the bank. Maybe you won't have to take court-ordered money for the next addict you represent? Maybe now you'll get some major celeb action with some real money? And get yourself some real suits next time?"

Truth was, I was feeling jealous that Roy was about to move on from representing me. I had to admit I'd been enjoying his company lately. Even Renata had forgotten about me, moving on, I'm sure to a new, well-needed job. I had put her name on the approved visitors list at the jail, but she never came. Only Roy did. And Dr. Barrett.

Roy kept on hemming and hawing and flubbing and flustering at my accusations about his opportunist motives, until I asked to be taken back to my cell.

In the end, neither Roy nor Dr. Barrett convinced me of anything. My mother did.

Because a few hours later, when the warden came to tell me that my mother had come to visit me at the jail, I told the warden to tell her she was *not* on the list, thanks for asking, and then I asked to call Roy.

I shouldn't have been surprised that my mother showed up. I had seen her inside the courtroom. She had been sitting in there when I walked in with the guard and Roy, and I acted like I didn't know her, and when the judge announced that the hearing was closed and visitors would have to leave, she didn't stand up and announce herself, or demand to stay. From the corner of my eye, I watched her leave, without turning my head.

So no, I wasn't surprised that she showed up at the prison trying to see me shortly after the hearing, but it did make me rethink the whole rehab idea after all.

When Roy showed up looking a little defeated the next day, I greeted him with, "So this rehab—it will be undisclosed to the public? They won't know where I am? For my safety, you know. I have a lot of angry clients right now."

"The whole arrangement will be strictly confidential. You'll be at a rehab facility 60 miles away—the best facility in the region, frankly. Dr. Barrett has arranged the whole thing. She's on the Board there. They are very experienced with confidentiality, et cetera." Roy pushed some papers across the table for me to sign.

I continued stalling. Maybe because I knew it was going to be the last time I'd see Roy for a while, and I was growing a little fond of him, in spite of myself.

"You collect anything, Roy?"

"Baseball cards, Kind of. I used to. You?"

"Nah. My mom, though. She collected something really weird. Those little bath soaps that you get in motel rooms? She'd have dozens of them at any given time all piled up in the closet of her bathroom. Sometimes I'd open that closet over and over again just to inhale the swoony smell of lemongrass and citrus and lavender coming out from the closet. Squares and circles and half moons of soaps spilling out of a basket in that closet. It was the weirdest thing—downright spooky if you must know."

"That's not such a weird collection. I'm sure lots of people those soaps. I have about five right now under my sink if you were to go to my house. Do I grab them off the housekeepers' cart as I leave any given hotel on the way out the door? I'll never tell."

Roy smirked a little—like we shared a secret. Which we did, of course. He just wasn't in on it.

"Ok, I'll do it." I signed the papers quickly before I could think too long about it. I knew my decision could have appeared too eager, but Roy didn't bother asking why the sudden change of heart. I wondered for a second if he knew my mother had tried to come here. Whether he had been speaking with my mother despite my requests not to speak to anyone about my case, and telling her far too much that was supposed to be strictly inside the attorney/client cloak of privileged communication. But no, he didn't even flinch when I mentioned my mother's collection of motel soaps. He was still clueless. I didn't want this thing to get any more out of my control than it already was.

If rehab was the necessary next step; if that's what Dr. Barrett was recommending, then so be it.

"I'm so glad you've come around, Thea." Roy's relieved breath wafted across the table, forcing me to lean back and wince.

"I haven't come around, Roy. I'm just looking out for myself. Same as you."

While Roy twisted his pen over the paperwork he'd brought me to sign, and then signed it himself, I thought about how when I was a kid, my mother seemed terribly permissive. My classmates would tease, "Your mom lets you do *anything*. You're so lucky." I'd watch how their moms would enforce bedtimes and safety rules. Bicycle helmets were a must. As were seatbelts, sugar-free snacks, and rounded corners. I could come home to the house on my own even at 10 years old, because my single mother was working. I had my own key, and there was always licorice in the kitchen cabinet and I could eat sugar cereal for dinner—

which was encouraged actually, because I wasn't allowed to turn the stove on while my mom was gone.

One rule—only one—*no stove.* I held tightly to that one rule. Cherishing it.

I had more freedom than anyone else I knew, but there was something uncomfortable about it even then. I couldn't quite put my finger on the source of the discomfort until I was older and understood better how my mother could have been acting ... should have been acting. Because I knew about my father and what he had been, it seemed incomprehensible to me that my mother wouldn't be more engaged in my life. Wouldn't try harder to make sure I didn't end up in the wrong crowd—smoking, or drinking, or using, or worse.

If I didn't know better, I might think she *wanted* me to end up like him.

As I signed my life away to the Philadelphia courts and Juniper Lane, I wondered as I had on so many occasions: *Why didn't she want more for me. For us. Why?*

"The mother/daughter relationship is so complicated," I said to no one, but Roy nodded as if it was to him.

*9 months earlier, October, 2016*

# Chapter 5

It was about a year before Audrey found herself in a losing race against a red pickup truck at the rural Pennsylvania gas station that she had started to realize: *Thea was in real trouble.*

Thea had dropped out of college the previous spring with only weeks left to graduate. She was starting a new business, and she hadn't been home to visit in almost 18 months, claiming her workload was simply too demanding, and she was acting, well odd, mostly.

Audrey had given up trying to talk to her second husband, Greg, about Thea. He seemed—at best—distracted. And at worst—not to care. Audrey had remarried when Thea was about 13, and Greg's daughter (and Audrey's step-daughter), Trudy, was a handful of precociousness. Juggling her back and forth between their home and Greg's ex-wife's home had become a full-time job that Greg seemed to think should take enough of Audrey's time that she wouldn't have to think about all of Thea's problems. Sometimes he seemed to think he was doing Audrey a favor—distracting her from a long history of bad decisions she would like to do over.

She had admitted that to him one night after too many glasses of wine. "So many bad decisions I'd like to take back." Which he had nodded and showed empathy for; but really when she mulled over the admission and thought about it later, she had essentially admitted to him that she wished *he* didn't have a place in her life. Greg must not have needed the same time to mull her words over, because he was pretty cold to her after that conversation.

Audrey believed that Thea knew on some visceral level what happened to her father. Well, that's what she told herself anyway.

*She knows. Of course she knows. She has to know.*

But then Audrey had to let that little green bloom of truth and self-awareness die on the branch each time she thought it. Because of course she had no idea what Thea knew. She only knew what she had told her. Which was that her father died. Many years ago. And that he loved her. Of course he did. How could he not? Even sight unseen. She had also said often that Thea was a precious gift in the face of such terrible loss and that Audrey had to get over it all very quickly. Was she negligent in not giving Thea more information? In not monitoring more closely how she felt about everything? Maybe. She was a single mother for a long time, into Thea's teens, and used that status to excuse a great many negligences over the years. Perhaps too many. Perhaps she had been in survival mode ever since she helped John fake his death.

John's drug dealer, Bruce, had showed up at the back door two weeks after Audrey brought Thea home from the hospital. Not long after the funeral.

She opened the door to him. She had been expecting him since John left. And she wanted that part to be over sooner rather than later.

"You Audrey?"

She nodded.

"Hmm. You're a little prettier than I expected. But fatter, too."

"You're looking for John, right?"

"You know I am little lady." He chuckled like he had just made a very funny joke.

"John's dead."

"Shit." He didn't make any move to leave the door.

"I will pay you whatever he owed you. I'm just hoping that you could leave us alone."

"Us? Who's us?" He looked over Audrey's shoulder. Thea started to cry as if on cue. "Oh, man. A kid, too? He really was a piece of shit, that husband of yours. Maybe I could help you out a bit? Babysit or something?" He reached across the space dividing he and Audrey and touched her hair.

"This is everything I have. $10,000. It's enough, right? It's enough to cover John's debt?" Audrey's accompanying shiver was understandable but involuntary.

"Why are you shivering? You sick or something?"

"I just had a baby. And John's gone."

"Hunh. You sure he's dead? Maybe he just ran out on you *and* me. Wouldn't that be a trip? You and me would sort of be on the same side then, wouldn't we?" More sinister chuckling.

"I had to identify his body myself. I work at the hospital where they brought him. I took pictures if you'd like to—" Audrey started to reach behind her for another envelope that wasn't full of money.

"Oh lady—come on. That's sick. I don't want to see no pictures of a dead body. Put those away."

"Ok—I just ... I really just want this whole thing to be over. I have a baby now to think about."

"What whole thing? Never mind. That baby's got some good lungs on it, don't it?"

Thea kept crying, and without thinking, Audrey turned to comfort her, using her name.

"Thea, Thea, it's ok."

"Thea? Weird name." The drug dealer glanced past Audrey at the still crying baby.

"Thea. Thea. Thea later." The slimey dealer waved and faked a lisp at Audrey's baby over her shoulder. "Listen, I'll be back to check on you and that baby of yours. You seem like you could use a little checking in on." And with that, he let the back door slam a divide between them, with him on the outside of the door and his final threat lingering inside the door with Audrey.

Audrey took one last hard look around the sagging rental home she'd shared with John for the last five years. Five long years of alienating what little family she had by standing by her drug addict boyfriend and then husband. Audrey's parents had died in a tragic car accident when Audrey was a teenager, and she'd been raised by an aunt and uncle with what they had reminded her always was a very meager life insurance policy. "Hardly enough to feed you, Audrey, not that we mind, of course," they'd say any time she was listening. Which wasn't often.

Audrey had managed a scholarship to the local college where she met and fell in love with John. There were signs, even then of course, that his drinking and partying signaled a deeper problem; but Audrey had ignored them by enthusiastically agreeing to John's marriage proposal shortly after graduation, anxious to start her own family, anxious for a chance to re-create the childhood she never really had.

Audrey had worked parttime typing medical records to put herself through medical school. She had gotten her first job as a pathologist at the local hospital about a year ago, shortly before she found out she was pregnant. John was high the day she told him. She knew that. But still, she'd been hopeful. Hopeful that the baby would save him, and so she had been squirreling away extra pennies, dreaming of the day when she and John would officially begin their own family.

Now most of that money had been withdrawn to pay John's drug dealer. And their family was down to only two.

With John's bill paid, and John pronounced dead, Audrey

suspected Bruce would lose interest in them. But she wasn't going to wait around to figure out how long that would take. As soon as Bruce pulled away with most of her last dollars, Audrey closed the door of her dilapidated house, grabbed her already packed suitcase, and left the house, turning the lock as she pulled it shut behind her.

Thea and Audrey headed due west and didn't stop driving until they hit Ohio, stopping there for no reason other than that Audrey was tired. She rented a cheap apartment and started applying for pathologist jobs.

She thought only briefly about changing their names. Maybe she was hoping John would find them some day after all, despite her order that he leave them alone. Or maybe she just felt badly making it impossible for him to do so. No matter the reason.

They stayed Audrey and Thea.

It took some time after the move to Ohio, but Audrey found work as a pathologist at a local hospital. With a baby and no family interested enough to move out to Ohio to help her, she was constrained to part-time schedules, and saddled with debt from years of living with a drug addict. Audrey and Thea struggled financially until Greg came along—a fellow doctor—but a more highly paid one than Audrey.

Greg was a surgeon with a generous salary. He also came with a toddler daughter of his own named Trudy who needed full-time care, since her biological mother was distracted trying to find herself a new doctor husband—an endeavor she seemed to sink her teeth into as zealously as a full-time job.

When they were first married, Audrey used to seek advice from Greg. She'd ask him over and over again if he thought she should tell Thea more. She had opened up to him. She had confided in him. One more of those decisions she was now starting to regret in hindsight. But she had loved him. Didn't she? And she was marrying him, wasn't she?

"Do you think it's wrong that you know more about Thea's dad than she does?" Audrey asked Greg one day shortly before they got married.

"Of course not," he replied. Greg said that he believed a husband and wife should have no secrets from each other. That was what made Greg and Audrey's marriage different—better—than the one Audrey had had before him. And the one he had had before her. And Audrey decided to believe Greg when he said that. Another one of those misguided decisions in hindsight.

Audrey's prior marriage became something barely spoken of—barely acknowledged—as if Thea was just dropped on this planet from two people who had nothing to do with Audrey or Greg. Audrey had never kept pictures of John around the apartments she lived in with Thea before Greg came along. It was too painful for Audrey to look at photographs of John and know she was keeping so much from Thea. So with Greg in the picture, it was even easier to forget Thea had another father. Or that Audrey had once had another life. Greg even adopted Thea—changing her last name to Brown—which he seemed to think was very noble of him—very altruistic at the time.

He came home one day, and said, "I want to adopt Thea properly."

Audrey started to say, "But, Greg." He kept looking at her furtively, like he was testing her. To see what she would say. So Audrey agreed on the spot to the adoption even though it wouldn't be legal. Pretending John was dead had become such a way of life by then that she could even take his daughter away from him and give her to another dad.

Still, it stung Audrey a bit that Greg knew and went through with the whole thing, too. All day at the courthouse,

Thea didn't look excited or gleeful; she looked at the door expectantly like John might just come bursting in through that door and stop the whole thing. Audrey watched her the whole time thinking this until she realized how ridiculous she was being. Thea didn't know what John looked like; she didn't know he might still be alive. She couldn't really be looking at the door for him.

When the judge called them all into her chambers, she made a big fuss over Thea and made a fuss over Greg, Audrey, and even Trudy.

"What a wonderful day for your family! What a special joy adoptions bring to my job. My very favorite. Helps me forget about some of the seedier aspects of my job," the judge said as Audrey focused on the shock of pink that stuck out of her black robe from a shiny silk top that lay underneath. Audrey thought about how *you would never know.* You would never know what people hid underneath their black robes, if sometimes a little shock of pink silk didn't make its way out like that one did, gradually throughout the ceremony, like it was demanding to be seen. All the while Audrey watched Thea look toward the door until she realized the sad fact that Thea wouldn't be looking for John at the door. It was *Audrey* who was looking toward the door and it was Thea who in turn kept looking to see what it was Audrey was looking for. When she realized that, Audrey made a conscious decision not to look away from the judge any longer, pulling discipline over her own want and desire that was bubbling up to the surface as well—like a shock of pink silk—the want and desire for John to come and save them.

"Thea is worrying me."

It was a breezy fall day in 2016 when Audrey found herself talking out loud to the only person who still seemed to be listening.

Her 10-year-old stepdaughter, Trudy, walked closely alongside the cart with Audrey in the supermarket, pulling items with high fructose corn syrup off the shelves while Audrey walked behind her unconsciously replacing them. It was a game they played. Trudy's mother let her eat junk food wrapped in lard, and when Trudy came home every few days, Greg and Audrey tried to help her detox. She was a willing participant, but still she tried to sneak some Oreos into the cart each week.

Audrey continued talking for little reason other than to hear her own voice. "She's dodging my calls—in and of itself not an entirely unusual occurrence, but you know what? It's becoming somewhat of a comedy. I call her. The phone immediately goes to voicemail. And then 2-3 minutes later, a quick text: you rang? What's up?

"I can barely remember the sound of my own daughter's voice. It's been literally months since I've heard it." Trudy looked up at Audrey from cartside, startled, and said, "You've heard my voice, Mom Audrey—oh, you mean Thea." Audrey realized Trudy had all but forgotten Thea existed. Since Thea left for college, she came home infrequently—and since Thea dropped out rather suddenly in 2015, she stopped coming home at all.

Audrey heard a ping on her phone just as she was thinking of how to apologize or cover up her faux pas with Trudy. She looked down and saw a familiar message. "Super busy today, what's up?"

Audrey had tried ringing Thea about four hours earlier. There was some relief thinking that maybe, just maybe today, Thea really *wasn't* available when she called. That she wasn't holding that phone that was her extra appendage and rolling her eyes grandly as she hit decline on its broad and shiny face.

Audrey didn't stop what she was doing to respond to Thea's half-hearted belated text because Trudy had embarked on a long story about a tragedy that occurred in school that day—something about a lost math folder and Swedish fish. There was something melodic and hypnotic about Trudy's stories when she was not driving Audrey to distraction. Audrey had tried explaining to Greg just the day before that she loved the sound of Trudy's voice until she didn't. He looked at Audrey with a familiarly empty smile that made Audrey long for attention. Sometimes she had to admit, she even missed the hyper-attention she got from John back in the day. There were times she missed the complete dependence he had on her. The way he often needed Audrey's around-the-clock care for days or weeks on end. The way she had to in turn be hypervigilant and on alert over John's whereabouts. The way she had to move money around or know at all times where her purse was or her money or bank receipts because she didn't want John to know where their latest bank account was located.

Sometimes she found things a little boring with Greg.

Even in those years with Thea as a young girl, there was excitement in Audrey's life. Granted, it didn't look like excitement back then. She wouldn't have called it that. She called it hard and shattering and demoralizing and hell. She called it a lot of things. She didn't call it excitement.

But it was. They had a fresh start—John wasn't in their lives but there was a constant belief on Audrey's part that he would show up. That he'd be clean. That he'd come back. That they'd live as a family again.

Audrey actually believed that for a long time.

Until she didn't.

Which was why she married Greg. Which in hindsight didn't seem like such a hot idea after all.

"Greg is really, really good-looking. And practical."

That's how Audrey described him to friends and co-workers when she met Greg around the time Thea was 13.

Even though people were looking for more poetic descriptions, more gushing talk, that was always all she could muster. He was a doctor in the hospital where she worked. When they met, he was 40 years old and recently divorced with a young baby. Audrey loved how adamant he was that he stay in his young baby's life. He wanted shared custody and he wanted to have Trudy for part of every week. Audrey didn't ask him how that was even possible with a surgeon's schedule. Her own schedule was fairly regular and as Greg starting asking her to do more and more of the caregiving, she took it on as a badge of honor. She didn't question that Greg seemed to want his daughter on the weeks when his call schedule was particularly busy so that on his off weeks, he'd have more time to himself. She didn't question whether his insistence on shared custody wasn't really about not wanting to pay child support rather than wanting to be in his child's life. She didn't think about any of those things until much later. Until she found herself marching up and down grocery store aisles with Trudy every few days, and spending more and more time with Trudy, and less and less time with Thea, who was simultaneously beginning to look like a sullen teenager, and not all that pleasant to be around anyway.

Audrey eventually had to accept that she had chosen a man because she believed he was the father she always wanted for her daughter—a belief fostered because of the father he apparently wanted to be to his own daughter. She also had to accept that all of her original premises had been flawed.

But still, how much would she have done differently? When Greg came along, Audrey had been on her own for 13 years. She was tired of being stoic and fierce and setting a good example for Thea. Trudy was lovely, and Audrey embraced stepmothering with all the zeal she thought appropriate. Thea didn't exactly take to Trudy very enthusiastically, but they had a cordial enough relationship until Thea left for school when she was 18. College was a destiny Thea started talking about almost immediately after Audrey and Greg got married and bought a new home in an affluent area of Ohio, where Audrey assumed she'd be applying to schools.

But then Thea turned 16, and started bringing home applications to schools mostly in Pennsylvania.

*Allman College?* Audrey asked with something akin to panic, when Thea revealed her absolute first choice college at a birthday dinner for Audrey. A few mom friends were gathered at a kid-friendly restaurant with their charges and were preening over Thea like she was an exotic gamebird. They all had toddlers and preschoolers—Audrey was in their circle via Trudy by proxy—and they thought it very exciting that Audrey had a daughter who was applying to *college.*

Allman College was a liberal arts school not five miles from the hospital where Audrey had given birth to Thea. Thea knew exactly where she was born because she had seen her birth certificate on many occasions—mostly in the context of Audrey trying to register her for various recreational sports over the years while trying to prove that Thea wasn't really a nine-year-old trying to gain an advantage by playing on the eight year old soccer team. Thea was spry and long legged, and while others brought their birth certificates to these things as a perfunctory exercise, Thea's was always scrutinized and read aloud.

*Cross County, Pennsylvania, hunh?*

Once Audrey caught a soccer coach scratching at the seal—for what reason she couldn't imagine—other than to check if it was real—and she grabbed it back from him with a "Hey! You can't deface her original birth certificate!" That particularly zealous coach had smirked and asked Audrey to coffee which she was tempted to take him up on and pour right in his overblown lap. But she didn't—pour the coffee in his lap or even accept the offer.

But by that time, Thea had seen her birth certificate so

often, she stopped squealing so much every time someone read its seal out loud as she had the first few times it happened.

*Pennsylvania—was I really born there?*

"Yes."

*Was it near Philadelphia?*

"Sort of."

*Was I born near the Liberty Bell?*

"Not exactly—more like Amish Country."

*What's Amish country?*

"It's quieter there than in the city. There's a large Amish population. A group who lives much more simply than we do. They don't drive cars or even have electricity."

*Are we Amish?*

Around the time that Thea stopped asking the same old questions, Audrey realized that their neighbors were now asking them for her, and Audrey also realized that Thea was always going to be looked upon a little skeptically in this provincial Ohio town while she was still being raised by one of the only single mothers in school—a transplant from a town they hadn't heard of in a state that wasn't theirs.

So even though Audrey had previously rejected dating prospects when she arrived in Ohio, she started actively campaigning for a new husband when Thea was about 10 or 11 years old. She started letting people fix her up. She tried hard not to visibly wince when someone had a cousin "who would be so awesome for you!" She said yes to coffee dates, but not with the rude soccer coaches.

She stopped waiting for John to come find them.

Eventually Greg came on the scene.

And by the time Audrey and Greg got married, Thea was no longer asking about Pennsylvania, she was telling.

*I'm going to go back to Pennsylvania to go to college. Where I'm from.*

And really, Thea's knowledge about Pennsylvania was so laughable, it seemed to have developed a kind of mythological lore as she moved about those early teen years that were made increasingly more difficult by hormones, blended families, and a new stepsister.

Audrey shouldn't have been so surprised when Thea announced to Audrey and Greg one night that she would be applying to college exclusively in Pennsylvania—"Getting back to my roots"—but still, Audrey *was* surprised, and even more flustered, when Thea said, "Mom, why don't you take me back to Pennsylvania and give me a tour when we go look at colleges—show me where we lived, you know, before Greg." Thea had looked over at him quickly then, with a disingenuous: "No offense."

Greg didn't answer Thea, but just looked at Audrey over his glass of water, waiting to see what she'd say, seemingly willing her to quash all this "before-Greg" talk with only his eyes.

"Thea, you know we only lived there briefly—we left when you were only weeks old. It's hardly where you're from."

She quickly changed the subject to ask Greg about some new hospital e-record system that was creating chaos in both of their schedules, and shushed Thea about the Pennsylvania college tour until later that evening when she knocked on her door and interrupted Thea's late night conversation with a friend. They were supposedly "finishing up their homework together" but the overheard laughter that trickled through her door seemed more to do with a boy in science class than any actual schoolwork.

Audrey whispered to Thea to get off the phone so they could chat. As she sat next to her on the bed where Thea was still curled up from her ended phone call, Audrey rubbed Thea's shoulders and stroked her dark hair, happy that Thea let her. They had done this on many nights when it was just Thea and Audrey, but Greg and Trudy's introduction into their lives left less and less time for Audrey/Thea time as the years went by.

"You understand why I have to go back to where I'm from, right, Mom?"

Audrey didn't answer. Audrey was always trying in vain to disavow Thea of that notion that she was from some other place. Some far away place. "You are from me, Thea," Audrey had always told her whenever she'd ask, "Where are we from, Mom?" But she would feel the same guilt always as she stroked Thea's long thick, dark hair. There could be no doubt where that head of hair came from.

Audrey would think sometimes about the John Doe on the gurney instead of her own John—confused in her brain sometimes about what had really happened—worried for a moment that her John—that *their* John *had really died.*

Then, when she'd remember what actually happened, she'd often wonder—had he died by now?

Had he succumbed to the disease that was killing him when last she saw him?

But of course, if her brain went there—if it tried to erase her guilt for all that had come next, she couldn't let it. She'd think instead: *I'd know. I'd feel it—if something ever happened to him, I'd know.*

*Our John must still be alive.*

While Greg was in the shower washing the hospital off after work one lonely night when Trudy was at her mother's, Audrey walked in and opened the shower curtain to talk to him.

"I'm worried sick about Thea."

Greg didn't flinch or stop washing his torso. "What else is new?" he sputtered out of the soapy stream.

"Greg. This isn't the usual worried about Thea thing. This is months without hearing my daughter's voice. Something is wrong with her."

"Don't exaggerate, Audrey. You talk to her all the time."

"No. I don't, Greg. She texts. She returns my voicemails with emojis and snaps. She doesn't pick up the phone anymore and just say, 'Hey Mom, it's me. How are you?'"

"I'm sure there's nothing to be worried about. Thea is Thea. She has her own agenda. She's selfish, you know that. And you have to stop letting her have all this control over you. She's a grown woman for heaven's sake, and a business owner. She's not going to just come home for your homemade cherry cobbler every other weekend, you know." Greg turned off the shower, and Audrey missed the hot steam in her face instantly.

The transition to cold made her shiver and Audrey sat on the toilet with her arms wrapped around herself and watched Greg towel off while trying not to cry.

For a fleeting moment, Audrey wondered when married life transitioned for Greg and she such that having a conversation in the bathroom while one partner was showering and then naked was not so much a turn-on, but rather an annoyance.

*When did we cross over that line from newlywed bliss to this state of "this could really end any day now?"* She wondered from her perch on the toilet.

It had been nearly a decade of marriage by that point, so really it could have happened at various landmarks along the way; but still, she was distracted by the realization that she missed the transition, one that her marriage to John didn't last long enough to make. The distraction was only temporary until she began her refrain anew.

"I just have such a bad feeling these days. About Thea."

"Nothing's new," Greg reminded Audrey. "She's been MIA ever since she first left for college."

"I don't know, Greg. I can't explain what's come over me all of a sudden." Greg was right in a way. The truth was, Thea had been distant ever since she left Ohio for her former birthplace in rural Pennsylvania to attend the same college that Audrey had. The same college campus where Audrey and John had in fact, met. Audrey never bothered explaining that to Thea—it seemed too sad, too pessimistic.

From the moment that acceptance letter came, Thea was so excited at the thought of returning "home," as she kept saying. Audrey knew there was a part of Thea that was rebelling from the family that Greg and she had created there in Ohio. Thea liked her stepsister, Trudy, but she couldn't help competing with her. Audrey knew Thea was anxious to leave, and she knew that much of what Thea was feeling was completely normal. Yet, Thea's obsession with Audrey's old alma mater was both endearing and also concerning. After all, if she was headed back and retracing Audrey's old steps, what else would Thea find?

And it bothered Audrey that she was leaving Thea completely ill-equipped for whatever it was she might find there. As Thea headed off to Allman College, Audrey thought briefly about telling her the whole truth about John, but it seemed a futile and dangerous time to tell it. Audrey didn't know what had become of John. He had never come looking for them, even though she hadn't really made it that hard to find them, and she certainly didn't want Thea going on a wild goose chase to try to find John while hundreds of miles away from Audrey. Audrey put any thoughts about confessions out of her mind as Thea embarked on her new adventure, leaving Audrey behind, still with hands full, what with Greg *and* Trudy.

At first, it seemed a renewed point of connection between Audrey and Thea, as Thea returned to Pennsylvania—the place Audrey and John had lived and met, in fact setting into motion Thea's whole existence. But, as the years marched on, Thea's departure had become a true exodus. She made her gradual exit from Audrey's life—apart from requests for money—which waned over the years as she became more and more independent, and eventually started her own business, (dropping out of college suddenly and with only a few months left before graduation).

Honestly, Audrey wanted to talk Thea out of dropping out; but then again, Thea had her reasons, and Greg just said—'Let her go—she's saving us a whole month of college tuition—and she's got a good head on her shoulders', which was a rare compliment from Greg about Thea. So Audrey tried to embrace it; she tried to hold onto it.

But now Audrey sat on the toilet and protested, "She hasn't even been home for a holiday in over a year. It doesn't seem like her. Doesn't seem like something my Thea would do."

Greg towel-dried his hair and then removed the towel just long enough to look at Audrey and shake his head, like he was dealing with a petulant, naïve child. Audrey knew what his expression was saying—because by that point, it seemed like *exactly* the kind of thing her Thea would do. Since she left for Pennsylvania, it was as if she couldn't really get far enough away. From Greg, Trudy, *and Audrey.*

The next day, Audrey dropped off Trudy at school, and went to the hospital before escaping her dark office and her distracting thoughts about Thea to head to a committee luncheon convened to talk about some allegedly pressing issues at Trudy's school. The conversation buzzed around Audrey, but since they were not saying anything new, she quickly left the conversation in her mind.

Trouble was—with these women—it was always the same. Always. The. Same. The salads they chose and the topics they covered. Husbands and children and the perils and exhaustion of having either one.

"Audrey, you look fabulous," Liz lied just before she started the lunchtime rituals. "My husband has now announced he wants sex every Wednesday. Can you believe this man?" Liz lamented above seared tuna over greens, which she had ordered as usual: "Rare, please. I want the tuna still swimming when you bring it to me." The women laughed every time like it was the cutest and funniest thing they'd ever heard.

"I scheduled a meeting with the new third-grade teacher to discuss why she refuses to teach cursive in class anymore," Marie scowled over cobb salad. "But hold the egg and bacon, please!" She had exclaimed familiarly when she had ordered.

"Marie, you do realize that's not really a cobb salad anymore," Audrey reminded her every time with the same wink.

Audrey stole glances down at her phone until she saw Thea's name pop up in a bubble next to her bright face in a photo taken at Mirage Lake—a place Audrey and Thea used to go to kayak on long weekends together when it was just the two of them. Before Greg.

Audrey winced at the image of Thea rather than the text itself, as that sweet young girl of all of about 11 was ....

Gone.

No more sweet girl, her texts were just heavy with sarcasm and disappointment.

*Not this weekend, Mother. I have an actual job.*

It occurred to Audrey as she read it, that there were a thousand other ways to give this response and none of them would hurt as much as Thea's chosen one.

Audrey typed short answers knowing that she was not hiding her texting from anyone and yet hoping no one was thinking she was all that rude.

The phones were common guests at these luncheons.

*Ok. Next wkend?*

*Oct 4?*

*Before Thanksgiving, please?*

Each one was met with an "N."

Not even a No. She was too busy even to turn Audrey down with a full word.

Audrey watched a long scroll of Ns next to the icon of her sweet Thea with the dark brown ponytail. The picture was such an old one, but still one of her favorites. Taken on the lake while she was in the kayak next to Audrey pointing to an osprey nest they thought had been destroyed in a recent storm. Audrey just so happened to have her camera out at the exact right moment—the moment Thea both saw that the nest had survived and decided that Audrey was the one she wanted to tell. Thea's mouth and her eyes were both smiling and her face was flushed. Her ponytail could only contain about half of her thick hair—the rest swirled around her head in a dark halo. Audrey had hit click at the exact right moment.

Of course the osprey discovery picture had no relation to Audrey's actual Thea these days. Her moments of carefree had always been few and far between. But now they were almost nonexistent. Still the picture served to distract Audrey during the lunch. Which was something she was craving more and more lately.

"Audrey!"

She jumped in her seat and moved her eyes back to the lunch table volley of complaints when she heard her name.

"Stop texting and give Marie some advice."

"What? Oh—I—Sorry—it's Thea." Audrey nodded down to her phone and the women ignored her in their customary way. "What were you saying, Marie?"

"Jesus, Audrey. You're in another world. I was saying I could kill Justin for making me take his mother to all of her doctor appointments this week. Seriously, he's dead. I could just kill him."

And suddenly even the ponytailed picture of Thea couldn't distract her.

Such a simple thing to say.

*I could kill him.*

Marie didn't mean it of course. But it stopped Audrey in her tracks anyway.

Because she could. And she did.

And everything she had been doing since, was really just a farce, including keeping the truth from Thea.

# Chapter 6

*Tell me the story you want me to know.*

I had said that to Nia Hamilton in October 2016 only a few months before my arrest, just like I said it to so many clients before and after.

*Nia is a black ballerina.*

This is what I told myself as she compressed her long slender limbs into my newest IKEA acquisition in the shape of a chair. It was Renata who convinced me to buy yet another chair for the office. "Miss Thea. No one wants to watch you fall from the front of your desk. And one of these days you will fall." And so I had shrugged and bought the chair that Nia the beautiful black ballerina was now sitting in.

You would think I'd have learned not to make assessments and judgments based on my first impressions and yet I subconsciously told myself in the moment between Nia standing and Nia sitting, that her assumed occupation as a black prima ballerina defied both stereotypes and political correctness, even though in fact it did neither.

As it turns out, this Nia Hamilton was an organic farmer. She sold lavender and herbs at the local market aside the Amish produce vendors in rural Pennsylvania. This is the story she wanted me to know. Although it took us some time to get there because she was preoccupied with the paperweight on my desk, picking it up and rolling it around in her hands and dropping it clumsily but still unapologetically several times before abandoning it to the opposite corner of the desk.

The clumsiness and indeed the lack of apology made me question my assessment of Nia as a ballerina even before she confessed about the lavender in the Amish markets. And I was not as shocked by my inaccurate assessment of her as you might think, because by the time we got there, she had already told me about the murder.

"My mother was shot by her lover when I was seventeen."

"I'm terribly sorry." I was aware before I said them that my words were dumb, but silence seemed worse and I realized I'd have to move quickly to fit in appropriate responses between her bursts of information delivery.

She spoke quickly with the tone of someone who had told the story of her mother often and easily. Of someone who didn't mind showing me that I wasn't special for hearing it. "My brother recently found and killed that lover, so he is being accused of murder in a trial that is expected to last for weeks. At the least. We have a very good lawyer."

I must have made a face that betrayed me as she chided me with an expression that said: *Shit, you, too?*

"We are not some welfare family. I hope that's not what you assumed? I have money. Lots of it. And it has been legally obtained." Her longer than expected reply gave me time to put my composure back on.

"Miss Hamilton, I make no assumptions ever. That is on my business mission statement." I pointed to the empty wall behind her and when she craned her neck to see, I refrained from giddily chanting, "Made you look!"

There was as good a chance of me hanging a mission statement on the wall as there was of me writing one. Nia's expression softened. "Ah. It's just that sitting there day after day in the courtroom with the prosecution painting my brother like some street kid stereotype is wearing me down. I wouldn't have fallen for that mission statement trick a year ago." I felt an apology trying to come out of me, but I suppressed it. I didn't want to make her feel bad ... but vulnerable? That was good business.

I sat quietly nodding, refraining from asking her what in the hell she was doing here. Surely, she knew I couldn't help her murderous brother jump bail with a catfish Facebook profile no matter how sympathetic a case she was trying and failing to paint.

The silence dragged on so long it became boring. I was just about to turn her down when she said, "I need to get away. I can't sit there for weeks on end and watch them vilify my brother. It's making me a bit stir crazy."

"Well surely you are free to go? Are you being charged in some way? As an accomplice?" She shook her head with frustration, before barking her response, "I know I'm technically free to go, of course, but how can I leave for a vacation with my brother sitting in jail for what he did? For protecting my mother?"

There was a pause, then. A dipping the toe in the cold water pause; a sip of the hot coffee pause; a moment swelling with caution and curiosity (would it burn or sting?) until I went in.

"Protect your mother," I said rather than asked, hoping to set a tone of trust rather than mistrust. Perhaps I would take this case after all. "Your mother is still alive?"

"Her boyfriend—he only thought he killed her. He left her for dead on the side of the road and my brother saved her life just before she disappeared. She abandoned us, leaving my brother to raise me on his own. My brother has been searching for both my mother and the monster that nearly killed her for over a decade. He found *him* first.

"My mother never so much as filed a police report against her old boyfriend—she just left. Left us all to clean up the mess. And now Jacob's defense is trying to argue self-defense—that when he ran into my mother's old lover, he was afraid for his life. Because of what he had done, and what Jacob knew.

"But the prosecution is arguing that there is no evidence of any such crime against my mother. That my brother is just using that story as an excuse—to cover up his bad behavior. As if Jacob is a common thug.

"We need my mother's testimony, you see. To help Jacob. But she's not here."

"Do you know where she is?"

Nia shook her head slowly.

I proceeded cautiously. "She's hiding even from you?"

She nodded.

"You understand I'm not a private investigator? I can't *find* your mother."

"If I wanted to find my mother, I would hire a private investigator."

"Fair. So why are you here instead?"

"I want you to create sightings of my mother. I want you to send the prosecution on a wild goose chase."

"But from what you're telling me, the prosecution isn't too interested in finding your mother. They are only interested in convicting your brother, no?"

"That's true. But Jacob's lawyer has said that if the prosecution had any evidence of my mother's whereabouts, and any evidence that she was in fact attacked by her crazy ex-lover, they'd have to turn that over to us. It's a rule, apparently."

"And you believe the prosecution is playing by the rules?"

"I'd like to believe that. I'd also like to find out."

"Where do you actually believe your mother is?"

"I have no idea. She fled long ago. Probably to her family's home in Dominica. We were born there—Jacob and I—and another sister."

"Ah, where all those pirate movies were filmed." I smiled, hoping for a point of recognition, but she grunted at me in disgust.

"Is that all you know of Dominica? Pirate movies and

Johnny Depp and stashed rum?"

I shook my head too quickly with embarrassment. "No. I've heard good things about that island. It's very eco-friendly, isn't it? Lots of volcanos and geo-thermal energy, and, I don't know—I paid only about half-attention in my high school geography classes. Cut me some slack, would you?"

Nia got a dreamy expression as she started describing her homeland to me.

"Dominica is a small island in the Caribbean. My childhood was full—hours of playing in lush green jungles, inside the bamboo and banana trees. We lived near a place—in English you would translate it to Tranquil Waters—small waterfalls fed into shallow warm water pools that served as our bathtubs. We'd scrub clean in nature's waters, washing off long days of play and hard work. My brother and sister and I. From the moment we could walk and reach the bananas, we worked on our grandfather's banana plantation alongside our parents. Those were beautiful times. Our farm, like most of the banana farms in Dominica, was a family-owned farm and a source of pride to the generations in my family who had been planting and growing and harvesting. Some years were hard, I remember those, too. We had hurricanes and then long dry seasons that threatened our yield. But we weathered many, many storms, figuratively and literally, in that beautiful place.

"And then the U.S. markets stopped buying our bananas. It was so much cheaper—I would learn later when I grew up—to buy bananas from Latin America where the farmers were paid nothing. Those Latin American farmers were barely kept alive on the wages they made just so corporate-owned farms could eat up our market share. Our bananas were too expensive and too rare for the new markets. Our way of living dried up quickly. It killed my father quite literally, and my mother came to the U.S. with her children to start a new life. Only, there wasn't too much work for a middle-aged ex-banana farmer from Dominica."

Nia drifted off at the memory of her early struggles, and I waited for what seemed an appropriate length of time before asking, "So you think your mother went back to Dominica? To start over yet again?"

"Put it this way, Miss Brown. I'm asking for sightings—but I do not, under any circumstances, want you to actually find my mother."

"I understand," I nodded. "You're still trying to protect her."

Nia shook her head violently. "No." She looked me dead in the eye and said, "Frankly I don't care where she is. She can rot for leaving Jacob and me alone to sort out this mess. I want the prosecution to believe Jacob's story—believe she is in hiding and that she was nearly killed by that monster. But I do not want to find her. Here are some suggestions for some sightings." Nia handed me a folder with some photos and basic information typed out.

"Create an account for her, but don't truly look for her. If you find her, I'm afraid I might kill her myself for all she's put us through since she left." I nodded as I leafed through the pages in the folder. Nia interrupted by taking my hand and thrusting a card and a pile of $100 bills into it, seeming to believe that the mere act could create some kind of binding contract between the two of us.

She wasn't wrong. I glanced at the card. "The Amish produce market on route 212?"

"Yes, the organic lavender farm," she said as she stood up and shut the door on me and the story she had locked inside with me.

The police had arrived very dramatically. None of this, "We only have a few questions, ma'am," like I'd seen in movies. Instead there had been a full-on recital of my rights (so that is *not* only for TV, hunh?) and then I had said, "Of course I need a lawyer, I don't even know what you guys are talking about," and I had barked some orders to Renata to "get my lawyer on the phone," but of course, since I didn't have a "my lawyer" I ended up with "this Roy," instead.

I went willingly with the police—I mean as willingly as you can go when two burly men and one even fiercer looking woman are "helping" you into a patrol car parked outside your place of business. Which is top secret and confidential and good paying clients will stop paying you if they find out the police actually know where your office is.

"I guess I always knew this was a possibility."

Roy nodded, causing me to believe he just might be done listening to me at that point. I was wrong about never seeing him again after I signed his court paperwork. He showed up one last time to see me off to Juniper Lane. We had a cup of muddy coffee together and I spent the time blabbering, grateful for real live company, even if it was only Roy.

"Then again, I don't try to sort through my clients' stories for truth. That's never been in my business plan and I'm not about to start now. It doesn't matter what my clients believe or what they want me to believe. It's only important that I help make possible what they want others to believe. That's how I make a living.

"Or rather how I make money. How I make a living is by living with what I do for money." I laughed at my own observation. Roy looked at me. Clueless.

I expected him to use that cue to pull out a bill, but he didn't. I wondered if my mother was footing his bill, and thought about the burden that would be on her. On so many levels. I swatted away the guilt that was trying to land on my shoulders. What helped alleviate that guilt was thinking about my mother in the courtroom before the Daubert hearing, watching from the sidelines and then leaving and letting the court do with me what it wanted. Permissive as always. Allowing my fate to be sealed by Dr. Barrett. Allowing her to say the very things I'd always wanted to be more than. These very specific things about addiction, and recovery, and Juniper Lane.

As I prepared to change my residence for the next 90 days to Thea Brown, c/o Juniper Lane, I conceded, "Well, I guess, everything up until now made this fate pretty much a no-brainer, hunh, Roy?"

Roy nodded, drained his Styrofoam coffee cup and stood up, hand outreached.

"I wish you all the best, Thea. This is a good result. Make the most of your time in Juniper Lane."

"A good result. Ok, then. Have a good life, Roy." But for kicks I didn't bother shaking his hand so he had to stand there awkwardly for a few moments with his hand out until he shook his head with frustration, turned and walked out, taking his bad tie and kitty litter smell right out the door along with him.

I got a ride to Juniper Lane from a state trooper. Roy told me that I am not a convict, but I had a hard time believing that as I looked around at the bullet proof glass and doors that wouldn't open from the inside.

I tried to accept this as a genuinely kind gesture on the part of the Pennsylvania taxpayers, as I lay my head back on the uncomfortable and sticky leather seat and dozed on the trip west from Philadelphia into rural Pennsylvania. There was a familiarity to the manure-scented air that wafted in through the musty car vents that woke me from my nap just as we entered the county where the posh rehab was located.

I stayed awake then and watched out the window the rest of the way, noticing that the bypasses and sprawling shopping malls of the Philadelphia suburbs had traded places with corn fields and hay bales wrapped in white tarps.

The trooper made a final turn into a gated driveway,

and while he barked some information into the intercom, I took in the manicured lawns and chiseled façade outside the place that would be my home for the next 90 days.

As we pulled up to the doors of Juniper Lane for the first time, a mosaic of colors reflected off the windshield and I had to squint and shield my eyes, causing the whole scene to bend and reflect in my vision like an old toy I used to have as a kid.

I went shopping with my mom every month to something she called the "dollar store," only I was annoyed to find out that the dollar store wasn't really a store of all things that cost just a dollar. But it was a discount store nonetheless, and I bought my coveted good with tooth fairy savings one particularly lucrative month when I was seven and it seemed my teeth were falling out with some frequency that resulted in reliable salary generation. My mother stood behind me as I walked up and down the aisles of the store searching for buried treasure amid the expired deodorants, and packages of multi colored straws. I found it in aisle eight; a red cardboard kaleidoscope with pictures on the side that looked like letters; but when I asked my mother what they were, she said they were Chinese symbols for words.

"What do they mean?" I asked her.

"I don't know," she replied.

I asked her over and over again, "But what do they mean?"

Finally she yelled a little too loudly in the middle of aisle eight of the dollar store, "I don't know!"

I forked over the $3.99 that the cardboard treasure cost anyway. And as I rode in the backseat with my mother in the front, I twisted the cardboard this way and that, holding it up to the window of her car, watching the letters and the light bending and interacting with each motion; but by the time we got home that day the toy had already lost its luster. And I realized something for the first time.

*Sometimes the mystery of a thing is better than the reality.*

# Part II
## JUNIPER LANE

# Chapter 7

The day after he warned Zak without a C, Ali, Cassandra, and the rest of the Wednesday group about the new patient, Will takes a longer than usual lunch to prepare for her.

Without fanfare, without much by the way of explanation at all, the intake director had come in the week before and gently placed a file on his desk that, while still closed, looked like every other file on his over-burdened desk. He started paging through it and became lost in a type of morose voyeurism very quickly.

The file tells the story of a girl named Thea. The same one Will had been following on the news since her arrest in December.

A young woman really—she is 23—but she looks so much younger in her photographs.

Prison photos are affixed to her file as a point of reference. A way to verify that the jail has sent the right girl to Juniper Lane when she arrives. Yes, she has been on the news, but because there were no cameras allowed in the courtroom, she had only been viewable walking into the courthouse with her face hidden by her thick dark hair striding alongside her slick-looking attorney, a young and ambitious public defender named Roy Letters, who seemed to have taken the case due to long-standing political aspirations. At least that's what the news kept saying about him.

Much was said in the news, including conflicting and contradictory reports.

It is hard to know what is real and what is not.

In her file, Will receives the first long and direct look at her wild dark hair streaked with gold, framing a pale complexion that makes her look like an odd mix of pathetic and fierce.

Thea has convinced the court, or rather Roy has—that she doesn't belong in jail. That the factory explosion, the death of Carmen Fierro, of whom very little is known, and the lies, the coverups, should not keep Thea Brown in jail. The theory is that whether or not these things can even be pinned on Thea—and the circular path of blame has in fact become more and more confusing—that even if there *is* a path from the girl to blame, that in fact the punishment is mental health treatment and not jail.

One of the commentators even worded it that way, "Her punishment should be the mental health system." And of course, Will felt vitriol against that commentator immediately, having been part of the mental health system for more than 20 years, as both a patient and an employee. He has different views about it. It is flawed, of course, but it saved his life.

And now he works daily to save others' lives through it.

Which is why he is being sent this new patient, and being asked to save her now. Through his championed landmark on the road to recovery: truth.

Despite his lies.

"I wouldn't say I consciously chose hypocrisy. It's not as if I weighed various choices and decided that hypocrisy would win the day."

This is what Will had said at the AA meeting the other night when, after his routine purge, some had come over and asked him how he made the transition from addict to counselor.

"I believe in truth and authenticity. That's the kicker. I

believe in all of those things and think they helped me win sobriety. Because that's how I look at it. Winning. It's not like I deserved it any more than anyone else. I guess you could say I was lucky because I had Audrey and she believed in the truth in the end. Yes, she did. She believed that it was absolutely true that I would never get out from under my addiction, my life, and Bruce, if I didn't get a second life. She didn't view it as a cop-out or a shortcut. It was the way. The only way."

Will had wondered over the years about Audrey's daughter and whether Audrey had passed all that conviction onto her daughter. And that was indeed how he thought of her: as Audrey's daughter. Not his. If asked, he would have replied that he "Contributed only my sperm to that venture. Nothing else."

Will knew that in all these years he had been gone, Audrey had been the one nursing her daughter through flus and heartaches, through the terrible 2s and the teen years. Audrey had been the one helping her with her homework and brushing out her hair and teaching her about boys. In fact, Audrey was probably advising her to stay far, far away from boys. Audrey was being mother and father to that girl—he knew that truth, too. And he never indulged in thoughts that he had a right to intrude on that or to covet it or to wish it weren't so. Will accepted that if he had stayed in their lives, if he had stayed to be that little girl's father, then that little girl would have a host of burdens that no one deserved. For these reasons he stayed away as Audrey had instructed on their last night together.

Will sits at his desk and stares again at the file on Thea Brown that he has been reading and re-reading nearly every minute since the director placed it gently on his desk with all the care that someone might give a newborn. Will hadn't even let his girlfriend, Margot, who was also on the Board of Directors of Juniper Lane, know about his new file, although he wondered if she had access to information that might have given her a heads up anyway. *She's got her hands full these days with that sister and brother of hers*, Will thought. He had been trying to give Margot the space she needed. In that space now came a new distraction.

Will feels a familiar feeling engage as he pages through the file. Ever since he got clean, he has discovered he has a sixth sense about people. He is hard to swindle, con, or even finish magic tricks on. He is observant. His five senses, no longer dulled by chemicals, have actually become even more astute; an additional sense has kicked in, providing a keen intuition—an almost foreshadowing—when something powerfully good *or* bad is going to happen. Will had known when Becca Robertson was close to relapsing, calling her on a day she said she had been about to head to the liquor store. Will had known Dylan James was loading a weapon that night he had called him and made him stay on the phone for hours. Will had known something special was going to happen the night he met Margot. In a similar way, Will feels something keenly about this new patient who is headed his way.

It is hard to wade too far into the file without getting stuck on the name. It's so unusual.

*Thea.*

◆

"I met Audrey at a bar—cliché but true. That it was a college bar and a sponsored frat party makes it no better." Will uses his long lunch to squeeze in another AA meeting two towns over. He is feeling particularly nervous this week with the imminent arrival of Thea Brown and her very unique addiction diagnosis. He hadn't intended to make yet another purge this week, but here he is.

"I grew up not far from the college campus where we met in rural Pennsylvania. I later found out Audrey had grown up not far from the area either. But we had never met before that night.

"After a longer than average childhood spent mostly bouncing between divorced parents who never seemed to time their vacation days from the office with the week they were actually supposed to have me, I ended up doing what the kids would now call a gap year, but what my dad called 'getting your shit together so you don't waste any of my hard-earned money on an overpriced college education.' I wasn't enrolled full-time in the local college, but many of my friends from high school were, and I made it a habit to hang out at the bar on the nights the college kids frequented it rather than the nights the "townies" did—as my group was called. I was trying hard to mesh in so closely with the college crowd that their aura would somehow rub off on me.

"The truth is, I didn't want to actually go to college, and in fact, I never did make it too far once I did, in fact, get my shit together and enroll in college. I had a pretty savvy business sense, and a mind for numbers, and I started doing the books for the college campus bar. I was making a little spending cash off the same books I was balancing, plus unlimited beer. The latter form of compensation proved to be my downfall. I started chasing the buzz I could no longer get from free beer with stronger goods run through the bar—also left off the same books I was balancing bi-weekly. That I was a customer of the illegal drugs running through the bar and a quiet accomplice to the funds left out of the bar's books, made me more qualified for the on-going position than the college education I was pursuing only half-heartedly by the time I spotted Audrey.

"I saw her standing in the restroom line across the bar when I was playing pool. She was talking with another girl behind her in line. The other girl kept letting her hair fall into her face like she was hiding from something or someone and I noticed Audrey moving the hair out of her eyes for her. It was so tender and intimate. Arousing even. But in a completely surprising way. I stared at Audrey for an extra second and when she glanced up at me, she locked eyes with me and didn't look away. Not until I looked away to take my turn. I shrugged off the discomfort I felt as I nailed the shot. Four ball in the corner pocket. I remember the shot exactly. I remember everything about the moment, oddly enough, as I was already using by then. But that moment—for good or for bad—it's frozen in my memory. Seared in my brain. Honestly, it's like I knew. Right then."

"That's so sweet. You knew she was the one?" a white-haired woman interrupts Will's story with her romantic ideations. He feels badly having to pierce a hole in them.

"Knew that I would ruin absolutely everything."

"Oh." The white-haired lady crosses her arms over her chest in disappointment.

"But like I said, I shrugged off that discomfort and I dove in anyway. That moment was key for me in my relationship with Audrey. Which is why I was so mad that she didn't even mention it at my funeral.

"Yes, I went. Working off the high Bruce provided me in a baggie in the diner that first day I left, I sat in the back of the big echoing church where Audrey sat in the front next to a coffin whose shiny veneer and loud brass detailing gave me the oddest sort of pride, even as I went completely unnoticed. Mostly because there was pretty much no one there. Audrey's friends and family—largely faces unrecognizable to me as I had become so disconnected from Audrey's life back then, took up a few—but not many—pews close to the front.

"After some prayers and singing that put me to sleep, I woke from my place of nodding off in the back pew as I heard Audrey's melodic voice ringing through the microphone.

"John Morris was self-assured. That's a nice way of saying he was cocky. I'd like to be nice about him now. Given all that's happened. I'd like to tell you nice things about him. I'd like that you remember him fondly. Kindly. With happiness and joy. If you knew him in the last five years—that's almost impossible. I get that. If you were a supplier or party friend of his, well, then there's no point even talking to you—you're as stupid as he is."

"'Was.' She cried when she corrected herself. I wasn't sure if she saw me sitting in the back; she didn't look in my direction at all as she spoke. I noticed that she wasn't pregnant anymore, but I don't remember if the baby was there in the church. It's all foggy. Ever since I got sober, I've been trying to remember if there was a baby in that church after all, and whether I caught a glimpse of Audrey's daughter that day. But I just can't remember."

Later that night, following the AA meeting, and after a long day at Juniper Lane, Will reads the file one more time before he turns out the lights and heads to bed. He touches his receding hairline as he counts the years since John Morris has been declared dead.

*Twenty-three years.*

# Chapter 8

*When I get out of here, I will never—in my whole life—have a linoleum floor.*

My counselor, Will Cann, and I are having lunch together in the rehab cafeteria after group therapy. The green speckled linoleum floor distracts me from the friendly banter Will has initiated. I look up from the linoleum to see Will staring at me.

It's been exactly a week since I arrived here in the trooper's car, and Juniper Lane is not nearly as disastrous as I would have imagined it being. I'm getting some of the best sleep I've gotten in years. I feel a little badly that I can't text my mother (my smartphone privileges are decidedly revoked in light of my, ahem, problems), but it's also peaceful in a way, and my assigned counselor is downright charming. He has a whole past he's only alluded to—that seems to involve some seedy druggie history that he's completely recovered from—that I sort of want to know about, but also sort of don't. It hits a little too close to home. But his rags to riches backstory also gives me some hope. Maybe everything really is forgivable. I'm not sure yet. This is all pretty new.

When I look up at Will, I realize it's my turn to speak. And I don't want him to think that nothing he is saying is getting through to me. Because so much of it is. The stuff we talked about today in group—authenticity and happiness and all that shit—that meant something to me. It really did.

But what he is talking about now—I can't for the life of me remember. Something about a Margot.

I take a chance, "So Margot's like what? Your sponsor?"

"No, Margot is my ... girlfriend."

His hesitancy throws me a bit—like he doesn't want me to know but why wouldn't he? Or is he just mad that I wasn't listening?

"What's she like? Is she an addict?"

"No."

"In recovery?"

"No."

"So she drinks around you?" I look down at the linoleum again.

"Yes."

"And you're ok with that?"

"I don't know what that means; 'ok with that.' I'd like to be able to drink around her, and with her, and over her. But of course, I can't. The fact that she drinks is pretty irrelevant to me. The whole world drinks without me. She's just another face in that world."

"Hunh."

"What?"

"Do yourself a favor. Don't tell Margot she's just another face in the world you're living in. You haven't said that to her, have you?"

Will smiles. His shoulders shake like he might unravel with laughter at any minute, but instead, he just takes a bite of his club sandwich. I don't even bother looking down at the bacon that slides out from between the toast toward the ugly linoleum below, because I fill up with a surprising surge of pride when he says, "No. I haven't. That's pretty good advice, kid."

Juniper Lane is a little cushier than I might have expected. I doubt this is the kind of rehab facility my dad would have tried and failed at back when he was alive.

For one thing, there are a handful of celebrities and recognizable faces here. I keep passing in the hall a guy whose face is on a string of billboards for a successful appliance chain all the way out near Philadelphia. Apparently he has some help getting that dazzling smile he shows off on the Schuylkill Expressway. Another is a soap opera actress whom I actually recognize, which embarrasses me so much that I ignore her. And another is a relatively famous musician, whose absence from the tabloid world I'm sure is a source of many new tabloid headlines. I wonder if they know he's here. He's actually what my mother would call a "major celeb," but I hate his music so I'm not nearly as starstruck as the others.

The staff tries to keep the major celeb away from us, mostly. He has a personal zen leader who follows him around all day just so he has someone to bark orders at. He seems addicted to power, if you ask me. Which no one has. The one place that seems to be the great equalizer is the rehab's cafeteria. It is in serious need of updating, with its peeling walls and linoleum floor. But it remains the only place to eat while the new wing of the rehab facility is under construction with some promised posher accommodations. There are signs up everywhere affixed to tarped off sections of the facility that read "Pardon our Mess! We're making things even better around here!"

Even though it's not all that bad, still, I'm hoping I'm not here long enough to ever eat anywhere else but this tired linoleum-lined cafeteria. I'm not all that anxious to see the plans to make an "even better" home for addicts.

The major celeb and I end up next to each other at the breakfast line one morning, and he looks me up and down, sizing me up in a way that doesn't really feel as much sexual as it does curious. "Why are you here?" He lifts his chin up and furrows his brow, looking at me like he's caught me sneaking in or something. Like he's the Juniper Lane security guard and maybe I crashed in here for the disgusting orange juice or gluey oatmeal.

"Same as you," I reply.

His eyes widen to a degree I would not have thought humanly possible before, and I become slightly alarmed, until he starts a low chuckle that gathers steam into a roaring laugh. Little beads of spit gathers at the corners of his mouth and threaten to spray me until I turn my head and duck. I turn to the sad-looking girl behind me, and offer her my spot in line, as I stay behind and heap extra cinnamon onto my sticky oatmeal.

I've decided to think of my 90 days as a luxury vacation away from reality. But still, it's hard to get too excited about actually being in rehab, a fate I've spent a lifetime fearing and avoiding. One of the reasons I'm not super gung ho about this place despite its luxuriousness is that the on-going construction is ruining *my* zen, so I have a hard time caring about the major celeb's. There is this incessant pounding that begins at 8 am and continues until midday. We are not allowed to take so much as an aspirin here without about a hundred pages of permission forms and doctor's orders, so I often start therapy sessions just after midday with a throbbing headache.

Zak without a C (I don't know why everyone calls him that, but I just keep going along with it) has some fabulous noise-deadening headphones and yesterday I bartered time with them for a promise that if I do get out, and if I do get to keep my business, I'll make a profile for him that will win him some actual awards on a dating site.

I don't have the luxury of analyzing either the ethics or the viability of this promise—because my head simply hurts.

I've caught Zak without a C emerging from behind the construction tarps here and there smelling like smoke. I hope all he's doing is bumming cigarettes. Today after lunch, I catch him red-handed, and I tell him if he shares his loot with me, I won't tell.

He looks disappointed, but he complies, forking over three Marlboro reds while saying, "I'm keeping the other four." He is so sheepish that I forgive him and tell myself it's only cigarettes that he's stealing, and we're allowed to smoke anyway so what's the big deal.

We take our loot out to the courtyard where some comfy chairs are arranged around a shallow swimming pool and we smoke until our lungs hurt.

By the pool, we are far enough away from the construction noise that it's only a dull rhythmic pecking in the distance. The sun is just past its midday height and it's making the trees and the grass and everything around us look shiny and new. Or maybe it's the nicotine high. No matter, I'll take it. Neither of us needs the noise-deadening headphones or anything else out here. I realize I've been trying to avoid the construction noise in the wrong place—inside rather than outside. I had thought so often to complain over the last week, but no one likes a whiny addict. I've learned that, at least, in my short time already.

"Zak—what's next for you after this? You going to really try to make it stick this time?"

I want to keep Zak without a C out here with me for the company and yet I can't think of any real way to get him to stay so I decide to make small talk. And I start with a question that I quickly realize threatens to push him back inside. But Zak's enjoying the view and the quiet as much as I am. He stays. But he also stays silent.

I decide not to push my luck and I stay silent, too.

I watch across the yard as the major celeb tosses a cigarette into the sand pile atop a tall ashtray and I think briefly about retrieving it. Not as a fangirl. But rather as an entrepreneur.

◆

I financed the early days of my business, Alibis, on the backs of people who couldn't get enough of celeb paraphernalia.

When I first got the idea for Alibis, I needed a way to fund my ambitious venture, and so I started small—I started selling my old clothes. The Michael Kors tunics, the Lilly Pulitzer dresses that I'd scrimped and saved to own with waitressing proceeds were suddenly hocked as a source of weekly income.

Each Monday I'd choose a few gently worn clothes. Sometimes I'd even find ones with the tags still on them. New With Tags!—I'd advertise gleefully. There was something quite rewarding about setting prices and controlling my weekly income. They were commanding a healthy sum of a few hundred dollars a week. But soon I was running low on clothes and I needed more money than I was making. I didn't have many expenses, but the web/technology upgrades that I needed in order to make sure my GPS and time-scrambling app would interface with Facebook directly, was still out of my tax bracket.

One night I had an idea to start a blog detailing where my clothes had been. I used a pseudonym –Holly GoFiercely, a play on one of my favorite characters and old movies, *Breakfast at Tiffany's*—and I talked about my star-studded life. From trips to the White House to a meet and greet with Justin Bieber, I posted photoshopped stock pictures on my blog and linked back to my Ebay site. People started responding in kind. And the traffic to my blog—and in turn to my Ebay page—grew like crazy. People started to outbid each other on clothes I had bought on sale at the King of Prussia Mall, and suddenly my weekly income was moving into the thousands. It occurred to me that there was no way people could actually believe these stories. They were so far-fetched and the comments on my blog even suggested the same. But people were able to suspend disbelief. I kept the blog going until I had enough seed money and then I shut it down. I hired a web technician who worked out of his home in the Philippines through a freelance website, and I got to working on my entrepreneurial venture ahead of schedule. After all, not only was I able to fund it, but now I knew my idea really did have meat. Because it was clear that people love a good story.

Even if it wasn't true.

# Chapter 9

Both the major celeb and Zak without a C seem to fully embrace my presence at group by week two. Ali, who is here for her third try at kicking painkillers, is starting to look a little haggard. She's stopped washing her hair, and it hangs stringy along the sides of her very pretty face. She has claimed a spot on the couch and no one challenges her. The greasy hair is a turn off, in addition to her sour attitude. She's still not too sure about me from the look of things. A new girl, Darcy, a heavy blonde who is apparently addicted to food and bath salts, sits on the floor against the wall, observing us all silently.

Everyone is pretty quiet today in group. Except Cassandra. She looks at me accusingly from her spot on the floor—legs outstretched as if they are useless, repeating one question too many times.

"But why are you here?"

"Because the court said I had to come here, Cassandra."

"No," she shakes her head at me with obvious frustration.

"But why *here*? *Here*? This is a place for drug addicts and alcoholics. What are you addicted to?"

"Well, it's for more than that," Will corrects Cassandra.

I agree with Will's seeming assessment that Cassandra might be a tad hypocritical. We all know she is basically in here because her husband is covering up the fact that she tried to kill herself, rather than actually helping her. But I keep indulging her questions because I'm feeling good this afternoon. Zak without a C got me a few menthol cigarettes, and the construction banging is done for the day.

"An expert witness who was hired for my trial said that I am addicted. To social media. And fake identities. It was a brand new theory and apparently the court accepted it as true and so voila, here I am!" I snap my fingers like I have somehow just conjured myself into existence. Into this very room.

"Did you do something bad? What were you on trial for?" Cassandra has a ghostly glow in her eyes.

I think carefully about how to answer that. Because yes, I've done some bad things. But what I was on trial for? That was ridiculous. It had nothing to do with anything. I pause for a few beats though, because I don't want Cassandra not to like me—even though I'm not sure I like *her* yet.

"I was framed for something, Cassandra. I didn't do any of the things they said I did. But still I agreed to come here, with my business out in the open now, because it's safer for me in here, than out there right now."

Cassandra nods hard at me. That she understands, and we have a moment of connection. I think about Renata, and how she came to me beaten and battered but without any of the ghostly resentment Cassandra carries around on her back. Cassandra apparently tried to escape her abuser by driving her car into a cement barrier. Renata did it by coming and asking me for a job. Everyone responds to tragedy differently. That much I've learned for sure.

"So what *were* you on trial for?" The major celeb is curious, now. He's been a little more engaged in all of our lives lately. I think he's either bored, or looking for some good songwriting material while he's here. I'm expecting to end up in a pop song when this is all said and done.

"Well, there was an 'accident.'" I put my hands up for the dramatic air quotes. "I had nothing to do with it, of course. One of my clients tried to kill her no-good husband who probably deserved it but I wasn't involved in all that. There was a factory accident and explosion and since my client ended up killing herself in the explosion, and the husband skipped the country—everyone was anxious for a real live scapegoat. That scapegoat turned out to be me. So my lawyer got an expert who told the court I had some brand new disease—a syndrome of sorts."

"You mean like battered woman syndrome?"

"Yes, Cassandra, like *that*." And then, a shroud lifts off Cassandra's eyes, and I feel like she and I will find somewhere to meet in the middle of the morass after all.

"So, thank you to Dr. Barrett for the very novel, very interesting opinion that landed me here with you fun people." I do a fake slow clap for effect.

"Dr. Elizabeth Barrett?" Ali asks from the couch.

"Yes, she was my expert at trial. Why?"

"No reason. I know she's one of the shrinks on the Board here, but I thought she doesn't really take patients anymore. I've been trying to get in to see her, but I can never get an appointment."

"Ali, I think Dr. Barrett has reduced her caseload substantially. You have a very good psychiatrist in Dr. Baransky," Will jumps in. He's been managing my file. And he knows Dr. Barrett was my courtroom shrink, and is still my shrink of record at this place. She has promised I'll get to meet with her regularly while I'm here, which I'm looking forward to. But I didn't know I was special. That she wasn't even taking other regular addict clients. I swell with a little pride at the realization. I try to hide it from Ali, though.

"Oh, Dr. Barrett's a hack. You wouldn't want her." I walk over and give Ali a playful punch on the shoulder which she says hurts, even though I know it was gentle. Will steps in like we are two children having a playground spat over the same toy.

"Ok, ok. Ok, you two. To your corners. Thea, no punching, playful or otherwise. Ali, you know Thea was just trying to connect with you, although she went about it all wrong."

I retreat to a folding chair in the corner of the room, begrudgingly as if punished, but still willingly. I'm constantly surprised by how important it is to me to impress Will.

Will is a recovering addict so we are supposed to be able to relate to him. Only he seems to really have his shit together, too, with a great job, a supposedly nice house in a neighboring town, and his beautiful girlfriend, Margot, who is a tax lawyer and also on the Board of Juniper Lane. I learned all this over cigarettes with Zak without a C in the courtyard.

"So tell us about Margot, Will." I decide to change the subject altogether.

I see Will squirm a bit when I do that and it makes me bold.

"Margot?"

He indulges us. He indulges *me*.

"What do you want to know? How we met? What her favorite color is?"

"No." I move off the uncomfortable folding chair onto the floor and fold my legs neatly into a pretzel shape, manually linking my legs around each other as I do. I pick imaginary lint off my leggings. "I want to know what you fight about. What you hate about her. And whether you tell her those things. I shared a lot with you guys today. I'm feeling vulnerable and in need of some reciprocity."

In the two weeks that I've been here, I've learned some key buzz words in dealing with Will, and I pull them all out now.

"Thea, I think honesty *is* important and I want you to feel safe saying things in this group to me and to your peers. That's why I ask you to share such personal things. That's why I agree to also share very personal things in here. But I have to be careful about keeping a line intact as well. I'm here to help you. To guide you. From the other side. I have reached a place of health. I want you to meet me here and not pull me back to the starting line. Does that make sense?"

"Yes," I answer honestly. "But I also really want you to drop the bullshit. From where I'm sitting, it looks like you keep a pretty healthy wall around you, maybe even from your beloved Margot. What do you do about conflict in your personal life, Will? Do you follow any of your own instructions?" I watch him carefully. He doesn't flinch.

"Your questions are fair—I'm not saying they're not."

Will stands up and for a moment I think he is walking out of group. Apparently I'm not the only one. All eyes lock on his back and he heads toward the door but then he veers left and makes himself a cup of coffee from the pot situated next to the door that leads both in and out of group.

"Margot and I have a very healthy relationship," he starts when he comes back to his seat and sips his coffee gently.

"There is no conflict—real or imagined. We are different, yes; I'm a recovering addict and my career revolves around people. She is a tax lawyer who can have as many glasses of wine as she likes on a Saturday night and still not be controlled by it or me. She likes numbers rather than people and she is very logical and pragmatic. We both love movies— sometimes choosing one we'd both like and sometimes conceding the choice to one or the other until next time. She eats pretty healthy although she has a weakness for those disgusting fried onion rinds they sell in gas station markets. She grabs them sometimes on road trips—and I can't even think about kissing her until she's brushed her teeth like four times afterward. She knows that and laughs about it and indulges me."

"You sound like a great boyfriend." Darcy breaks her silence while rolling her eyes.

"I am," Will replies, seemingly ignoring Darcy's sarcasm. "I've made mistakes, of course. Like any relationship, there have been missteps. By both of us. I'm happy you all are inspired by my recovery, but I'm not here to predict nirvana or perfection for any of you on the other side. You understand that, right?"

"Missteps. What missteps? Did you cheat on her?" Ali asks from her reserved spot on the sofa.

When Will shakes his head, Cassandra asks in a whisper from the floor, "Did you hit her?"

Will shakes his head more viciously that time. "I did not. Never."

"So what did you do?" I poke and prod. As endearing as I am starting to find our counselor, I want to see the warts pop up on good old Will's face. I want to expose him a bit, too. The appearance of perfection doesn't sit well with me. If nothing else, founding and running Alibis showed me exactly how easy it is to put a false face on for the world.

"I forgot her birthday."

"You forgot her birthday." *How's that for a cop-out.*

"That's *it*?" I unfold my legs and notice Darcy rolling her eyes at me—or Will. Who could tell?

"Her birthday is very important to her because her mom was a drug addict and so is her older brother. So she was really left to raise a kid sister on her own. Her birthday was never celebrated as a kid. As an adult she has finally begun celebrating her day of birth and it was something she confided in me early on in our relationship. It was a vulnerability that really needed protection from both of us. And I knew that. Yet I missed it anyway."

"Shouldn't you have made a big red heart around the day on your calendar? Or set an alert or something?" I ask.

"I was at a meeting. With my sponsor. I was in such pain that day I couldn't trust myself to celebrate anything or to go near a restaurant or even outside of my sponsor's apartment until I got my emotions in check."

"Why? What was the trigger? Her birthday?"

"Well that's just it. There doesn't have to be a trigger and there wasn't that day. I should have been able to hold it together for one day—her birthday—the day she needed me to hold it together, and yet I couldn't and it made me spiral even further out of control."

"Did you explain all of that to her? Didn't she understand? I mean it's not like you just blew it off." *Margot is starting to sound a little unreasonable to me. Not so perfect after all.*

"She understood. But it didn't make it hurt less. It was a reminder, you know, of how this relationship is going to be; honest and raw and thus uncomfortable. Not pretty. Nothing like the fairy tales."

Darcy pipes up again. "I'm sure it was fun for her to tell her friends that her boyfriend blew off her birthday because he was trying not to go on a bender. That kind of information doesn't really instill confidence or endear the boyfriend to the friends and family."

"Well that's just it. She has co-workers, colleagues, business acquaintances. But she doesn't have any real friends and her family is a little—well, self-centered. So she has me. Just me. She was counting on me. And I couldn't come through."

We all look at the ground, even the major celeb, unnerved by Will's vulnerability for a moment, until Will summons us all to stand—even Cassandra. "Come on, stand together in pairs with arms outstretched."

"What are we going to do—some corny trust games where we all lean into each other and fall?"

Ali drawls the word "fall" out into syllables in a way that makes it sound particularly sexy. I glance over at Will to see if he notices.

He isn't looking at me or Ali.

He is looking at Zak and leaning in to him and sniffing him.

"Zak are you high?"

I exhale a short chortling laugh.

*How could Zak without a C be high?* This place is like Fort Knox. I can't even use my mouthwash. The rules and the drunks are starting to annoy me, frankly.

"I am not," Zak says properly, chin jutted out comically.

*Oh. Maybe he is high.*

"Ok, so why don't you start our honesty exercise by telling the group exactly why you look like hell."

"You want honesty? Ok, because I live in hell now. I liked my life out there. I really did. And I left my really great life out *there* so that I could live in *here* now. With you assholes. Who, for all I can tell, don't seem to have an actual drug problem like I apparently have. And it's hell in here. So it's clearly rubbing off on me. And that's why I look like hell. Honestly."

Zak waves his arm around the room which seems to throw him off balance a little and he staggers and then falls into his seat.

"Wow. You *are* high. You're a liar," I hear myself say out loud.

Zak shoots me a vicious look. Will shoots me an even more vicious one.

"What?"

"Zak just explained to the group why he looks and feels like hell," Will says looking around the room with an arm gesture that mimics Zak's without the drunken swagger and fall at the end.

"Sooo. The point of this exercise is to let everyone lie? And pretend it's the truth?" I am starting to wonder if maybe Will, like Zak, has fallen straight off the wagon. "Yippee!" I clasp my hands together mockingly. "Well then. Good news! I am the Dutchess of Windsor. When I get out of here, like tomorrow, I am headed to my castle to eat twinkies and drink all the wine I can get on my hands on. Because I— unlike you hot messes—am not a drunk. I'm just eff'd up in a variety of other fun ways, apparently."

Will looks at me with something I am tempted to interpret as a smirk.

"Um. You're about halfway there," he replies.

"Hunh? What does that mean?"

"Only the last part of that was truth, Thea. That you're not a drunk, that you're eff'd up in a variety of other fun ways, as you put it. The rest of it—all lies."

My mouth drops open angrily and I throw my hands up incredulously. "What the—? Zak just lies to the entire room about whether he's high—he gets a free pass—and I'm not allowed to fantasize about being royalty for two minutes—how does this game even work?"

"Ok, it's not a game. It's about finding our truth. Zak's truth has nothing to do with him getting high or not today; it has to do with what he believes he left behind and how much he hates being here. It's not about what we want to be true for him—it's about what his truth is.

"Same for you, Thea. And I know for sure that your truth has nothing to do with being the Dutchess of Windsor."

"Oh you're so smug with your life lessons," I shoot back at him across the room, and as I say it, I put myself back into a life-sized pretzel and I close my eyes and fake a yoga pose and chant, as I think over and over again:

*What is my truth?*

*No seriously—what the hell is my truth?*

*Om.*

*Om.*

# Chapter 10

I watch Will from my perch on the bench near the construction site as he heads toward me. I am waiting for Zak without a C to emerge with the stolen cigarettes from around the corner, which only half explains why I am on edge with stunned nervousness as Will approaches with her.

Zak had to go back into detox for two days after his stunt in group. He went willingly, because Will told him he was lucky not to get thrown out. I had heard that a few of the construction workers were fired who were found to be smuggling in some joints. But still the loud construction waged on, and Zak without a C headed straight from detox to the tarps for free Marlboros.

"Thea! I want to introduce you to someone," Will's voice is too high pitched as he makes the introductions. "Margot, Thea. Thea, Margot."

"Nice to meet you, Thea," she smiles politely with her lips in a tight line, pretending we don't already know each other, so I go along with it.

"Nice to meet you, Margot. Where are you kids heading off to?"

"I have the weekend off, and Margot and I are headed to the mountains for a little fresh air. You guys behave yourselves. I'll be back in time for group on Monday. Ok?"

I like the way Will is asking my permission. I give it, without looking at her.

"Sure, sure. We'll behave." Zak arrives as if on cue with the cigarettes and offers them around to the group.

"I promise. Only legal drugs today," Zak reassures as Will and Margot decline and I gratefully accept. Will smirks and they head out of our sight while Zak and I light up.

"She's pretty, isn't she?"

"Well, that's an understatement," Zak exhales.

"What's her story, do you think?"

Zak shrugs. "No idea. I told you already—she's a hotshot lawyer and she's on the Board. She and Will have been seeing each other for a while now. She's trying to get more money into this place." Zak waves backward to the tarps and jack-hammers behind us. "Word on the street is that this is all her doing. She's been single-handedly securing the money for all these cushy updates. She makes so much money as a lawyer that she does all of *this*—" he gestures toward the tarps again—"for *free*. You heard Will talk about her screwed up family life? I guess her mom was an addict or something and now this place is her cause. Never hear anything bad about her. And Will likes her, so you know—"

"Yeah, I know." Will's seal of approval could pretty much redeem anyone these days. I already agree with Zak on that point.

# Chapter 11

A few days later, Will and Margot are back and while sitting in the courtyard, I catch a glimpse of Margot behind the construction lines. She's wearing a hard hat, apparently inspecting some of the work or the workers. She sees me, but doesn't acknowledge me, and so I flag down Daniel, who is rolling by, for some company.

Daniel is in a wheelchair but it is not clear why. I've seen him move his feet to the music streaming in through cafeteria speakers and in the elevators. I've seen him stand up, stretch, and then fall back into the wheelchair. One time he even caught my eye as he was doing it and gave me a wink. But still he sits in that chair day after day and no one seems to want to know why.

I have come to assume it is some sort of garden-variety self-punishment imposed out of guilt. Maybe he killed or maimed someone in a drunken car crash.

*Who knows why people punish themselves the way they do?*

At any rate, Daniel's isn't my burden so I don't take hold of it by asking him about the chair. I just push him occasionally when he asks and offer to pick stuff up for him when it falls on the ground.

Daniel and I make small talk until I see Margot emerge from behind the tarps. I think maybe she'll ignore me, but she doesn't. She comes walking right over to me and Daniel.

"Hello, Thea. Daniel."

"Hello, Margot."

"Thea, are you getting all settled?"

I nod. "Will's great. He's helping me a lot." I smile broadly, wide with enthusiasm. It's meant to be comforting.

She gets a funny look in her eye. Not quite jealousy, but something else.

She walks away then and I think, only, *Well, we have a secret, you and I, don't we? A delicious roll it over in your mouth, across your tongue, and suck the flavor out of it, secret.*

*I won't tell.*

I nearly say it out loud and I notice that as she walks away, she looks back at me with a carelessness like she wants to tell me to go ahead and tell him. Like it doesn't matter. But it matters to me. Secrets are my business—my life—and I keep them with pleasure.

But still, I wonder as she walks away, *Was she playing me then, or is she playing me now?*

At dinner that night, Will finds himself trying to focus on the fuzzy lines criss-crossing in the corner of Margot's dining room ceiling. Margot's home is a converted, renovated farmhouse that sits on a modest piece of property in the same county as Juniper Lane. She bought the house before Will knew her, and renovated it before she met him as well. He's seen before and after pictures, and is always impressed with the work and money Margot seems to have put into this project—her home. Thick wooden beams decorate the ceilings of the living room and dining room that are joined by only a half wall, giving an open feel to the home and creating the illusion that the humble farmhouse is larger than it is. Sometimes when it is just Will and Margot in the home, he feels small.

Tonight the wooden beams and the ceiling loom higher than usual above him and he focuses on the corner of the ceiling without meaning to. "Is that a spider web?"

"No," Margot says without looking up. "It's a cobweb. Nothing as lovely as a spider web—it's just born of dust. Of too busy a schedule and not enough time to vacuum."

"Hm. How do you tell the difference? It looks like a spider web."

"Are we really going to spend dinner time talking about my bad housecleaning skills?" Margot smiles wryly at Will and he tries to keep his eyes on her and away from the corner of the ceiling above her—the area hovering directly in his peripheral vision—a place he can't quite turn far enough away from.

"There's something about this new girl that's bothering me."

Margot sits waiting for more as Will drums his fingers on the distressed wooden planks of the dining room table next to his steak-filled plate. He grilled two steaks for Margot and himself outside of her patio door, and he can now smell wine on her breath across the table, so he knows she snuck a glass in while he was outside—as is her usual custom. She likes to unwind at the end of the day with a glass of wine, but when Will is over, she sneaks the glass instead of drinking it openly. Will thinks about telling Margot that she doesn't have to sneak it, that he can handle her drinking a glass of wine at night without falling off the wagon. But something about her wine-soaked exhales tonight, and the way they are making his pulse quicken just above his drumming fingers, stop him from telling Margot there is no need to sneak a glass of wine before dinner.

Will sits back in his chair and looks up at the ceiling again. He focuses squarely on the cobweb. He squints at a piece of dark dust in the middle, imagining it is a spider somehow appearing in this wrong web and eating an errant fly.

He shudders at the daydream, trying to dismiss it while still debating its origins.

*Who is the spider? Who is eating whom?*

Margot reaches over and pats Will's hand. She presses down firmly, and he realizes the drumming is getting annoying, and she is trying in a gentle manner to get him to stop.

"What is it, Will? Are you afraid that she doesn't belong there at all?"

"She has some real anti-social traits. There's no doubt about that. A lot in that expert report seems misplaced. But a lot of it seems dead on. It's more than that, though—"

Margot nods, as if that is the right response. Her nod empowers Will to keep going.

"According to Dr. Barrett's file, her bio is so confused, almost a patchwork of lies. She says she was a waitress, a startup founder—even an organic lavender farmer at one point."

Margot raises her eyebrows.

"I know, I know. But Dr. Barrett believes a few core things. That she grew up in this area. That her father was an addict, that her mother tried and failed at helping him over and over again. That she dropped out of college over a year ago and has been particularly lost ever since. And that she is obsessed with social media. Completely addicted.

"She's trying to get something from me. Some sort of validation. Affirmation. She won't let her mother come visit, so obviously she's not getting the validation she needs from her. But why from me? Why is it so important it come from me? She seems on a campaign, almost. To make me like her. It's not the usual projection or transference I see from the residents. It's different with this girl. She's very determined."

Will chooses his words carefully, dancing around a topic he isn't sure he is ready to discuss. "She seems certain that addiction was foretold for her. Because of her—in her words 'dead addict of a father.' And she feels that her mother did little to change that course for her. So she had to take things into her own hands. Develop fancy internet apps that would trick Facebook and Instagram. She had to cyber-stalk her clients' philandering husbands. Connect to people only through the virtual world. It's as if she just replaced—"

"Replaced one potential addiction with another," Margot finishes, and Will nods. Before quickly shaking his head again.

"But then there are some days—I'm just not even sure she needs to be 'cured' of anything. Maybe she got a raw deal. Maybe she doesn't belong here at all, and we're actually doing her a disservice keeping her cooped up with all these addicts whose ranks she's always been afraid of joining. I just keep trying to figure out how she got here and whether there's anything *for* her here."

Margot nods again, and then responds, "I'm going to go get the potatoes." She takes an extraordinarily long time to get the potatoes from the kitchen, and when she comes out her teeth are newly reddened and the smell of wine on her breath—even from across the table—overpowers Will, so he just looks up at the cobweb again after Margot starts speaking.

"Well, just remember, Will. The girl is accused of being a pathological liar. So, no matter what? You have to be careful. With her especially. I know how hard it is for you to maintain emotional distance from your patients."

"It is," Will nods in agreement and returns his attention to Margot. "But with this girl, addiction treatment is even more difficult. We can't frisk her for the sources of her addiction. We can't remove needles and bottles from inside the liners of her luggage and makeup bags. If Barrett's opinions are to be believed, then she's addicted to lies. How do you even remove that variable to try to cure someone? It's disconcerting to say the least."

"You'll do it," Margot says dismissively. "I have the greatest of faith in you." She lifts her water glass to Will in an ineffective toast.

Will moves his focus from Margot back to the ceiling again, and remembers a line he had scrawled in the margins of Thea's file earlier that same day.

*What if the only way to help this girl is to help her accept that while addiction is in her genes, redemption is as well?*

Will keeps focusing on the small dust speck in the middle of the all-wrong web, until he's sure he can make out eight legs, and he pictures the creature eating his imaginary prey with blood the color of red wine splattering violently and trickling down on Will sitting at the table below. Bathing him in it.

Throughout the entire dinner, Will realizes, of course, how careful they both are not to say her name out loud. Neither of them says it. Neither of them says the word: *Thea.*

*Thea means truth.*

Will leaves Margot's early that night, and heads to an AA meeting. He doesn't purge his story. He hasn't needed to do that as frequently lately.

Instead he looks around at the smiling, nodding group, and says, "There are times I feel like I'm moving, high above the fray, like a rock climber gathering a foothold on the empowered stories I have told others while simultaneously dodging the stories I've told myself like sharp barbs along the way. Picking my way up the wall without any pause or care that might slow me down—or worse—send me flying back down the wall in a mass of crumpled failure.

"Failure. I think that is what you call it when you refuse to believe what is true."

# Chapter 12

I sneak into Will's office on the twenty-second night I am at Juniper Lane. It is surprisingly easy. Which is a good thing as I spend relatively little time planning the break-in but an inordinately insane amount of time preparing to brag about it afterward in group.

I don't want to get the guy fired or anything—but I relish the idea of finding a little dirt on him; a flask or one of those airport bottles of booze stashed between patient files. Maybe a porn magazine or a half-eaten candy bar. My bar is low. I just feel like there is something to discover about Will Cann.

I used my Giving Key necklace—the one with the word "Courage" on it that I'd shoplifted at a county fair years ago. No, it's not a real door-opening key, but it is thin enough to fit between the door jamb and the wooden door. For a state of the art facility, Juniper Lane's security features are somewhat lacking in my humble opinion.

It takes about 3-4 minutes of jiggling and filing the key inside and out of the door jamb before the door knob pops in my hand. I smile soundlessly and find myself looking around, not out of fear, but rather pride. I almost hope I will get caught. I want someone to stare incredulously at what I have done. One thing I miss in rehab? Not booze or soft sheets—or even work. I miss the way I impress people through my work, and the feeling that gives me. I miss the validation of my various social media communities. Likes and shares and virtual high-fives for all the various identities I generally have running simultaneously—for clients and myself. Here in rehab no one is all that impressed with me—and certainly not with what I do for a living. As far as they are concerned it seems to be the reason I am here in the first place and Will's insistence that we all be treated with such frustratingly exhausting equanimity—right down to the major celeb—makes for a lot of egalitarian views in group that frankly I find a bit misplaced.

I push the door open carefully and slowly, waiting for a loud creak that might give me away or get me noticed. But nothing happens other than an open door.

I walk inside and carefully shut the door behind me. Again nothing but a closed door as a result.

The office feels smaller than I remember from previous visits for our regularly scheduled chats. I make it to the chair I usually sit in, in fewer strides than I remember. I take a seat in my customary chair and notice, even though it is upside down at this angle, that my file is the one on top of the others on Will's desk. I pop out of my chair to reverse positions; I move behind the small desk to sit in Will's seat and glower at the chair in front of me as if my alter ego was there and I am going to talk some sense into her.

It's then that I spot the poster on the back wall of Will's office. It's not visible from my usual seat, or even from where I make hasty exits from Will's office, as his door is usually wide open during our sessions and blocking the wall behind it. Neither he nor I ever bother to close it. He has a pretty generous open door policy, apparently unwilling to be locked in alone with any of us reckless addicts. The poster I can now see is situated on a wall that is only visible when Will's office door is closed. *Which seems to only be when he isn't in it,* I think somewhat sardonically as I squint to try to make out the poster's words across the room.

Even though my eyes are getting used to the dark office

with only a bit of hallway light streaming in, I still can't quite make out the poster's quote as my eyes adjust. I reach out in front of me where there is an old-fashioned desk lamp with those beaded attachments hanging from the lampshade. It looks oddly out of place within the otherwise institutional looking décor. I rub my hand underneath it to watch and listen to the beads clang against each other. I wait until they stop moving like a carnival pendulum ride, before I turn the light on, and it's then that I read the poster.

*So Will is a modern theatre fan?*

*Or maybe just a hopeless trend-follower as that musical's lines seem to be on the lips of everyone these days.*

And just which *Hamilton* quote has he chosen? It isn't surprising at all, of course. The painful obvious irony helps my eyes focus across the length of the room on the words I probably can't actually see, but know are there nonetheless. Will has chosen to adorn the wall with that very popular quote about having no control over who lives long enough to tell your story.

*No control.*

*Will, the recovered heroin addict turned counselor and champion of truth-telling, certainly has taken control of his story. But what about me?*

I've let my obsessions get the best of me. I've lost control at several key times in the last few years, and now I'm hiding in a posh drug rehab facility because of those decisions. This whole trip is in fact an abdication of everything I have been trying so hard to have for myself. Autonomy, reinvention. A new story. A life beyond the clichés. I rub my fingers underneath the crystal beaded lamp until I feel the off switch. I close the lights on the *Hamilton* poster, the institutional décor, and my open file.

I sit for a few moments in Will's chair, and then I head out, softly closing the door behind me just in time to bump smack into her. She has seemingly appeared from nowhere. I wonder if she has been watching me. I wonder if she has actually *let* me break in and break back out again.

"Margot."

She raises her eyes at me in response.

"It's late, Thea. Better get to bed now."

*Jesus. This passive aggressive shit is starting to get old with this woman.*

"Actually, I think I'll head to the library and read for a little. I'm having trouble sleeping tonight."

She locks in on me as if we are in a silent duel and I consider whether or not to raise my weapon before the count of ten.

Lucky for Margot, I'm not exactly known for my cheap shots, though. I step back a pace. Margot doesn't make the short list of people I want to tell my story, after all.

I feel Will's door latch softly and soundlessly behind me and I stare down at my socked feet, breathing deeply and stalling for time, hoping Margot will shoot first. She doesn't.

She has the will of an ox, that woman. No wonder Will loves her.

I raise my weapon finally. "Maybe I'll skip the library tonight, though. I need to rest my mind and my body, right? What is it Will always says? Oh that's right. Sleep can be better than sex. Let me try out that theory." I wink at her and watch for only an extra moment as she works her face into an expression-free façade. When I get to my room, I stare at the ceiling too long, realizing I am not nearly as happy about my shot across the bow at Margot as I would have been a few weeks ago.

*Maybe this place is getting to me, after all,* I think, as I drift off for some good sleep.

Will makes up work-related excuses and eats at his own house for a few nights in a row instead of watching the cobweb on Margot's ceiling.

Will has to admit that Margot scares him.

But she also scares him less than other people do—and for different reasons.

If he had had a close friend (which he doesn't) to ask him why he keeps seeing her given all the drama that has passed between them, especially recently, that would be the short answer.

The longer reasons would include the way she smells, the way her face lights up when she sees him at the end of a long day and the fact that she has shared some very personal details about her life before and during him that seem the sort of things people share only when they really decide to trust a person. So he trusts her, too.

Will and Margot met at a fundraiser nearly two years before Thea Brown had arrived at Juniper Lane. It had been a black tie dinner to wine and dine donors of the new Juniper Lane construction project. Will was invited by the Executive Director of the facility, and while he usually shunned such events because of the obvious temptations, that night he had one of his intuitive feelings that it was an event worth attending.

He found himself near the bar and next to the most beautiful woman he'd ever seen, an hour into the event. "Buy you a drink?" He'd smiled, enjoying for a moment the feeling of asking a beautiful woman that question. Since he'd been clean, he had mostly dated women who were also sober, by choice or necessity. There was something delicious about ordering this woman a glass of champagne, and slipping a $5 bill into the bartender's tip jar just before asking for a plain seltzer for himself.

She had looked at him, but not asked. He decided to answer anyway. He wanted this woman to know him. "I'm strictly sober. Started at Juniper Lane as a patient 20 years ago, and now I'm one of its biggest advocates.

"Will Cann. Nice to meet you—"

"Margot," she finished for him. "Will. It's so nice to meet you. I've heard about you. You have quite a story. And quite a reputation. I'm on the Board of Directors. Pleasure to meet you at last. I've heard so much about your amazing treatment record. It's counselors like you that make this place the success that it is. The extraordinary staff at Juniper Lane makes necessary the renovations and expansion we're trying to do. I'm honored to finally meet you in person."

"Oh. I'm embarrassed, now. I've heard your name as well at Juniper Lane. Nice to put a face to the name."

"Don't be embarrassed. I never expect anyone to know who I am before they actually meet me in person. That would be arrogant."

Will laughed, "I suppose it would be."

They never left each other's sides that night, despite the fact that Margot was supposed to be mingling with the donors and Will was supposed to be leaving early before the wine-scented air did him in.

Will asked Margot out again for the following night, and they began seeing each other regularly, although platonically, while Will tried to figure out what on earth Margot saw in him, and why she kept saying yes, every time he asked her out.

One night, a few weeks into Will and Margot seeing each other, she asked him to come meet some of her colleagues at the law firm where she was a partner. They were the closest she had to friends. And she wanted him to meet them, to cross over into that area of her life. The problem was, she said, they were meeting at a BYOB tapas restaurant. And there would be drinking. She left the decision up to him.

Will wanted to meet her friends and he wanted to show Margot what a healthy person he was. The decision to go seemed like a double win.

But when they got there, there was something oppressive

about the dinnertime conversation—not the drinking per se but the heaviness it brought to the crowd. Will could tell he wasn't meeting any of them. He was meeting their representatives; the versions of themselves they were comfortable showing off. And it felt so awkward to be showing them his true self—spilled water on the table and all—while all he got from them were loose-limbed drunken well-fed representatives.

Instead of just politely excusing himself and going home early, he had to go and have a heart attack.

Well, it felt like one anyway. Pains shooting up and down both of his arms—which was the bad arm to have pain in? Right? Or was it left? And beads of perspiration dripped down his forehead throughout half the meal in such quantities, he had to keep cleaning himself up with his dinner napkin. Margot seemed oblivious to his pain as she chatted up her table neighbor, until Will grabbed her leg under the table trying to be discreet and she looked at him with a shy smile as if they had a secret all their own until she saw his sweaty red face and asked, "Are you all right?"

Will managed to shake his head as he leaned in for a low whisper, "I think I'm having a heart attack. I need to get to the hospital."

Margot got up right there and excused them both gracefully as Will stood by her side mute and drowning before they headed to Penn General where Will got hooked up to about five machines that were whirring and whizzing right along with his static-filled brain and heart.

The hospital staff assigned Will to a gurney in a large room off of the ER, which had a curtain as a partition and would be the "only private room you will be getting at this time, Sir," according to the head ER nurse on duty. When the ER resident on call came to read Will's charts, he said that Will was not having a heart attack, but that they would keep him there for a few more hours to monitor his rhythms. The resident looked disappointed and for a moment Will felt sorry that he hadn't brought him something just a bit more exciting that night than vanilla-flavored anxiety.

As the resident left he pulled the curtain closed behind him, and Margot exhaled with relief. "You see, that's all it is. Anxiety. Nothing we can't work with."

Will reached up and brushed hair out of her eyes while his own welled up with the realization that a little thing like anxiety wasn't going to scare this woman away. That maybe she would never know, would never really understand the worst of him. But that what she knew right now to be the worst of him was ok with her. She could handle it. Something that felt like love grabbed hold of his heart.

He was still nursing that feeling, trying to figure out what to make of it, what would develop from it when he got out of the hospital, when Margot climbed off her wooden splintered seat onto the edge of the cot and rubbed Will's head and kissed his forehead. Will's brain started to feel fuzzy at her touch. He actually had a stab of worry that the nurses had accidentally put painkillers or narcotics in his IV even though he had expressly told them he was an addict during admission.

Will pulled Margot's head to his and kissed her gently. He felt her hips move farther from the edge of the cot finding a place alongside his own.

"What do you think?" Will nodded toward the closed curtain in a gesture that felt more romantic before he expressed it, than it did once it came out.

"I don't think anyone's going to be checking on us," Margot laughed in response.

They kissed for a few minutes, and Will noticed that she made no move to pull or tug at the jeans still tightly wound around her long legs, and so he accepted that this was just going to be their funniest, messiest make-out session until Margot climbed on top of him, and opened her jeans zipper, a triangle of black silk visible through the opened gapping jeans.

They continued their magnetic dance until Margot leaned in to Will to kiss him fiercely, pushing her jeans down and away from the black silk, which he caressed as her heat and wetness wrapped itself around his fingers even through the silk.

Finally she adjusted herself to kick off both the jeans and the silk underwear, and Will lifted the scratchy hospital blanket that formed the last barrier between them. His flimsy hospital gown was open where it needed to be and so was she.

He pushed himself toward her slowly, and she found him easily.

As much as Will didn't want it to be true, the hospital cot and the nearby curtain partition made the whole episode awkward and he was more tentative than he would have imagined being with Margot for the first time. He didn't enter her as much as she closed herself around him but it was enough. In the background, he heard the beeping of the monitor, and the low chatter of the ER all around them. He thought of the chaos that was surrounding them, the births, the deaths, the blood and life fluids spilling out all around them and he thought, *This is how real feels.*

The messiness of life and death is no reason not to make love. The messiness of life and death is no reason not to give into this.

As Margot raised and lowered herself on Will rhythmically, he caressed her back and kissed her ear softly, and he whispered, "I'm sorry. I imagined it so much more romantic than this."

She laughed low as she whispered back: "Shame on you. You should know by now never to measure reality against fantasy. Shh. Here we are."

He exhaled quietly and added with conviction: "Yes. *Yes.*"

# Chapter 13

The day after Margot caught me breaking out of Will's office, I raise my hand first in group, insisting that I want to start.

"My mom killed my father."

I say it with a smirk so maybe it loses some of its dramatic value, because no one gasps, and Will says only, "Stop it, Thea."

"Stop what?"

"Stop being dishonest."

I give Will a long stare out of the corners of my eyeballs that is meant to mean "you're not so smart, you know," but it doesn't work. He keeps at me.

"Ok, Thea, Tell us the truth, then. Did your mother really kill your father?"

I give a long sigh before deciding to play along.

"No. Heroin killed my father. But she was always kind of a pain in my ass, so I can imagine that she drove him pretty nuts, too. You know, back when he was alive." I look around the room a lot as I speak, but settle on Will with these words. Just because.

Ali sits on the couch, and really looks like she has given up showering altogether. Her hair is so greasy it is hard to look at her, but I have to because she asks, "Are you on heroin, too?"

And I study her expression to understand whether she means "too" as in like my dad or "too" as in, like Ali. I wager on both. "No. Heroin is not my particular drug of choice."

"So what is?" From Zak without a C.

"Well. Apparently, dishonesty."

"Pppah." Cassandra makes a sound that is one syllable away from being a hiss. I am not sure what to make of it so I ignore her and keep going.

"My dad was a heroin addict. I don't even remember him. He died before I really knew him, and my mom, she just went right on with our lives. Like nothing happened. So for some reason, everyone is just SHOCKED to learn that I have become enamored with creating false lives for other people. For a living."

"Wait. For a living?" Morgan, the soap opera star looks interested in me now. She's still relatively new, and I realize I haven't really talked about my business since she joined in group. "Yes. I run a company called 'Alibis.' Alibis helps people create viable and confident social media profiles."

"So, like fake profiles?"

"Well it's more than that. Anyone can make a catfish profile. I make them real. I can make posts that look as if they have come from anywhere. And from any time."

Morgan suppresses a yawn, and since I'm worried that she's not quite impressed enough, I break into a full-on marketing pitch. "Let's face it—people have long been hiding their demons under masks. Fifties housewives are said to have had the highest rates of alcoholism, et cetera. But now, with social media—facebook, snapchat, Instagram, all of that—the masks are public. They are accepted.

"Painfully so. It's hard to stomach your own marital discord when your best friend is updating her profile pic every other day to include her adoring spouse. It's brutal to rise each day to begin yet another shift at your minimum wage job when your high school prom date is posting pictures of his recent trip to Bali with his third wife. Who looks like she might well have been his daughter in another life. Or this one. I help people create the kind of masks they need to get by. But I make them look—real."

"Do you miss it?" Cassandra asks.

"I do. I really do," I admit.

"So you're really and truly addicted to social media?" Ali asks.

"I don't know," I concede for the first time since I've been at Juniper Lane. "I guess the real question for me has always been: even if I am, is that so bad? Is it ok if the soft glow of a smartphone powering on in the morning gives you the same release that a drag, hit, or pill gives you as an addict? Is it ok if you turn to an addiction like mine to avoid an addiction like yours?" I look at Ali as I say it, and then uncomfortably turn my attention back to Will instead.

"I'm not actually addicted to opiates or heroin. But I worry that I could be someday. Because my father was an addict. And he died. And we never got over that, not really. Some days I fear I'm just one bad decision away from ending up just like him. So I try to keep my bad decisions to a minimum and I focus on other people's bad decisions instead."

Morgan pipes up with interest. "So this company of yours? What do you charge?"

"I'm not sure I'll be able to keep it open when I get out of here. I'll let you know, though. I'll give you my card before I leave." I wink at her.

Will raises one eyebrow and eye at me and I see him do it out of the corner of my own eye.

"Kidding." I roll my eyes at Will in response. "Of course I'm not handing out cards. And of course, I'm not keeping my business open after I leave. Apparently, you see, I'm addicted to this life. And that is indeed bad. That's why they sent me here. Only I have to become a model citizen doing something else. Something other than my business that I've poured my heart and soul into. Any ideas?"

"What did you study in college?" Cassandra asks without

looking at me.

"Psychology." I give my routine answer. "I guess I had some ideas about a career as a psychologist. But I took it in a different direction, ultimately, and never graduated."

"Maybe you could go back to college?" Cassandra replies.

"Nooooo." I make my reply drag on for a few syllables for emphasis. There would be no way I could go back to college.

*Even if they'd let me.*

*Thea Brown would not be going back there.*

# Chapter 14

Will is still mulling over Thea's breakthroughs from group that day when he arrives at Margot's house for dinner later that night. He sees the light on in the back end of Margot's house, even though the front stoop light is uncharacteristically dim and the limestone-faced entranceway is dark when he walks in.

He lets himself in without hesitating like he has many times before and heads back through the house toward the light. When he arrives at Margot's home office, he stops in the doorway to watch her for a few moments before breaking the spell. She is bent over a pile of papers, scribbling notes in the margins of the top sheet, and shuffling back and forth between the top and bottom, reading and writing intently. The desk light is the only light on. Will imagines her having been in her office since the afternoon, when the outside sunlight would have made any other house lights unnecessary. He realizes she must have been in here for hours, earnestly working and reading and making sense of the pile of papers in front of her, whatever they are, with such intensity that she missed sunset. Missed the darkness overtaking the house that made her front stoop dim, and the rest of the house dark, save this small corner basking her in warm glow. Will sees that she is still in work-out clothes and has only a touch of pink in her cheeks that could have been

either natural or some light makeup applied for her afternoon of working from home. Or maybe—Will treats himself
to a daydream, just in case he stopped by to surprise her
like he is doing now—she applied a light sheen on her lips, a
light glitter on her cheeks and eyelids that remain visible
only to him as her face stays bent closely to the papers below
her.

Will leans against the doorframe and enjoys watching
Margot for a few moments in silence, smiling to himself,
enjoying the citrusy aroma of the room, an essence that is
all Margot, until he feels a small tickle in his throat, and suddenly he coughs.

And Margot screams.

"What the hell?" Margot jumps out of her seat and papers
go flying everywhere.

Will is now in the middle of a coughing fit, so he holds
his arm over his mouth and bends to help pick up papers
with his free hand.

"No, no," Margot shoo's Will's free arm away with hers.

"What are you doing here? How long have you been
standing there, for God's sakes? Were you trying to scare
the bejesus out of me?"

Will takes offense at her tone and the fact that it ruined
the few moments of pleasure he had just enjoyed standing
and watching her work. He wants to tell her that, to explain
how lovely she had been and how he could have stood there
for another hour just watching her, smelling her, enjoying
her. But she has ruined everything with her yelling and
horror and flying papers.

When he stops coughing, Will tries to help Margot pick
up the papers properly, with two hands, but she just snaps
at him even more harshly.

"No please—just get out of here and let me clean up this
mess. And gather myself. I feel like I was just robbed or something. My heart is beating a mile a minute. Please don't do
that. Like ever again. That was so creepy."

Will walks out of Margot's office defeated, all the momentary pleasure he had just received by standing in the doorway watching her in the soft glow evaporates. He walks to the front of the house and starts turning on lights to brighten the dark house and bring everything into present time.

"Maybe you're right about the girl."

For dinner, Margot has made Will's favorite, a Creole stew that was her grandmother's recipe from Dominica. Fresh fruit lines a plate on the dining room table. But no bananas. Never bananas. Margot will never buy bananas in the United States, she always says. The Latin American bananas lining every grocery shelf in the States is the reason her family-owned banana farm in Dominica went bankrupt when she was a young child. There is a straight line between Latin American bananas and her mother's drug addiction in Margot's mind. And there is no talking her out of it. Will has tried. Instead he has simply given up bananas as well.

Margot isn't very talkative over dinner, and Will knows she is still mad that he surprised her while she was bent over her work, so he is startled when she finally breaks the silence at the end of the meal, to tell him he might be right.

"What do you mean—I'm right about the girl?"

"Maybe she doesn't really need to be cured. Maybe in fact there is nothing wrong with her. Maybe this thing she has—this obsession that created her business—is really just, you know entrepreneurial spirit. What's wrong with that?"

Margot leaves Will then, walking back into the kitchen, leaving her words in the air and he grabs at them hungrily.

"That's right," he calls after her. "Why is society always trying to zap from people what makes them different, special, unique?"

Will is buoyed for a few moments with Margot out of

the room, swirling his ice water in his mug like it is a wine glass. He puts his nose down and inhales deeply the fresh lemon and the scented water. Margot returns and cocks her head to the side and Will sees himself through her eyes for a moment with his nose furrowed in ice water, trying desperately to explain away a young woman's addiction as if it is important to *him* personally to do so. He feels embarrassed; although there is no recognizable judgment in Margot's face, he feels it nonetheless.

After the dishes are cleared, Will drains his ice water and makes an excuse about having to go. Margot looks at him with no surprise in her face, nods, and simply kisses his head lightly before retreating to the couch to tuck her legs up under her and bury her head in a book.

"Have a good night, get some rest, and try not to be so hard on yourself," she says as Will closes the door behind him, and he thinks, *I love you, Margot Hamilton.*

# Chapter 15

Cassandra plops her cafeteria tray next to me on the bench by the pool area. We aren't supposed to bring those trays out here, and I know security has been a little lax with the construction mess next door, but I still admire Cassandra's moxy. I am in fact surprised by it, so I am a little more confused than usual, when she says, "Let me read your numbers."

"I'm not reading anything. What are you talking about?"

"No, your numbers. Let me read you."

Cassandra's moxy seems to extend past cafeteria tray tables today. She grabs my hand and starts drawing a star on it with a sharpie marker.

"Hey! What are you doing?" I wince but I don't pull my hand away and just that small permission is all she needs. Offer and acceptance has been achieved.

I leave my hand in hers.

"When is your birthday?" I pause a moment as I do lately when personal questions like that are asked of me. These things are difficult for me. Even with all the work I'm doing here at Juniper Lane.

"February 29, —"

She glances up.

"Leap-year baby."

"Indeed."

"Special, you know."

"Ah, that's what they all say," I murmur, trying to distract myself from the discomfort of the sharpie pen digging deep into my palm.

"Well, your birthday is one of your five core numbers in your numerology chart, and it reveals much about you."

"Un hunh, keep going." I stare down at my palm.

Cassandra carefully presses numbers into my palm. They tickle a bit, But I grip my other hand to help me focus not on pain or tickling but on the numbers themselves.

Cassandra writes 2 and 29 and then 11, 9 and then 2 again in various spots of the almost three dimensional star in my palm.

"Two and nine and their sum, eleven, are all going to be very important numbers for you." She writes and re-writes numbers in various spots on my palm; then on the bottom of my upturned pinky finger, she makes a circle with her finger softly, before drawing a circle with the number 11 floating above the palm star.

"My husband doesn't let me do numbers for anyone anymore."

Cassandra rarely mentions her husband, but when she does, it's usually like this. To give concrete examples of what an ass he is.

I nod, both to agree with her and to selfishly encourage her to keep going.

"Nine is a powerful number. I'm not surprised at all that it's yours."

"What does it mean?" I try not to reveal my breathlessness.

"You are intuitive. A healer of sorts."

"Like a doctor, do you mean? Are you really trying to suggest that I head to med school when I get out of here?"

"No, not exactly—I'm talking about a spiritual healer. A shaman. Do you know what that is?"

I shake my head.

"I studied medicine, you know. Before I was married, I studied not just medicine, but healing. Traditional and non-traditional. I lived in New Mexico, among the Native Americans and I studied with a shaman in a small Indian tribe located outside Albuquerque. I was also somewhat of a hobbyist sculptor and the tribe took me in and let me practice with them. I refined my techniques and mastered my sculpting and even started making pieces on commission, but my greatest lessons took place with the tribal shaman. He thought I had promise. He thought I should take my healing powers and infuse my art with them. I wanted to pursue his advice, but when I met my husband, he told me it was all very impractical, and that I should focus on getting a job with a "real doctor." That's what he said. I got married. I gave up my art altogether. I moved east with him because he got a chance to head up his own congregation. I got a job working as a receptionist for a pediatrician. And I gave over all my money to my husband so he could invest in his dreams. So he could be successful. I miss reading numbers. My husband never lets me speak of any of this; he thinks it's like believing in the occult."

Cassandra looks over her shoulder like she might find him. "I think he believes there is a little witch left in me that he hasn't quite beaten out." She smiles angelically through the gruesomeness of what she is saying.

"Shamans, however, are not about black magic," Cassandra says with an apologetic tone I have not suggested she needs. "They are deeply spiritual. They can drift between the living and the dead and can bring healing to both sides because of their transitory power."

I have never heard Cassandra speak this many words to anyone, and I am afraid of breaking the spell, but still I interrupt, "Can anyone be a shaman?"

I am considering revising my résumé substantially in light of this interesting conversation.

"Of course not." I feel wounded from the harshness of

her words until she softens them. "But *you* could be. Becoming a shaman requires a sickness they say. A great sickness of the body or the mind. A crisis, if you will, that pushes the shaman to her absolute limits. That pushes her in fact closer to the realm of the dead than the living. At that point, the shaman overcomes and brings back to the living all that she has learned from her crossover."

"Shamans talk to the dead?"

"Not exactly. Not the way you are thinking. They learn from the dead. And they heal the living with all that they learn. They are the greatest healers among us. You have powerful and repetitive numbers that suggest that you could be a very great healer once you survive this sickness of the body and mind that you are suffering from."

I hold onto Cassandra's words while she holds onto my hand tracing the numbers and the lines of the pinnacles of the star with some hypnotic repetition until I glance down and study the center of my birthdate star, and have to acknowledge that, of course, this is all complete bullshit.

# Chapter 16

Will is drawing words on the whiteboard in our room at group.

*Authenticity.*

*Self.*

And we are playing a game like Pictionary where we draw images on small pads of paper on our lap that relate to the words he is drawing.

It doesn't make much sense to me, but it seems to have the group pretty engaged. Even the major celeb, who rarely takes anything seriously when he deems to show up to group at all.

I'm drawing a portrait of stick figures on my pad of paper in response to Will's latest written word: *Family*.

I draw a woman, a man, two girls, one taller than the other, and a dog, all standing outside a giant house. I start sketching a BMW in the driveway.

The major celeb looks over my shoulder. "But that's not your family, is it?"

"Sure it is."

"But I thought it was just your mom and you?"

"Why? Cause that's all I've been talking about here in therapy? That was then, this is now. Keep up." I chuckle a bit, as I continue sketching.

"I'm just trying to suss this all out," the major celeb says.

135

And I laugh so hard at that—because who says that? *Suss this out.* The major celeb is cracking me up.

"You remind me of someone I knew on the outside." I hit his arm.

"Did you like him?" the major celeb pleads.

"Very much."

*Tell me the story you want me to know.*

His name was Lonny and he was gay. I knew this as soon as he sat down, but he didn't seem like he wanted me to know that just yet, and so I kept the information to myself.

"My girlfriend is really pressuring me to get married."

"That's what girlfriends do if you keep them around long enough, Lonny. Occupational hazard." I laughed a little but he didn't. He squirmed in his seat. He moved his hips back and forth—I'm not sure I ever saw anyone squirm as well as Lonny. Unlike Roy the public defender, I really tried not to take very many notes, especially in the initial interview when a potential client was as nervous as Lonny was.

Sometimes I thought about asking Renata to eavesdrop through the thin partition and take notes for me during the initial interviews. But I didn't want to rely on anyone that much. I didn't want to let my guard down and trust that Renata wouldn't become distracted by a phone ringing or a spider crawling or a weak bladder, or a PTSD memory from the crazy gangster ex-pimp of hers. It was something I was always struggling with; craving a bit more from her, but over-protective and distrusting of letting myself need anyone too much.

To that end, the initial client interview could be challenging, and Lonny was no exception. What with all the tentativeness and furtiveness. Lonny was sure taking the cake in the challenging category. The way he was moving his hips in the too small Ikea grand opening sale se... almost obscene. I was starting to worry that there would be a hole worn through the plastic when he actually stood up. I had to work hard not to stare at his hips.

I had a rule against interrupting my clients, too. I knew they didn't want to be interrupted. It would be a form of judgment. Even if the intention was to break awkward silences or help them tell their stories, it would be highly arrogant to put my own words in their mouths. Even though that's what they came to me to do. Put someone else's words in their mouth. Someone else's life in their day. They didn't want that with me. They wanted me to know the truth. They wanted me to know them. Otherwise, all that pretending? It can swallow a person up whole. Unless one person in the world knows your truth—the way you express it—you are doomed. Believe me, that is something I have learned from my mother.

One of the few things if you must know.

So back to Lonny. In the middle of all his squirming and silence, I just sat and stared at him. Not an uncomfortable stare, one that had a little head cock and a smile. I had practiced this stare. My clients were often uncomfortable around me. I liked to joke with Renata that it was my spell-binding beauty that did it; but she was ever honest with me and would just return a, "You're pretty. But they are scared. That is what keeps them quiet. And that is what keeps them talking."

Damn that Renata. She was so freaking smart.

"Who is that?" Lonny pointed to the photo on my desk, which I kept facing out toward my client chair. My clients were a little clueless. They fell for that one every time. Like a child you are trying to distract with a lollipop just before vaccine time, I kept that photo pointed out toward them. The dark-haired raven beauty smiling with her equally dark haired and equally beautiful toddler. The lilacs were in bloom in the picture. And they were brightly colored. A strange color. Not lilac colored at all. In a box of imaginatively named crayons, you wouldn't pull out the lilac one, or even the purple. You'd pull out the blue and the red and try to swirl them around and around until the tips of your crayons broke and you could kind of make out the red-blue color which had not set into purple but rather had kept the integrity of the colors making it up.

And then you'd still not quite have it.

"My mother and me," I answered matter of factly.

"How old are you in that picture?" Lonny asked.

"About four."

"My first memories are around that time. And they are with my mother as well."

I had answered questions about that framed photograph on more client visits than I could even recall. But Lonny, like so many other clients, was acting like he was the first one who had ever noticed it, had ever shown interest in it, like he was finding a point of connection with me. I let him believe that.

"Are they?" I encouraged with an upswing at the end of my sentence. I leaned forward a bit more intimately.

"My mother was so beautiful. I wanted to be like her. I wanted to look like her. I'd climb into her shoes when she was getting dressed to go out. She loved to take her time to dress to go out. And I loved to watch her dress, but I didn't love what it meant." I nodded as if I had a mother who loved to go out, too.

"My father—if he caught me in my mother's shoes—would lose his mind. Screaming and cursing that I was a faggot and better get myself out of those right now." Lonny reached over and picked up the photo; I made no attempt to stop him.

"So my mother would bring me into her closet when he was working late. She'd let me dress up in all of her dresses and shoes, and she'd paint my nails and help me put makeup on, and if I worried—'but what about Dad?—she'd shush me and say, 'Dad's not here. I am. Be happy for a little while.'"

He rubbed his finger along the red-blue lilacs. "Be happy for a little while. She'd always say that. It was our thing. Neither one of us could be happy when he was home—what with all the screaming and yelling and ..." his voice caught in his throat, "he was so mean to her. But we'd be happy for a little while. She'd say that and she'd dress up and I'd dress up and then she'd scrub my face and my nails and help me back into my regular clothes and she'd go out to dinner with my father and I'd stay with the babysitter. And I'd yell out after her—'be happy for a little while'—and she'd just look at me sadly and say, 'Ok. Thank you, Lonny. I will.'

"She hated that man. I hated him, too. Only she got to leave him and I got to stay with him."

He held onto the photo.

"She died when I was eight. He remarried within a year. My stepmother has never really liked me very much, let's put it that way."

I wanted to say, "Well Lonny, your dad sounds like a real jerk," but I knew better than that. This story could be taking an entirely unforeseen direction: Lonny could be crazy about his dad now. Lonny and his dad might have found some common ground, some understanding. He might not be here at all to hide who he was from his dad.

After all, I had started the interview believing Lonny to be gay and now realized that Lonny may well be transgender and unhappy in the skin and clothes he seemed to be trying to crawl out of in that plastic chair right in front of me. Or maybe I was wrong altogether and Lonny loved being a man in his own skin and only wanted to decorate it every now and then with makeup and pink feather boas. This was why I learned early on not to interrupt clients. Things never ended up the way you thought they would.

And that was true about Lonny, too.

"I need a fake profile. But it needs to be believable."

I nodded my head. "Yes Lonny, I'll be happy to do that

for you."

It was always hard to walk the line between letting a client know that I was well versed in what they needed, while not saying out loud: *You're hardly the first person who's coming into my office with this problem you've convinced yourself is so freaking unique.*

It was a misconception of some that Alibis was in the business of creating catfish profiles: profiles that had no relation to the client's real personality, look, or lifestyle. In reality, what many of my clients wanted was a place where they could hide from their faux lives. The ones that had become the prisons. The ones that had no reflection on their very souls and beings. The husbands and wives trapped in marriages that were stifling wanted the ability to pursue love for the first time ever. Lawyers who hated their jobs wanted to be erotica authors part time.

And transgender, homosexual, and cross-dressing clients wanted to leave behind their "ordinary" lives and be authentic for a little while. So it seemed at this point in the client interview that Lonny wanted something usual: a profile without real pictures but describing his real life, his real personality, to give him a vehicle to meet some like-minded partners. Go on some dates. Allow him to be happy for a little while.

I was planning a great new profile for Lonny when he finally replaced the photo back on my desk.

"Ok, Lonny. Let's talk specifics for your new profile."

"Well it's not for me. I want you to make one for my girl-friend."

"Oh. Ok, well shouldn't I talk to her then?"

"No, I mean ... I want you to create someone who can seduce her and make her leave me."

I nodded more vigorously to cover up the fact that I'd made a misstep. It wasn't a costly misstep, but it could have been. On the other hand, the fact that I'd screwed up seemed to have empowered Lonny for a moment. I thought about adding, "So you can finally come out to your father, Lonny? So you can finally be happy for a little while? The way your mother so desperately wanted for you when she was alive?"

But of course I didn't. I was a trained professional, no amateur. No way to know for sure if Lonny would have admitted what he wanted for himself out of this arrangement. No way to know for sure if Lonny would even have known at that point. I wrote down an email address and handed it to Lonny. "This is a secure and unique email address I will have set up for you and you alone. Your eyes only. I'll need the initial payment in all cash today. No checks please. We'll arrange further details and future payments through this email address. I'll never use your full name again in communications. Once payment is wired as per the details I'll send here to this email address, I'll get the new profile set up with access. It will look like it has been active for the last at least four years with pre-dated posts, and additional posts will be made from a town about 45 miles from here. It won't be one of those generic pop-up overnight catfish profiles that you could make yourself."

Lonny nodded at me and accepted the slip of paper with the fake email address on it.

As he glanced down at it and then at the lilac landscape again in my photo, he opened his mouth to speak and closed it again. I waited again in silence with my head cocked and my smile plastered on my face.

"How do I know?"

"Know what, Lonny?" I wasn't about to help out here. I wasn't about to make any further missteps.

"Know if this is all legit before I pay you?"

"Well, Lonny. I'm guessing you wouldn't be here if you didn't hear that I was legit. It's not like you came here because of a billboard on the turnpike, right?"

I smiled maternally at him, wondering only briefly who had sent him here. All of my clients were word-of-mouth clients by that point. Connected to each other by dishonesty;

my own grassroots network of protective custody.

Lonny pursed him lips and smiled, too, seemingly remembering fondly whoever it was who had sent him here. My mind went quickly to Beau, a terribly handsome cross-dressing gay man who had come to me about six or seven months earlier. He had wanted to catfish a few prospective dates. He was actually a fun client. Until he found a boyfriend. He had showed me pictures when he came to close out his accounts. Pictures of a handsome man who, now that I thought about it, had looked remarkably like Lonny sitting across from me, only with a pink bob-shaped wig.

"But here's the thing, Lonny. You need to pay me $1,000 today no matter what you think. If you want what you're asking. Before you get it. Because that's how I work. And you don't have any real way of knowing if I'll do what I say I will, just like I have no way of knowing if I can trust you either. So we're both in the same boat, right?"

And there it was. Lonny gave me the relieved nod as if I had just made sense. Which I hadn't of course. But he wanted to believe I was trustworthy so badly that he was willing to listen to my little well rehearsed speech anyway. If he was lying, I could lose money. Maybe even get into legal trouble. If I was lying, he could lose his dignity. Hardly the same boat.

Nevertheless, he reached into his pocket and pulled out an envelope of money: $1,000 in big bills, likely counted carefully at a bank teller window only a few hours earlier. It seemed that Beau very well may have been the one. I had charged him $1,000, too. Some clients were less. Some were more. Given my hunch about Beau, I had taken a gamble and quoted $1,000.

"Ok good, Lonny. Glad we can trust each other. I'll be in touch. Have a great day." I dismissed him, and got to working on the new profile right away.

Before he left, though, I didn't bother telling Lonny the truth about that photo with the dark-haired beauties set against the blooming lilacs that had provided his break-through.

*It was just the one that came with the frame.*

# Chapter 17

Will has summoned me because Audrey called and wants to see me. She's tracked me down after all, in this place where no one is supposed to be able to find me. Well, that was inevitable, I guess. But still.

"So did you talk to Audrey yourself?"

Something I can't quite place floats across Will's expression.

"No, she left a message—for the Director. They'd like me to respond and frankly, I'm not quite sure how to do that. So, Thea, what do you want me to say to Audrey?"

I drum my fingers on the arms of my chair for a few moments, stalling, collecting my thoughts, so I don't screw it all up. "My mother was always too busy to come in to volunteer in school."

Will leans back in his chair, apparently exasperated by the fact that I won't answer his questions head on. But I decide to answer another question altogether. One he'd asked in group earlier that day. He had asked, "Thea, why do you think you agreed to give that woman—Carmen Fierro—an alibi when you just admitted that she was running away from her husband? You had to know she was capable of a lot more than she was letting on—maybe not factory explosions, but still? Why did you help her?" It had put me on the spot. And sitting here in Will's office now, I think of something I wanted to say earlier, but forgot under the pressure of all those eyes on me at group therapy.

"It was a simple thing, but sort of impactful at the time. For a woman who should have been obsessed with ensuring that I turned out ok, turned out differently than my addict father, she was disengaged at all the wrong times. It drove me nuts."

Will is scribbling.

"No, not literally nuts. Don't write that down, Will."

Will stops writing.

"You know, she was limited. She was distracted. She was not there. That was it. That was the initial point of connection between Carmen and me, if you must know. That was it. She admitted to having the exact same kind of limited mother when I first met her. And we bonded over that fact. Small connections can lead to big ones, don't you think?"

"Wait. We're talking about Carmen again? The one you gave the fake alibi to? The one who blew up her husband's factory and landed you in jail? So you bonded with Carmen over your respective negligent mothers, and that's why you felt compelled to give her an alibi? A fake identity?"

"Oh, Will. You're so cute. Compelled? Trying to trick me into admitting some addiction you know I don't really have? Come on, you don't believe in all of this, do you?"

"But you have addiction in your family history, Thea. You've been quite open about that. You can't ignore the genetics here. It would be irresponsible to ignore the genetics here." Will taps his pencil on the notepad too hard and the point breaks. I feel uncomfortable as he gets up and takes a long time sharpening his pencil again.

My thoughts drift.

*Why does Will always write with a pencil anyway? Does he make that many mistakes?*

When he comes back, he splatters the lead remnants off the notebook onto the floor and resumes where he left off.

"You can't ignore where you come from, Thea."

I watch Will tap his pencil for a few moments before I tell him a story of one of the first clients I ever had.

◆

*Tell me the story you want me to hear.*

She had a dogeared copy of the *Life of Pi* paperback and she had a haunted echoing hollowness to her eyes. Like she could see through me. Like she knew more.

"My husband doesn't love me," she said without pity, remorse, or anger. In fact as I sat in front of her, I tried to decide what emotion she was actually feeling. The hollowness of her eyes had made its way to her voice, also.

"He keeps leaving me for her and then coming back. I need to stop the cycle once and for all. I need him to stay or leave. To choose. For himself." I figured out the emotion then. It was fear.

"How do you think Alibis can help with that, Mrs."—I waited but she didn't help me fill in the blank. She just handed me a heavy garment bag and said, "You need to make this dress disappear. It's hers."

I took the garment bag from her to avoid being rude but I didn't do it with any conviction whatsoever.

"Well with all due respect Mrs.—" still nothing—"couldn't you just sell it or burn it or give it away or get rid of it?"

"I don't know how to get rid of it."

I refrained from asking the convenient question: "What kind of medicine are you on?"

Instead, I asked, "So why bring it to me?"

She was still hollow-eyed, as she said, "I'm really just trying to break the cycle."

"And so you want me to do *what* exactly?"

"Destroy the dress. After I leave. It has to be after I leave."

"And then what?"

"He'll stop. He'll choose. Once and for all. He'll stop letting her choose. Her and this dress. It seems to have some kind of ... power over him."

I looked to the garment bag on my desk that was shifting all the other items wildly to the left. "Well, this isn't really, what I—you know—*do*."

"You alter time and place with your business, no?"

"Well, yes, but through an app. On social media. It's not *real*, you understand that?" I had sort of a spooky feeling about this client.

"I think we could have a lengthy discussion about what is real and what is not, Miss Brown. Would you please do this for me? Get rid of the dress. I'll pay you, of course."

She placed an envelope on my desk, and I tried again to get her name. "Do you really believe this dress has some sort of *power*, Mrs.—"

Still nothing.

She tapped the book repeatedly—the *Life of Pi* paperback—that was still in her hands. "Have you read this book?"

I nodded. After all, I had seen the movie. That counted, no?

"When there are two explanations for something, we are always drawn to the more interesting one, the more mystical one, no?"

I wasn't sure who the "we" were in her question.

"I don't know ma'am." I had given up on her name now. "Frankly, I tend to think the right answer is the *least* interesting answer most of the time." She smiled then. A warm smile that belied the emptiness in her voice as she answered, "Then I feel sorry for you."

"For me?" I didn't say it but surely she heard in my laugh the additional words, "You're in love with a man who can't give up his mistress and you are willing to blame the whole mess on a dress, and yet you are sorry for me?"

She must've heard what I didn't say because she responded, "He made me believe in all of this." She tapped on the book again. "Once you find someone who lets you believe in the extraordinary, it's hard to let go and accept only the ordinary again."

I had told Roy and Dr. Barrett the story of the woman and the strange dress. I was so disappointed when Dr. Barrett used the story to enhance her so-called expert report.

*Delusional.*

*Confused about reality and fantasy.*

*Addiction has blurred the lines of reality for her.*

In our meetings at Juniper Lane, she apologized. She said she didn't think I was delusional at all. That she had to say those things to save me. To get me here.

I believed her. But still, just to be safe, I didn't bother telling her the rest of the story. That I never ended up destroying the dress after the strange woman left it behind with a thick envelope filled of money. That the whole episode kind of creeped me out, and in fact, I didn't even tell Renata about what was in the garment bag that hung conspicuously on the inside of my office door when she arrived to work for me, because I didn't want her to think I had lost my marbles.

I didn't tell Dr. Barrett that, before her, in fact, I had only ever revealed the story of the dress to one person: a client who came in after the garment bag had been hanging on my door for about three or four months. A tall, extraordinarily good-looking man who was setting up a fairly ordinary shadow Facebook account to try to track down an old love from over a decade earlier. He asked what was in the garment bag, and on a whim, I opened it up and showed him a peek of the dress inside. He admired the dress and its odd color.

I rewarded his interest in the dress by letting him have it and adding some surcharges to my Facebook stalking bill.

Of course I suspected who he was even at the time. The philandering husband of the unknown Mrs. had come to claim the dress that belonged to his mistress, obviously. And there were two explanations for how he had arrived in my office. One was that the dress had lured him there with its mystical draw that his wife seemed to feel quite strongly about. Strongly enough to pay a complete stranger to destroy it rather than burning it herself.

And the other, more ordinary explanation, was that the husband had tracked his wife to my office and come looking for the dress pretending not to know who it belonged to when he admired it, even though he had an easy and quick name for its unusual color as soon as he saw it: *lemongrass.*

Will brings me back from the memory. "Thea, you have to stop ignoring where you come from. Don't you think it's time to sit down and talk with your mother? About all you're learning in therapy? Show her how far you've come?"

"The thing is, Will. When things happen in life, I have always picked ordinary explanations. When there are two explanations for something—I have always tended to the more ordinary. But now? I'm starting to believe in more extraordinary explanations. Do you know what I mean?"

Will's expression tells me he gets it. He's sitting up straighter. And he looks hungry, like I'm going to feed him something he's been wanting all along.

Only I don't know what that is, so I end our session instead with the best advice I can come up with for Will at that moment.

"But that makes me uncomfortable, you know. It's like this kaleidoscope I wanted from the dollar store so badly when I was seven and lots of other things I've wanted since then. Be careful what you wish for, Will. That's what I've learned in life."

Will looks momentarily disappointed, but he recovers quickly.

"Thea—I'll tell you what. Before you decide whether you're ready to see your mother—you want a day pass? I can arrange that. I'll take you and few of the group—not Zak of course—but some others, into town tomorrow."

I nod.

Will says he'll drive me into town and we can get a malted or something.

Like this is the 50s.

*This guy.*

*There's something about him that I can't quite put my finger on—but something that I really like.*

◆

*Audrey.*

That night, Will shows up at Margot's an hour before their dinner reservation, distracted by thoughts of Audrey Brown.

She has been calling and asking to see Thea. If Will has any weird feelings about coincidence relating to this 23-year-old daughter of a dead addict from the local area, the fact that she has a mother actually named Audrey doesn't make it any easier to shake off some very strong feelings surrounding Thea Brown.

But then again she lives in Ohio, Audrey Brown. She wants to make the road trip in to see Thea who has been refusing to see her mother for some time now. The Director delivers these messages to Will with increasing frequency, as Thea's stay at Juniper Lane goes on. Will refuses to speak to Audrey himself. He keeps passing her on to the Director, and to Thea's shrink, Dr. Barrett.

Will tries not to let his own fears and reservations inter-fere with his treatment of Thea, so he doesn't talk to Audrey, or investigate who she might be. He continually brings Audrey up, asking Thea if she is ready to meet with her mother, yet grateful beyond words that she isn't.

Margot had called just before his session with Thea ear-lier in the day and offered to cook them dinner that night, but Will told her he wanted to treat her to a night out. Given the overlong session with Thea that followed, Will had made a later than normal reservation, and so he had expected Margot to be home by the time he arrived.

Will lets himself in and calls out to Margot, fearing he'll surprise her like the last time, but he hears nothing.

Will wanders around the house sheepishly, feeling a little out of place, even though he has a key. He rarely comes here or stays here without Margot. There seem to be too many sand traps here. Bottles of liquor that are lined up in the dining room cabinet for guests, always seem to catch his eye when he walks by them. He never really wants to be alone with them and test his luck.

Will finds himself hurrying past the dining room without looking at the bottles as if he has caught them *in flagrante delicto*—embarrassingly—as he heads to the back of the house. He arrives at the doorway of Margot's home office nervously, as he thinks about the time recently that he startled Margot there, but he is relieved to find the room empty. Piles of papers remain scattered across the desk but Will doesn't bother crossing the threshold. He turns instead toward the staircase, and slowly walks up the steps. He hears the creaking noises under his shoes as he heads upstairs to the bedroom. The house is so silent, it makes him uncomfortable.

Will starts humming to himself, and when he gets to the top of the steps, he just barges right into Margot's bedroom, pretty sure he won't find her there ignoring him. At least not if she is alone.

The bedroom door opens soundlessly, revealing nothing but an empty room.

Margot's bed is made and everything is meticulously in its place. Will steps onto the plush ivory shag rug and immediately looks down to see if he's made any footprints with his outside shoes. Margot doesn't allow any shoes in the house and he feels a bit rebellious walking across her virgin rug tracking in the dust and dirt and grime he's brought with him as he crosses over to her dresser where there is a ceramic tray housing all of Margot's most intimate things: a pair of earrings, a brush, her perfume. Will picks up the brush to smell *it*, instead of the perfume bottle.

He's always found Margot's perfume too overpowering although he's never told her so.

It's her hair that he loves to smell. Occasionally when they have the luxury of spending the morning together, Will pulls her back into bed after she showers, wrapping around her, and burying his nose in her freshly washed hair, inhaling deeply and feeling a familiar drunken high from the endorphins that just her natural scent triggers. Before she starts applying products and makeup and perfume and the layers that keep him away from her.

Margot never seems to understand why Will resents all that stuff that is for the world and not him. The part of her that she still shares only with him—unruly hair and the scent of Margot, the scent that comes from deep within—he loves those things the best. When he tries to tell her that, it comes out all wrong. When he says "don't tame your hair" or "don't put any makeup on tonight" she seems to take it as an insult instead of as the ultimate compliment, so he holds it back.

Will is still standing, sniffing her brush with his outside shoes on her rug, when he hears Margot's car pull up in the driveway.

As guilty as if he'd been fumbling through her underwear drawer or liquor cabinet, Will races downstairs, and quickly takes off his shoes to leave them by the door and situates himself on the couch awkwardly, announcing himself quickly and loudly as soon as she pushes the door open.

"Hellooo!!! I got here a bit early so I just let myself in."

"Oh, hi honey." Will sees the passing glance of frustration and annoyance cross over her eyes but it's fleeting. "How long have you been here?"

"Just got here."

Will pats his own knee that is crossed uncomfortably over the other leg, and pushes up from the couch with guilt before making his way over to kiss Margot hello. He tries not to look behind him, up the staircase to her bedroom with its ceramic tray of treasures that he had just been fondling.

Before he kisses her, Will notices Margot throw out an accusatory glance that was focused not upstairs on the bedroom, but rather over his shoulder in the direction of the home office.

◆

The next morning, after a rare sleepover at Margot's, Will gets up before her, and comes down the stairs to make them both a cup of coffee.

He wanders into her office mindlessly while the coffee is brewing. He can't help think about how possessive Margot has been over this room recently.

*I didn't think we had any secrets left from each other.*

Her odd behavior is starting to make him wonder. Make him worry.

As he wanders across the threshold of Margot's office, Will sees the familiar stack of papers. He walks over and touches them. He starts to thumb through them with one ear cocked, listening for footsteps from upstairs.

It's all just legal papers and briefs. Margot's tax law practice is thriving, and her increasing success seems directly proportional to the amount of unintelligible and boring words on the papers she brings home. She often brings work home with her, and Will finds himself glancing longingly at papers on the desk, wanting so badly to share something of her work with her. Share with her the gift she gives him over and over when she acts as a sounding board for him about patients and other Juniper Lane business.

Will is about to ignore the papers on her desk the way he does so often when he sees them, when he catches a glimpse of something else peeking out from under her latest estate planning client file and red post-its.

He gingerly moves the top layer aside with one finger to reveal the document underneath. A blueprint.

Will tilts his head and tries reading the papers sideways without much luck. Margot is in charge of the ongoing construction at Juniper Lane on behalf of the Board. He knows very little about the construction except what he hears from Margot, that it's ahead of schedule. That it's more costly than anyone imagined. That Margot's fundraising efforts have doubled lately.

Will can't make out the details on the blueprints or the papers at the bottom of Margot's pile, without moving everything else on her desk, which he decides not to do.

Instead, Will heads back into the kitchen, pours coffee into mugs and takes the coffee upstairs to share with Margot. She drinks a few sips, and then crawls sleepily out of bed, grousing that she has an entire day ahead of her with contractors and subcontractors and has to "crack some heads" to keep costs under control with the new addition that is costing as much as a "fair trade bloodless diamond mine." She laughs loudly at her bad joke.

"I'll be late tonight. I have a Board meeting. Oh—and by the way—would you mind taking my car into town with you today on your day trip? Get the oil changed and a car wash? I'm swamped, and it really needs it. Just throw everything away at a garbage pail at the car wash. Nothing inside the car is anything I'm keeping, so don't worry about making judgment calls."

"Sure," Will says distractedly thinking again about how Margot is so open about the construction usually, and yet the blueprints and piles of documents are hidden on the desk downstairs.

"Margot." She stops on the way into the bathroom, and looks over her shoulder by way of response. "I don't have to worry about my job, do I? I mean, if this is all costing too much, are there going to be layoffs or any other staff cutbacks

I should know about?"

"Oh Will," Margot smiles, returning to the bed, and leaning over him, initiating a long and soothing goodbye for the morning. "You'll have a gorgeous new office in the new building. You have nothing to worry about. I'll even help you christen it." Margot drapes one smooth leg over him and any concerns Will has about the new addition to Juniper Lane go right out of his head.

Will slides into Margot's car and cringes. For a beautiful woman who seemingly has her life together, she really keeps her car like a train wreck. Gum wrappers and empty coffee cups litter the floor of the passenger side. There is a stack of empty bill envelopes bound together with a rubber band on the passenger seat itself and Will tries not to look at the impressive number of retail accounts that seem to be represented in left-hand corners.

It is no secret that Margot likes to spend money and Will has often wondered—albeit only briefly—if she could really afford her lifestyle, and if so, *how* she could afford her rather luxurious lifestyle especially while she was footing the legal bills for her addict brother, Jacob, and now her sister, who was tucked away in jail, after the debacle involving her no-good boyfriend, Wolf.

Will shudders thinking about the chain of events that happened after Margot's sister started dating Wolf.

And as Will flips through the bill envelopes ready to be discarded from Margot's car, he can't help but wonder, what with the way Margot has been acting lately, if maybe she isn't being entirely honest these days. Or maybe she's just preoccupied by her sister's legal troubles.

At the car wash, Will empties out Margot's messy car, and thinks guiltily about how self-absorbed he's been since Thea arrived. He's been much too busy and distracted to really ask Margot about her younger sister. To let her talk. To let Margot vent.

*Maybe Margot just needs to talk about Nia.*

With hair and makeup completed, Margot climbs into Will's car, adjusts the rear view mirror, and gets ready to start her day, grateful that he agreed to clean out her car for her. She wonders if he'll ask questions soon.

She's almost ready to tell him the truth.

Almost.

Margot didn't come from money. Quite the opposite.

Margot's life had long been surrounded by drugs and addiction. This was why she was always so adamant about using her experience to benefit Juniper Lane in particular. Margot was appointed to the Board of Juniper Lane because of her hefty résumé as a successful tax lawyer and an experienced development volunteer for several local community organizations, including a women's shelter and a food bank. Her fundraising skills were renowned in Eastern Pennsylvania and Margot was humble but aggressive at the black tie dinners where she was a frequent guest, mingling and recruiting new deep pockets for causes important to both the community and to Margot herself.

She didn't exploit her story—but she let it be known that her interest in these causes was not superficial. After the family banana farm had gone bankrupt in Dominica; after their father had succumbed to shame and despair and shot himself on the plantation grounds as it was being sold off to another family, Margot's mother had moved her and her older brother, Jacob, and Nia (then a mere infant) to the United States to start over. But Margot's mother, a struggling single mother, with few economic prospects when she arrived in America, had succumbed to drugs and died when Margot was only 17, leaving Margot to raise both herself and her sister, Nia. She wasn't shot by an ex-lover; she didn't escape to Dominica. She wasn't missing. She was simply ... dead.

By the time their mother died, Jacob was long gone to drugs by that point, and an absence in Margot's and Nia's lives much more often than a presence. Nia was eight years younger than Margot, and had formed a much stronger bond to Margot than she ever did to their mother, allowing Nia to all but forget the harrowing conditions the girls had lived in when their mother first died, conditions that were actually considerably better than when their mother was still alive and using.

Margot never forgot the kindnesses of the food banks and local churches who supplied the girls with meals for years on end, while Margot finished high school, and toiled away at community college between waitressing shifts at a local diner. She never forgot the kindness of strangers who filled their pantries with cereal and rice, and brought baskets loaded with new coats and socks and comfortable sweatpants and sweatshirts and the occasional toy or doll for Nia, at the holidays, allowing Margot to pass them off as deliveries from Santa Claus.

As Margot finished up her studies at community college, securing an economics degree, she took a job assisting a local tax preparer, continuing to wait tables for extra money that she saved for Nia to go to community college herself. Nia had just entered high school, and while she showed little interest in studying in high school, she showed lots of interest in boys, and Margot treated her sister's chastity as a full-time job, taking her to the local clinic for birth control when she was 15, and lecturing her for hours on end about the dangers of sex, not the least of which was another mouth to feed.

After Nia graduated from high school, she announced that she had absolutely no interest in college. She got a good job in retail that she actually seemed to love and to Margot's surprise, Nia showed some real possibility of success in her chosen field. With Nia settled, Margot took her meager savings and took the advice of her tax preparing boss: she went to law school at night.

Margot's unabashed determination, work ethic, and fierce smarts got her an interview with a local law firm that was looking to grow its corporate tax department. Margot quickly became indispensable and Nia continued advancing as a buyer and then a manager for the local retail store where her employee discount still seemed to be her favorite perk ten years in.

Within a year or so after Margot was appointed to the Board of Juniper Lane, she was just starting to relax a bit, having put enough years between her and Nia's background that she believed they really had started over: they had redefined themselves as something other than the unfortunate daughters of a dead drug addict. Sisters of a living drug addict.

Descendants of a failed banana plantation in Dominica.

And then Nia brought the Wolf home.

# Chapter 18

Will picks me up in his girlfriend's car for our day trip, which looks like it's just been recently scrubbed clean, so I joke, "She wasn't hiding a body in here, was she?"

Will doesn't look very amused.

We take Ali and Cassanda and the major celeb's zen leader along, too. Will makes me sit in the back of the car. I wonder if he thinks it's weird for me to sit up front, like I'll misconstrue things, and I want to tell him not to worry. I really *don't* think of him in any way other than my counselor, but I don't want to make it weird, by actually saying that out loud.

So I continue to crack jokes instead as we head into town to the diner.

"So, Will, why the new car? Are you like in hiding or something?"

"Hiding?"

"It's ok." I lean up from the back seat and whisper, "I won't tell anyone."

Will looks a little repulsed, like I'm coming on to him or something, which I'm not: *good lord, he's old enough be my father for heaven's sake.* I decide to dial back the jokes a little bit.

As I sit back in his girlfriend's luxurious car, I think with some curiosity: *Mr. Honest Will acts like he still has some secrets he has been holding out on us.*

When we get to the diner, it's got a serve yourself coffee machine, and Will lays his cell phone on the table, and everyone heads over to make coffee. But I've been promised a malted, and so I stay put and wait for the waitress to come and take our order.

With his back turned to me at the coffee machine, I eye Will's phone on the table. *How long could it go missing before he would notice? I could head to the bathroom and scroll through the messages, maybe get a little quick info about that mysterious girlfriend of his.*

*If his Facebook is logged on, I could scroll through his newsfeed. If he even has Facebook.* My hands twitch with the memory of the feel of a Facebook scroll. I close my eyes and open and close my fists. Suddenly I don't care about Will's messages or Will's secrets. I want to look through any newsfeed and see the concert photos, luxuriate over the VIP event check-ins, jealously examine the Bora Bora vacationers while I pick apart pictures of fake boobs and botoxed expressions. I want to update my own, by now completely outdated, profile picture and watch my screen notification page light up with the validation of a thousand likes.

"Thea."

I startle—opening my eyes.

Will had arrived back at the table with his coffee cup in hand.

I'm holding his phone, which I've discovered is password protected, and wonder: *hell, did he leave it on purpose, just to see if I'd do this?*

"What are you doing, Thea?"

I put Will's phone back down on the table with a "nothing, nothing." And suddenly, I am the bad guy here. The one without any control.

*I won't be finding out what secrets Will holds.*

*Not today.*

# Chapter 19

"How did your Board meeting go last night?" Will asks over lunch.

Margot has to come into Juniper Lane over her lunch hour to do some more head-cracking on the construction site, and they are eating from cafeteria trays in Will's office.

"Well," Margot looks over her shoulder, and noticing the door was open as per Will's famous "open door policy," walks over to close it before finishing. "The Board seems to think Thea is actually good for business."

Margot's laugh is uncomfortable. It makes Will equally uncomfortable.

"What do you mean, good for business?"

Margot lowers her voice to a whisper to supplement the effects of the closed door. "Have you been following the news coverage of her, Will?"

"Not lately," Will says truthfully.

The news coverage of Thea from the beginning had been confused and biased. They had little information about her or her business, Alibis, most of the records having been sealed by court order as a condition of her plea bargain. And so, left with a dearth of actual facts, the news had started making things up. She had gained a sort of celebrity status. Without a full name or a photo, they had made a cartoon avatar of her that they used in all the stories about her. They exaggerated the information they were allowed to use from court documents, which were mostly redacted to remove personal information such as surnames and business names and other identifying information. Somehow her first name had been left in, so they generally referred to her as Thea B and between the rapper name and the anime cartoon avatar, she had achieved a pseudo-hero avenger girl status in the media in recent weeks. Will had stopped watching when that happened, fearful that all the misinformation would somehow taint his treatment plan, which was progressing nicely.

Thea was starting to accept that maybe she really *was* substituting social media for opiates. And maybe she really *did* need to keep a cautious eye on her genetic predisposition toward addiction, but also be open to her own role in choosing a different path for herself. She was still refusing to see her mother, who called constantly, and whose calls Will had directed the intake director to send to Thea's treating psychiatrist, Dr. Barrett, until further notice.

He was still scared to death, of course. The idea that he might have to talk to Audrey Brown from Ohio at some point terrified him. The idea that Audrey Brown might be—

God, he couldn't even wrap his head around it, and so he didn't.

Will just kept focusing on Thea, and occasionally, he'd say to Margot, "Do you think it could really be *her*?" Margot would just wave her hands in the air and say, "Come on, what are the odds? What are the actual odds? Just treat her like you would treat any patient of yours, Will."

And so he did.

Thea was focused on next steps when she got out. Giving up social media for good, preparing a real résumé and applying for some tech jobs, since that seemed a real translatable skill that she had.

So, no he hadn't been watching TV, or keeping up with social media, and he'd been keeping the news away from the group as well, afraid that if Thea learned what an exciting business Alibis was still being described as in the outside world, she'd be reluctant to keep talking about giving it all up just yet.

Thus, Will makes all television choices for the whole group. Mostly what they watch together are soap operas on repeat. The newest resident, Morgan, seems intent on criticizing daily her temporary replacement and the admittedly ridiculous story line that she has undergone some "temporary" plastic surgery while she is in hiding from a disreputable mobster ex-boyfriend. "They'll be reuniting me with Raphael when I'm out and I'll get my face back again." Morgan frames her own chin with her hands to illustrate her unmistakeable beauty, and Will's group shushes her as they follow along with the soap opera. Even Thea.

Will has ignored the outside coverage of Thea B, but it's clear that Margot hasn't.

"Well, Will, you know I don't like to let the Board influence me, but I have to say on this point, I wouldn't mind having Thea around here a little while longer." Margot turns red with what Will assumes is embarrassment and he raises both eyebrows at her words.

"Oh come on, Will. Weren't you just telling me she tried to break into your phone yesterday? How far along is she really?"

"True. But, Margot, at the end of her 90 days, I'm not really sure we can keep her. And certainly not for construction money."

"Stop it, Will. You make it sound so dirty when you say it like that. Let's talk about something else."

"Ok."

And so he asks about her sister. "How's Nia doing?"

Margot sighs and drifts off somewhere Will can't quite join.

The Wolf was Wolf Holland.

"As if that's even his name," Margot had said as she shut the door on him after a night she had considered excruciatingly long. Their first meeting: Margot and Wolf.

"Margot, shush!" Nia said in a loud whisper. "He hasn't even gotten into his car yet. He'll hear you."

"Oh for heaven's sake—do you think he doesn't *know* that his name isn't Wolf?"

Nia had invited Wolf over for dinner and to meet Margot.

"Me? He wants to meet me?"

"Yes! That's how polite he is, Margot. I thought you'd be thrilled."

Margot was feeling many things; thrilled wasn't one of them. Wolf was a retired Wall Street tycoon. Allegedly. He had just moved to Pennsylvania from New York. Allegedly. He had never been married and had no family to speak of. Allegedly. And he was over the moon crazy about Nia. Allegedly. Margot couldn't help thinking in lawyer-speak when her suspicions were up. And her suspicions were up when it came to Wolf Holland.

"Nia, Come on. What do you even know about this guy?"

Nia and Wolf had been dating a few weeks. He had come into Nia's retail store and she had helped him pick out some clothes. He paid his rather large bill with cash, which actually impressed Nia, rather than horrified her as Margot cautioned her she should feel. And after a few dates, when Nia had apparently fallen short on new things to tell Wolf about herself, she had given him (in Margot's opinion) far too many details about her tax lawyer sister who was on the Board of Juniper Lane.

Now Wolf was interested in writing a hefty check to Juniper Lane. "I just want to give back to my new community." He had dripped the words on Margot over dinner.

"Are you really going to turn *down* his money, Margot? I thought that's what you do. You're constantly raising money for that place. I thought you'd be ecstatic. I thought you'd love to impress that boyfriend of yours." Margot threw the dish towel across the room at her sister. Part of the bargain of allowing Wolf in her home had been that Nia had promised to wash all the dishes and clean up after the dinner that Margot cooked (Nia was a god-awful cook). Margot had reluctantly wasted some of her favorite dishes—plantains and Caribbean chicken—on Wolf Holland and had even more reluctantly taken up drying dishes after he left, as she listened to her sister try to keep defending her new boyfriend.

"I don't know, Nia. I know you're a grown woman, and you can make your own decisions now. But it's hard for me. I'm so used to taking care of you. And I'm used to trusting my instincts. My sleaze radar is up very high right now."

Margot had barely gotten the dirt cleaned off her trail from Jacob's drug trial when Wolf showed up, and she had no interest in Nia bringing more unsavory characters into her life now.

Margot's older brother, Jacob, had followed their mother's path pretty predictably, and Margot had cut him out of her and Nia's life right after her mother died. When he called her from jail nearly twenty years later, she was only surprised because she had assumed he was dead by then. He called to tell Margot that he had murdered his own drug dealer. A noble crime in his opinion. Margot had to fight back a softening feeling in her gut, when he pleaded through the line.

"Please, Margot. Help me. I heard you're a lawyer. You must have lawyer friends. Contacts. Someone who can help me out of this place. Margot, they're talking about the death penalty. And I got a court-appointed lawyer who's got his own head up his ass. I'm done for."

Margot didn't want her brother to die. But she didn't mind him living in jail, where he'd likely clean up and stay away from her and Nia. Most importantly, Nia. She was still so impressionable. Margot wasn't incredibly proud of herself for the decision, but she had decided to call in a favor from Dr. Elizabeth Barrett, a fellow member of the

Board at Juniper Lane.

Ever ambitious, Dr. Barrett appeared to be on the Board for all of the opposite reasons of Margot. Dr. Barrett was an addiction researcher, who was published in all sorts of scientific journals and was highly sought after for lucrative speaking engagements, especially as she had started branching off into some controversial, but potentially marketable research on a growing field of "social media" addiction. It all seemed too speculative to Margot—a sexy way of talking about addiction—a subject that had grown decidedly less and less sexy in recent years as heroin and opiate abuse had become an absolute epidemic, touching affluent neighborhoods with such gruesomeness that they could hardly call drug addiction a ghetto problem any longer.

But this social media addiction seemed to be something the rich, white people liked talking about more than heroin. It was interesting and novel. Dr. Barrett had this idea that people could become so addicted to social media, it might actually be a gateway to chemical dependence. This theory was one the rich white people liked even more.

*It's not our fault that our kids are shooting heroin.*

*It's Mark Zuckerberg's fault.*

Dr. Barrett had been seeking introductions to some of the more high profile defense attorneys hired to get the rich and famous acquitted of their DUIs and drug crimes. She had a theory that they'd rather cop to a social media addiction than a heroin addiction, but so far she hadn't sold any defense attorney on her expensive theories. And Margot had cautioned Dr. Barrett on more than one occasion that there was a potential conflict of interest, or at least an appearance of impropriety using her information about the former and prospective patients at Juniper Lane to approach their attorneys to solicit clients.

At the time Jacob called Margot, Dr. Barrett had been secretly studying this underground company, Alibis, and Margot asked her for the contact information, claiming she wanted to check it out for herself, before letting Dr. Barrett loose to talk to some of Margot's own attorney contacts. Dr. Barrett was so peacock proud, that she handed over everything she had—and Margot went to meet with the founder herself.

Margot wasn't sure how much Thea would investigate into her own background, so she used a realistic alias: her sister's name. Margot couldn't risk having her own name smeared in this mess at all. No one at the firm or Juniper Lane had connected her to Jacob yet. His trial was just another drug and murder trial, nothing extraordinary, nothing high profile enough outside the criminal justice world to even touch Margot. If anyone tracked down Nia because Margot used her name, well, she'd take care of it. She always did.

Margot had paid Thea to create some fake discovery via social media that was "leaked" to the prosecution which they had to then turn over to the defense. Together, Margot and Thea made it look like Jacob's mother was still alive, was in hiding, and had a homicidal drug dealer ex-boyfriend, the same victim of Jacob's crime. The evidence wasn't enough to exonerate him, but it was enough to create mitigating circumstances that made the state give up their intention to seek the death penalty. Jacob was now serving 55 years to life in state prison and was dried out and far enough away from Nia and Margot to allow Margot to take a good long exhale. Margot didn't tell anyone about her part in the leaked discovery. And she hadn't expected to have any further dealings with Thea or Alibis.

Until Wolf showed up.

"Ok, Nia," Margot had said that night she met Wolf, ignoring her better instincts. "I'll take his money, but God, if he brings it here in unmarked bills, just allow me a couple of 'I told you so' a few times, ok?" She laughed and then left Nia with the rest of the cleanup as she saw Will's number light up her cell phone on the counter.

Wolf's money did not show up in a leather attache case, but rather as a large check with a lot of zeros, from the ridiculous name of "The Wolf Foundation."

Margot was twirling the check over and over on her desk, still trying to decide whether to deposit it into the Juniper Lane trust account or not, when Will showed up at her office to take her to lunch.

"Look at this." She flipped the check around and showed off a bit. She really was quite proud of her fundraising skills. Her ability to solicit other people's money was a big part of her identity.

Will leaned in and whistled. "Whoa. That's some check. Who'd you schmooze to get that one?"

"Ugh. I'm not sure I'm comfortable with this, to be honest. My sister's new boyfriend."

"The Wolf Foundation, hunh? Odd name."

"Odd guy. He's supposedly new in town. Former Wall Street guy. Has lots of money. And likes spending it in a pretty showy way. Nia's crazy about him. Wolf Holland. What a name, right?" Margot rolled her eyes, as she came around from behind her desk and leaned into Will for a delayed hello kiss. He looked past her, didn't lean in like she was used to and she almost tripped, she was so off balance. Margot put her hands out on Will's chest to steady herself.

"Hey, you left me hanging there. What are you daydreaming about?"

"Oh. Margot. I'm so sorry. Nothing. I—nothing." Will kissed her and they headed out to lunch just after Margot stopped at the bank to deposit Wolf Holland's large check.

A week later Margot was rethinking depositing the check after Nia insisted putting Margot on the phone with Wolf. "A tour? That's, well, a little unorthodox, to be honest, Wolf."

Margot was holding Nia's phone away from her face, as if holding it too close might allow Wolf to see the outrageous expressions she was making. Nia kept moving her hand across her throat signaling to Margot to "cut it out" which she kept mouthing as well.

"I'll have to look into it, Wolf. I'll let you know, how about that?" Margot handed the phone back to Nia and then proceeded to wash her hands. She refrained from running upstairs for a complete shower. She was having trouble understanding how her sister could stand that sleaze. She wished for a moment that Nia was still 15, and Margot could tell her who to date and who not to. Wolf was insisting that in light of his "sizeable donation" to Juniper Lane, he'd like a tour of the facility, particularly the newest construction that had recently commenced to really see his dollars in action. Margot wanted to explain to him that his donation, while important, was a small fraction of the money she solicited on a yearly, or even a quarterly basis, and that the construction that was underway had been in the works long before the Wolf Foundation came onto the scene, and would have plowed on even without Wolf's "sizeable donation."

But really, Margot just wanted off the phone, so she pretended that she'd investigate Wolf's ridiculous request with the other Board members. She had absolutely no intention of doing so.

"Get rid of him, get rid of him, get rid of him," Margot stage-whispered to Nia, increasing her volume with each repetition, trying to make Nia nervous enough that Wolf would hear, so she'd actually hang up on him. Which she finally did.

"Nia, please. Do me a favor. Do not mention my job or my Board positions to your future boyfriends. Don't even mention you have a sister. Sheesh." She collapsed onto the sofa and started playing with the remote, until Nia said, "Who says there'll be another boyfriend? Maybe Wolf is the *one*." And Margot let out a low laugh as she kept changing the channels—a laugh that stopped abruptly when she looked over at her sister and saw that she was actually serious.

Will couldn't get rid of that nagging feeling he had after Margot told him about Wolf Holland. His post-recovery sixth sense gave him feelings about these kinds of things. And he had a feeling about Wolf Holland.

More than a feeling. He remembered.

Bruce Holland, his former drug dealer, had had an elaborate tattoo of a lone wolf on his upper bicep which he flexed when he was threatening his customers, and one day Will had the audacity to ask about the tattoo. Back when he was John Morris.

"That's me—the lone wolf. And when I finally make enough dough to go legit, I'm going to change my name. Legally even. Wolf Holland. Bruce sounds like a common thug. Wolf—that sounds *sophisticated.* Don't you think?"

He had laughed then and so had John Morris. Will had been so high, he wasn't sure if he was even remembering the conversation correctly. But the way his intuition was flaring up, distracting him, he knew he couldn't ignore it—no matter what the truth really was.

After he'd gone clean and become a new person, Will had done a little research and had discovered that Bruce Holland had been sent away after a drug deal in New York had gone bad. The news provided a bit of relief for Will as he set up a new life not that far from where his old one had been.

Maybe Bruce had gotten out of jail recently and come back to his old stomping grounds? Bruce Holland could well have become Wolf Holland after he got out of jail, right?

Will knew he had to tell Margot. He had to warn her at least. But if he was right, if Wolf Holland really was Bruce, he'd probably know that Will was supposed to be dead. He could blow Will's past wide open, and Will would be in danger of losing more than Margot. At that time, Margot knew only that Will was a recovering addict with a vague, dark past, not unlike many of the patients that came in and out of Juniper Lane. She knew that he was a success story, like Margot and Nia, and she respected him for overcoming his past.

What would she think if she knew the truth? That he had, in fact, run away from his past like a coward. That he'd stolen another man's identity for a short time—albeit a dead one—and then reincarnated himself, leaving behind a pregnant wife and a rather large debt to his dealer? Would she still be impressed? Or would she be so shocked by his cowardice that she'd turn him in?

And more than that, if Will's cover was blown would Audrey be at risk? Her daughter? How many lives would be torn apart if Wolf Holland was who Will believed him to be, and if Will had to admit to Margot why he knew?

Then again, Will had wondered after watching Margot deposit a large check from The Wolf Foundation into the Juniper Lane trust account, how many lives would be torn apart if Will stayed silent.

At a Board of Directors meeting of Juniper Lane in early 2017, right around the time that Thea and Alibis came under fire due to a bizarre factory explosion outside of Philadelphia, a letter from one Wolf Holland was entered into the record.

Margot was present and so was Will, as the designated staff representative. The staff took turns attending the monthly Board meetings, to apprise the Board of new developments at the facility and to be on hand to answer questions.

"He's one of your solicitations, isn't he, Margot?" Dr. Barrett asked, causing Margot a rare moment of fluster.

"Oh, not exactly. I—"

"But he says right here, he's been impressed by your efforts and of the entire Board to bring Juniper Lane into the current century, with its state of the art advancements, and he wants to be an integral part of the institution's future."

"He says the recent donation is only a small amount of the funds he'd like to commit over the next 2-3 years. He'd like an opportunity to review the strategic plan, the financial projections, and to tour the facility itself before putting his commitment in writing. Kudos to you, Margot!"

Margot rubbed her temples, and tried to find the right words to address Dr. Barrett. That Dr. Barrett was excited to take Wolf's money without a second thought, and in fact, to give him unprecedented access to the facility, didn't surprise Margot one bit. That Margot was having trouble finding the words to shut the idea down, did.

Will jumped to her rescue.

"Speaking as a staff member, I'd like to express some concerns about allowing a virtual stranger access to Juniper Lane and potentially breaching the confidentiality of this place just because he has deep pockets."

"No one is suggesting otherwise, Mr. Cann," Dr. Hunter spoke up from his assumed place at head of the table. Notwithstanding the fact that he hadn't published a single thing in over a decade, seen a patient in even longer, or raised a dollar for Juniper Lane in years, Dr. Hunter still assumed a position at the head of the table each and every month, his spot apparently secure—at least in his own mind— by the seed money he'd helped raise for the facility when the cornerstone was being laid nearly four decades earlier.

The rest of the group gave Dr. Hunter what Margot thought was a rather exaggerated display of respect in light of the absence of any real or recent contributions. But every now and then he piped in with something that at least allowed Margot to piggy back on his cloak of respect.

Like now.

"Exactly. I fully agree with Dr. Hunter's position that we conduct a more thorough investigation into Wolf Holland's background before a) accepting his money, and b) allowing him access to the records and facility of Juniper Lane. Thank you, Dr. Hunter, for your wise counsel on this issue."

Dr. Hunter didn't even have the dignity to look surprised. He just nodded along with Margot, and added, "You're quite welcome."

Margot pretended to make some notes on the side of her agenda while saying, "I'll head up a background investigation, and submit a full report to the Board next month. Can we move on to the next item on the agenda?"

"Ah yes, the paper towels in the cafeteria are non-absorbent. Is that right, Mr. Cann?" The Board Secretary, Beverly Vose, continued reading from the agenda, and Margot stifled a laugh as she looked away from Will, who had to advocate for this line item on behalf of the staff who had, with all that was going on at Juniper Lane, actually gotten their backs up about the non-absorbent towels in the cafeteria. Margot had eaten there, and even spilled things there. She knew it was true. She also knew that sometimes the most trivial things can take on incredible importance when they feel like the only things you can, in fact, change.

She cleared her throat, stifled the laugh, and leapt into the on-going passionate discussion about paper towels.

◆

"Is Nia still seeing Wolf?"

"Yes. Ugh. Why do you ask?"

Will felt every bit the coward that he was, starting this conversation while in bed with Margot late one night the week after the Board meeting.

He'd been avoiding Margot's house, afraid he'd run into Wolf and Nia. He'd been making excuses, claiming work, and other obligations for the past few nights. Margot had showed up that night with a tray of her famous creole lasagna and a new black negligee. He had wanted to tell her about Wolf while they both still had their clothes on, but those plans changed quickly. They'd skipped dinner and jumped into bed. Now they were finally getting around to the lasagna, albeit on microwaved dishes in bed, and Will was trying to find some strength from the sex and the food to tell Margot what he knew.

And why.

He stalled.

"Your birthday is next week. How would you like to celebrate?"

Margot lit up with recognition. It was so important to Will that he stay healthy enough to be present on her birthday this year—unlike last year. This would mark the second of Margot's birthdays that they'd be together. That was significant on several levels.

"Want to rent Pirates of the Carribbean?" Will teased. It was a joke between the two of them. She hated that her homeland of Dominica was known only by the reputation of those movies. She had shared with Will the most beautiful memories of lush clear water, warm waterfalls and pristine beaches. She had memorized the recipes of her grandmother and cooked them for Will whenever she had the time. Creole dishes and plantains and spicy rice dishes. Once Margot had promised to take him to Dominica to visit, but they hadn't made any firm plans to do so. Occasionally, they jokingly discussed taking advantage of Dominica's economic citizenship program, a program put in place after the demise of its economy due to hurricanes and the collapse of the banana industry, to encourage investment in the island. To encourage business people to "buy" citizenship for the hefty price of $100,000 USD.

"Or we could just smuggle you in." Margot had laughed when they'd brought up the whole subject of going to Dominica one day. "Nia and I already have dual citizenship. I really want to show you the country one day."

But that was a while ago, and now with Jacob in jail and Nia dating Wolf, Margot was distracted, and it was hard to think there would be a moment to discover the Caribbean alongside Margot any time soon.

*Nia. Wolf.*

Will stopped stalling.

"Margot I have to tell you something about Wolf."

Margot pushed her plate of uneaten lasagna to the middle of the bed, creating a barrier between her and Will, as she listened to Will unravel his past—the real past—in which he had run away from his life. The one he had, up until that point, only revealed in anonymous groups far away from his current life and Margot.

That night in late January 2017 was the night that Will revealed the past in which he had left behind a wife named Audrey, and a drug dealer named Bruce "the Wolf" Holland.

And a daughter that Audrey had always promised she was going to name Thea.

*Because Thea means truth.*

Will unraveled to Margot a series of tenuous connections that seemed in fact quite strong by the time he was finished. Wolf might well be the drug dealer returned from a stint in New York's jail system, rather than the financial district. Will's former drug dealer might very well be the man seducing Margot's sister with money obtained from suspect ways.

It was the first time Will had told his story outside of an AA meeting. The catharsis was overwhelming. But of course, Margot didn't appear to share his relief.

"I have to go." Her plate of lasagna toppled upside down on Will's bedspread as she jumped up.

"I understand, Margot," Will was panicked. "Just, please Margot, understand that Audrey and my daughter—they would be greatly harmed ... I think, by any of this coming to light, I promised Audrey back then—"

Margot continued dressing, waving her hand to cut Will off. "I have no intention of telling anyone about your past. I just need to go talk to Nia. I need to tell her about Wolf. That what I thought was true. I'll tell her I hired a private investigator or something. I want that man out of all of our lives. I knew that. We'll address all the rest of this later. Or not. I don't know, Will. It's a lot. Just grant me that little truth, ok? It's a lot."

Margot left Will in the bed and he found himself remembering the fateful night that his pregnant wife had walked out of his bedroom, leaving him sad and desolate in his bed, with a wish that he could just start over.

◆

Three hours later, Margot and Nia were alone in their home and they weren't arguing about whether or not Wolf was a drug dealer or whether Nia should continue seeing him or not.

Those points seemed rather irrelevant by that point.

Wolf Holland was dead.

And he was bleeding all over their living room floor.

Margot had come home and surprised Nia and Wolf. They weren't using their time in the home to have an intimate evening. Instead, Wolf was using the solitude to go through Margot's office documents looking for Juniper Lane files and when Nia confronted him and told him to stop, he had knocked her across the room, just before Margot came in. Wolf was surprised enough, when Margot walked in, that Nia was able to get to her feet and run upstairs to escape him, leaving Margot and Wolf alone in the open living room.

Margot took in the scene that greeted her as she arrived, and assumed Nia had run upstairs to call the police. "So what's your story, Bruce? Yes, that's right. I've been doing a little investigation into your past. I'm not all that impressed by what I've found out about the Wolf Foundation. Are you hoping for new customers among the recently dried out and recovering? What exactly *are* you hoping to gain from all this?"

"You got me all wrong, Margot. I just want a little credibility, a little legitimacy. You and Nia did it. Right? You went clean and got yourselves respect in this town. I want the same thing."

"Nia and I didn't *go clean*, Wolf. Our mother was the addict. Not us."

"Well, don't be so sure about your sister. She likes to smoke a little here and there on the side, you know." Wolf put his hand up to his mouth and pretended he was smoking a joint and ducked his head in the direction of the upstairs where Margot thought that Nia was taking just a bit too long to call the police.

Margot decided to get rid of him. They'd call and get a restraining order, press charges for anything she could think of. They needed this dirtbag out of their home and out of their lives. If what he was saying was true about Nia, Margot needed to get her into a program as soon as possible. She couldn't risk Nia sliding into her genetically foreshadowed destiny. Not at the hands of this loser.

"Ok. Come on, Wolf. You've overstayed your welcome. Looks like my sister's mad at you, and I'd like you to leave." Margot pulled her cell phone out of her pocket and started dialing 911. "I don't want to have to call the police, Wolf."

The hairs on the back of Margot's neck started to stand up as the phone rang in her hand. What if he wouldn't just leave? What if he was dangerous? Had Nia already called the police?

"You've reached 911," Margot's phone yelled the announcement at both her and Wolf.

"All right, all right, I'm leaving. Relax. I told you. You got the wrong idea about me." Wolf started to head toward to the door, but Margot wasn't taking any chances.

"I'd like to make a report of an intruder in my home. A man is here and won't leave. Please send a police officer to 29 August Lane if you haven't heard from me in five minutes." She clicked off her phone.

"My god, you're just as dramatic as that sister of yours. I didn't do anything. I'm leaving." Wolf started putting his coat on and walked leisurely to the door, but his relaxed pace looked like a put on. He seemed genuinely nervous, but then his eyes fell on the flat screen that was still on in the living room not far from the front door.

*Thea B appeared at a preliminary hearing today. She is accused of aiding and abetting the late Carmen Fierro in the Fierro factory explosion last month.*

Wolf pointed at the screen. "Thea. Funny. Haven't heard a strange name like that in a long time."

Wolf was only a few feet from the door when Margot heard Nia come bounding down the steps behind her. "Don't you dare leave, Wolf."

Margot turned around to face her sister with exasperation. *Was she still going to stick up for this jerk?*

"Nia—Wolf is leaving. I've asked him to leave."

Margot saw then that Nia was holding a pistol up and pointing it at Wolf.

"Whoa, whoa. You are nuts sweetheart. Don't tell me you actually know how to use that thing?" Wolf chuckled, but still looked nervous.

Margot had gotten the pistol years ago when they'd still lived in dangerous housing projects under very unsavory conditions.

At night, in the early days after their mother's death, Margot and Nia would lay in the house's single bed atop a filthy mattress pretending they were somewhere else.

As the rough sounds of fights and occasional gunfire echoed just steps away from their flimsy door, Margot would stroke Nia's hair and tell her stories about their family's banana farm far away in Dominica where the water didn't drain from rusty pipes into roach infested sinks and tubs, but rather from clear blue waterfalls into even clearer blue shallow swimming holes.

"Can we go back there?" Nia would ask sometimes.

And Margot would say, "There's nothing left now. We'll have to find our own banana farms right here. And we will." But in the meantime, she bought them a pistol for protection. And she taught both herself and Nia how to use it. They didn't keep it loaded. And they kept it locked in a small safe in Margot's closet these days. They were a long way from both the banana farms of Dominica and the bullet-hole rid-dled walls of the housing projects, but as she stood with the gun pointed at Wolf, Nia looked every bit the scared child she had been back then.

Margot couldn't help wondering if the inordinate delay just now had not been Nia calling the police at all, but rather Nia finding and loading the gun. As her sister stood there with the gun pointed directly at Wolf's chest, Margot noticed Nia's face was swollen and green—something she hadn't seen when she had first arrived home; all she had seen was Nia scrambling up the steps away from Wolf.

"Nia, did he do that to you?" Margot reached her hand up to her own face in empathy, feeling the rage course through her at the sight of her sister's eye that was retreating behind swelling—swelling that was increasing every moment they all stood there. Margot's rage only expanded as Wolf reached inside his jacket she'd allowed him to grab on his way to the door and pulled out a gun of his own.

"I wouldn't take a chance that I'm a better shot than you, Nia." Wolf's voice was all sour and no sweet now.

Margot took charge of her feelings, controlling the rage and fear to call out to her sister a few feet away on the steps. "Nia, why don't you put that gun down. I called the police and told them to send someone if they don't hear from us in five minutes—that five minutes is over now. I'm sure the police are nearly here."

Nia stayed still. The guns stayed pointed at each other.

Wolf stayed still. The television blared in the background.

Margot wondered if the police were indeed on their way.

*Thea B will remain in jail as she has not been able to make bail as of yet. Her company, Alibis, which provided social media hacks to private clients, is certain to go up for trial as well.*

Margot shivered at the television report, wondering

briefly how much was actually known about Thea Brown's private Alibis clients. She wasn't distracted for long, though.

Wolf brought her back to reality, when he said, "Thea, Thea, Thea later." Wolf waved at the television with his free hand, and pretended to lisp a goodbye chant at the news channel. "Last time I heard that name, I was saying, "Thea later," to a woman and her baby daughter after their dead-beat druggie husband had gone and ODd, leaving her with a big bill to pay off. God that has to be 20 years ago now. Good times. Wouldn't it be funny if that little baby Thea grew up to be a criminal, too?"

Wolf was getting more comfortable the longer he was standing there and Margot knew he was trying to distract them both with his blabbering.

*God, this guy is vile. How could Nia have fallen for him?*

In addition to her disgust, Margot bristled at the characters in the story Wolf was telling about Thea Brown, trying to wrap her head around how and if a story of a little girl named Thea with a dad who overdosed, was connected to the story she had just heard from Will for the first time.

*If Wolf is who we think he is, could Thea Brown be—*Margot pushed the thought out of her head as she focused on the gun standoff not feet from where she was standing.

"Nia, put the gun down."

"That's right, Nia. Listen to your smart sister. I'm starting to think she got the brains *and* the beauty in this family."

Nia's shoulders slunk and Margot was thankful for the first time for Nia's low self esteem. "Nia, you can't do it. You know you can't do it. Just put the gun down." Margot pointed at the first step. Nia stepped down and placed the gun gingerly down on it. Wolf started to cackle as the gun hit the step—but the cackle caught in his throat mid-laugh, as Margot grabbed the gun and shot Wolf in the chest before he even had a second to adjust his aim.

She shot him two more times in the chest as he lay bleeding on the floor, while Nia cried and gasped from the steps.

And then when no police came, Margot called 911 again, and calmly said to the operator. "My sister has shot an intruder. I need police immediately."

Nia stood speechless until Margot hung up. "Margot! I didn't shoot him." She sounded like she wasn't quite sure. Margot walked over and placed the gun down and went to the kitchen sink to wash residue off her hands. "Nia, are you using? Has this low life got you using drugs?"

Nia looked down at the ground in response.

"I can't help you if I'm in jail on trial for murder, can I? I'm going to get you out of here."

"Out of Pennsylvania?"

"No—out of the US. I'm going to get you clean and away from influences like this. I'm not failing you like Jacob failed us. Like our mother failed us. We're going to do this for real now, Nia."

In the next few moments while waiting for the police, Margot and Nia discussed the steps that would be needed to get Nia back to Dominica where Nia could presumably start a new life and get help.

One thought plagued Margot as she and Nia planned.

*There was no rehab facility of the caliber of Juniper Lane in peaceful, beautiful Dominica.*

*There had never before been a need.*

Sitting in his office, Margot hears Will repeat his quiet question, "Margot. How's Nia? How's she doing?"

Margot sighs. She decides to drop the subject of whether Thea Brown is good for business or not. She looks over her shoulder again, as if needing some more reassurance that the door is still closed. "She's Nia. That's my best answer right now, Will."

# Chapter 20

After the whole episode in which Will caught me red-handed, holding his phone at the diner, I have to get a little more serious about treatment.

I don't have to see Audrey, but I do need to think seriously about what my life is going to look like when I leave Juniper Lane in a little over a month. That's according to Will.

From my point of view, I know Will doesn't really have a clue about me. What I haven't figured out exactly, though, is why he cares so much about me and seems to care what happens to me when I get out of here.

The major celeb is getting out of here in about three weeks—even before me. He has started to pack his things. He told me recently he hates his zen master—that he hasn't made him feel very zen at all. I jot down a number and a name on a piece of paper and I tell him, "When you get out of here—look her up. She was always the best zen master for me when I was outside."

"Don't you want to hold onto her?"

"No, she needs bigger and better things. She deserves it. Treat her well, ok?"

The major celeb hugs me and I hope he finds Renata and pays her well and treats her well, and she never regrets that day she came to work for me. I certainly don't.

◆

As Day 90 is looming over my head, I start to accept that even though I might have gotten into Juniper Lane under questionable circumstances, maybe I can benefit from what's happening inside of these walls.

I know now from my digging and eavesdropping and even from prodding Dr. Barrett a bit during our weekly sessions that Will's girlfriend helped me get in here. She and Dr. Barrett convinced Juniper Lane's staff to take me on as some sort of charity case.

"Margot is extremely dedicated to addiction causes and this facility. You're quite lucky she took such an interest in you and took you on as a cause," Dr. Barrett says somewhat indulgently in one of our more boring sessions.

I haven't told her or anyone else that Margot was masquerading as a drug addict's sister named Nia Hamilton less than a year ago. Not even Will. I don't want to puncture any illusions he has about this woman just yet. I've put the pieces together to see that she has gotten me here, and has also made sure I know it. Maybe as a payment of sorts. Maybe she's hoping I'll stay quiet, and so I do.

But there's a piece of this puzzle I haven't quite figured out, and I'm determined to do so before my 90 days are up.

Dr. Barrett let it slip that Margot had requested specifically that I be treated by Will Cann; she phrased it as, "She really does think—personal feelings aside—that he's the best of the best. And she was adamant that you get the best of the best. Lucky you, no?"

Why did Margot risk me telling everything and blowing her whole cover to her boyfriend by getting me assigned to Will? Seemingly she brought me here for the very purpose of bribing me to keep me quiet. Why then would she have put me in front of Will, Mr. Honest Abe, day after day? Why would she have risked that? Unless Will already knows Margot hired me and Alibis back then?

But no, Will had introduced us that first day I saw her at Juniper Lane. He didn't know we'd ever met, and she was cautious to keep up appearances that day: *"Nice to meet you, Thea," she had said with syrupy sweetness.*

He didn't know and she didn't want him to know. But still, she wanted me to be treated by Will.

*With all the other qualified counselors at Juniper Lane, why Will?*

And when I catch glimpses of her in her hard hat behind the tarps at Juniper Lane now and again, I can't help but think: *Margot Hamilton clearly is good at dishonesty. So what else is she hiding?*

# Chapter 21

Will notices that Thea is starting to look a little depressed in group.

The advances they've made together don't seem as positive this week. He knows that part of the problem is that Cassandra has left. Headed back to that heel of a husband of hers.

Everyone tried to talk her out of it.

Even Will. Even Thea.

At group the previous week, Thea had been aggressive with Cassandra. When Cassandra said she was planning on returning to her husband, Thea walked over and sat down face to face with her and said, "Cassandra, no. You can't do that."

Cassandra sat so still. She looked at Thea and placed her hands on her own belly with a sad resignation that made Thea and everyone else in the room gasp. "Cassandra, are you—"

"Yes. I'm pregnant."

Will had shuddered, wondering when she had learned that piece of poignant news. Had she known when that sociopath had beaten her up most recently? Had she known when Doreen recommended a psych evaluation? Had she known when her car crashed headfirst into the highway divider?

"Cassandra. You have choices. You don't have to go back to him." Thea had taken Cassandra's hands in hers and pleaded. A few tears made greasy streaks on Thea's cheeks, but Cassandra remained dry-eyed and stoic. "Those are just empty words. It's his baby. He has rights. And no one else—"

She stopped suddenly.

"No one else, what, Cassandra?" Thea had asked.

"I'm embarrassed to admit this—but I used to hope that maybe I'd be rescued while I was here. A white knight. A new dream. But no one's come. No one's going to rescue me. This isn't a fairy tale. It's real life, Thea. Real life." Cassandra had wiped away Thea's tears as they sat there together.

"That's what we're both here to learn, no? You're not the Dutchess of Windsor. And I'm still the local pastor's somewhat unbalanced wife. I'll be ok, Thea. You don't worry about me, ok?"

"But Cassandra, you don't have to stay with him. Just because you're pregnant. You can leave." Will had joined in Thea's plea.

"I've learned so much in here," Cassandra had replied. "I'm grateful. So very grateful. I know my truth, now. And here it is: I'm not strong enough to do this alone. Not yet. That's my truth."

Will had sighed with resignation as had Thea. Thea had nodded as she held Cassandra's hands in her own until the end of group, and when the session was over, she turned her back on Cassandra as Cassandra left group at Juniper Lane for the last time.

Will looks around the room at the dwindling group.

Thea has claimed Cassandra's former spot on the floor, and looks lost without her.

It is not helping anything that the famous musician is checking out in just a few days, too. In fact, the recent absences have made the waning group more sober lately. Ali is still here as is Zak without a C. But they seem rather static in their treatment. Morgan has resumed her character on the soap opera and Will notices that there are no new residents checking into Juniper Lane lately.

He mentioned it to Margot recently, but she was vague with her responses. Will realizes she hasn't been loitering behind the construction tarps at Juniper Lane as much as usual. There's an odd feeling inside the Juniper Lane walls that change is imminent. A change more dramatic than a new cafeteria. A change more dramatic than replaced linoleum floors.

After group, Will and Thea sit in his open-doored office for a one-on-one session, and he decides to take a detour with her, trying to distract Thea from Cassandra's exit from Juniper Lane and her heartbreaking decision to return to her husband.

"Do you want to talk about your family in Ohio, Thea? Is it just your mom?"

"No there's a stepdad and a stepsister. They're lovely. We don't need to talk about them, Will."

"A stepdad?"

"Un hunh."

"Is that his name?"

"Is what his name?"

"Brown. Your last name. You and your mother have the same last name, but you mentioned a stepdad. Were you born with the name Brown, or did you get it from your step-dad?"

Thea makes a few seconds of solid eye contact before looking away. "I really don't want to talk about my stepdad in Ohio—ok, Will?"

Will's intuition/sixth sense is flaring up, like something is about to happen and he can't quite prepare himself—can't quite put a finger on it.

He wonders if he will be able to handle whatever it is

that is coming his way.

And more important, he wonders whether he will be able to handle it ... *sober.*

# Chapter 22

"I strongly recommend you sit down with your mom very soon, Thea."

"You're kidding, right?"

I've been floundering the last few days. Cassandra's departure affected me much more than I expected. The major celeb's imminent departure has bummed me out, too. Will has been trying to get me to talk more in group, but he's also been giving me a little more space lately. Until today. Today Will has summoned me to his office to discuss Audrey's nonstop incessant calling to check on me. I have left explicit instructions that I do not want to see anyone.

But now she's gotten aggressive. She says she's headed to Pennsylvania. To talk to my treatment team. I ran to Dr. Barrett immediately when I heard that. Dr. Barrett says she has explained in no uncertain terms to Audrey that she will not be permitted to see me, or to gain access to my file. HIPAA regulations, blah, blah blah. She has *assured* me.

But Will? He's still trying to get me to talk to Audrey. I can't figure out why he's so invested in this.

"Of course I'm not kidding. She's your mom."

Something flashes in his eyes as he says this. I try to read it. Fear. Excitement. It looks a little misplaced actually.

"Aren't you here to remind me how all of my problems are a result of my mom? I've done all your honesty exercises in group. But where's the exercise where I lie on your couch and tell you what a sorry and broken little girl I was? A dead addict for a father. A distracted, disengaged mom left behind to raise me on her own. How else was my story supposed to go, except for downward? Oh. That got you, right? The great Will Cann has an Achilles heel. How nice to finally see."

Will had winced visibly at my sad tale. I feel a little guilty.

"It's a sad story, Thea. But your mother has a point of view, too, no? Part of your healing may come from hearing your mother's point of view. Experiencing your childhood from her perspective. I'm worried that you will be undermining all the hard work you've done in here if you ignore your mother's point of view out there."

I lean back in my seat with an exaggerated movement. "Well, Will Cann, be careful. You are starting to sound like someone who gives too big a damn about his soon-to-be-released-to-the-world client." I am blushing as I say it, and I look up at the ceiling in feigned dismay to hide my visceral response to Will's paternal reaction.

When I look back down at him, Will leans far back in his seat and stares up at the ceiling for a period of time that is much too long.

I squander the silence waiting for it to end, and then when it does, I am unsatisfied. Because of who ended it and how.

"You need to discuss exactly how you feel with Audrey, Thea. It's more than courtesy at this point. It's imperative to your recovery that you speak with her. She's your mother, Thea."

I stare at Will's flushed face and even though I can't see it from this angle, I feel the quote from the Hamilton poster behind me across the length of the office shouting at me from across the room.

*Who will tell my story?*

*More important, what is the story I want you to know, Will Cann?*

Something that feels like a collision in my brain starts to affect my breathing. I try counting in my head. I notice I'm unconsciously scratching at my arms again the way I did when things got a little heavy in jail with my incompetent public defender, Roy.

Everything feels like it's about to spiral out of control.

I leave Will's office in the middle of our meeting. My head is spinning and I feel nauseated. I head directly to Dr. Barrett's office and bang on the door. She's not there. Her secretary tells me I need to make an appointment for later unless it's an emergency.

"Is this an emergency, Thea?" she asks.

I can't answer. I can't even talk. My throat feels like it's closing up, and that's an emergency, right? I nod my head, speechless, and the secretary tells me to sit down and put my head between my legs, and she'll call 911. I wave her off as I find breath and words.

"No. No. Just let me make a personal call. Can I do that?"

She looks over her shoulder like she's breaking a rule, but hands me her phone anyway.

I dial the number, surprised I can even remember it after avoiding it for so long now.

When she answers, I say simply, "Mom. I'm here. At Juniper Lane. And I need you to come see me. ASAP."

# Chapter 23

Greg Brown is in the hospital cafeteria in Ohio when he ignores his wife Audrey's call from Pennsylvania. She has left rather suddenly, apparently on a quest to finally see that daughter of hers face to face. In Greg's opinion, Audrey is just too obsessed with her daughter, Thea, and her dead but not dead husband. It's a little too much. And Greg has played the role of understanding new husband just long enough. He is bored with all of it.

They had an argument before she left. He said things that were unkind, but things he doesn't feel like apologizing for just yet. Audrey said things, too. That he was selfish, self-absorbed. Other things. Things that meant he would be wanting an apology from her. First.

As he ignores her call, he sits with his back to the cafeteria entrance, and he faces the large windows that look out on the parking lot. On the other side of the building is a grassy park and a large marble fountain built by the city to honor lost WWII veterans from town. Apparently three brothers and two cousins of an affluent old money family in town had the misfortune of dying together in that war. They got themselves a monument and a legacy. It would have been a noble view if only the cafeteria faced it. Which it didn't.

Greg often wondered who the planner was who picked the location for the cafeteria. It was the area of the building with the only floor to ceiling windows, and thus the best chance for an actual view. And yet the windows faced the parking lot. Brick and stone walls faced that park and its monument. No one from the hospital got to view it from the inside. Maybe that was part of the plan. You had to go outside to appreciate it. Walk the park. Throw a stick or two to a dog. Breathe the clean air.

No one inside these cafeteria walls knows much about breathing the clean air outside during daylight hours. They are soldiers of their own kind, standing arm to arm inside fighting the good fights. When Greg gets home each day, Audrey asks him the questions he knows she thinks she should ask: *How was your day? Any interesting cases today?*

But he can't share the bloody chaotic mess of his day with her. Only his fellow soldiers can share those feelings, memories, and emotions. He doesn't even know where to start with Audrey. Yes, she is a doctor, too, but her job is literally bloodless. Working with the cadavers in a practically solitary confinement, self-imposed and one that she loves, she is not fighting the same war he is fighting in the surgical operating room, day after day, year after year.

*Surgeons get a bad rap,* Greg thinks to himself as he pokes his white green lettuce with the plastic prongs of a fork several times before the plastic pierces through and he can bring the lettuce coarsely to his mouth.

*Surgeons get a bad rap,* he repeats to himself with subsequent mouthfuls.

*Maniacal, egotistical, self-centered.* When in reality they are simply self-assured.

No he didn't share much of his day, and thus his life, with Audrey, but only because it might scare the shit out of her. He doesn't even know where to start.

Greg pokes the white iceberg again several times and is in mid-thrust when he feels a familiar hand on his shoulder. He knows just the touch of her palm before she greets him.

"Hello, Dr. Brown."

"Hello, Dr. Lane," he smiles and moves his tray to make room for her.

Peggy Lane pulls up a chair and squeezes in the same side of the table as Greg and stares out at the parking lot view. "How are you?" She breathes out the words while she blows on her cup of hot soup. And as she does so, under the table, she kicks her foot out of her rubber surgeon's shoe and rubs it lengthwise up the side of Greg's leg. He lets his breath out and stops stabbing at lettuce, relaxing in his chair for the first time since he sat down.

"Want to grab a drink after work? Trudy's at her mom's tonight." He doesn't look at Peggy while he asks the question but rather keeps looking out the window.

"Sure. I can get away—how about you?"

"Always," he says. *Always for you.* He reaches over and gives her thigh a squeeze before standing up, masking the front of his bulging scrubs pants with a tray full of wilted lettuce as he heads out of the cafeteria.

◆

Audrey is sitting at a diner near Juniper Lane trying to work up the nerve to actually finish a road trip from Ohio she started the day before. She tries to call Greg, but it goes right to voicemail, and she imagines him staring at the phone and hitting "decline" as she has seen him do on countless occasions when the phone rings with a number he doesn't want to accept in front of her.

Audrey picks at the leftover chips on her lunch plate, notices her cell phone register the noon hour, and wonders what Greg is doing right that moment.

Possibly, he'd be picking at a salad for lunch. He had been trying to eat better: the "green diet" he'd proudly proclaim to anyone who was watching him put the salad on his tray. Sometimes Audrey had lunch with him in the hospital cafeteria if their schedules allowed, which they did with diminishing frequency lately. Greg was busy. Always busy. Thirty minutes on the treadmill every morning before his shift started, counting out fish oil pills and standing in line for decaf for breakfast. And then a full shift at the hospital.

*And the women.*

Audrey had to admit to herself that Greg was addicted to sex right around the time they had stopped having it.

He had been wildy crazy about sex when she first met him. In the car, in the hallway, quietly or loudly. He loved sex, but not intimacy.

Audrey understood this to be true and accepted it as normal behavior, the way a woman who has lived with an addict for a very long time is apt to do. She went along with it because frankly, she hadn't had sex in a very long time and really loved being desired and wanted. She wanted what he was doling out at the time.

*So I may have misled him*, she'd tell herself on countless occasions.

The sex never evolved. Even after they got married. It never evolved from wild to intimate. It never resembled anything like two people who knew each other and enjoyed making love to each other. It mostly just looked like sex, with one of the parties acting a little bit like he didn't want to know the other.

She had pushed down the unconnected feeling she got when he came home from the hospital and asked her to change into something sexier, or looser, or tighter. She ignored the voice that said they were heading in an uncomfortable direction when he asked her not to mention Thea or Trudy when they had a free night. Too often Greg wanted to pretend they were childless, and single and free.

And then when Audrey couldn't ignore the voices any longer and simply said, like she was supposed to be able to do, "No, Greg. No. I'm not comfortable. I want to talk tonight. I want to be heard. I want to hear you," his eyes had ignored her and interrupted her as he said too quickly, "No problem,

Audrey. No problem at all."

And after that, they didn't have sex at all. And the very fact that it stopped so quickly and so abruptly made her know that she had been replaced. Even before the whispers started within the hospital grapevine. Even before she knew.

And of course she knew why.

Because she had asked for it to be this way.

She had said, no. So what could she say, now?

Sitting in the diner, picturing Greg hitting decline on her call and knowing that he wasn't missing her one bit as she headed off to try to save Thea, she thought:

*I can't be mad at him.*

*I've done this.*

Audrey had gotten involved with Greg the same way she had gotten involved with John Morris, by ignoring the voice that was crawling up the back of her spine, and leaning around her neck, lifting her hair with its cold and calloused hands, and whispering into her ear unbidden and unwelcome:

*I am addiction.*

*Were you looking for me?*

*No matter.*

*You have found me.*

◆

Audrey stretched her back away from the fake leather chair at the diner and rubbed a knuckle into her lower spine with more violence that she originally intended to. Her bones were starting to ache in the middle of her back in places she couldn't quite reach.

Greg hadn't bothered to pick up an hour earlier when she tried to call, but suddenly his texts had become a bit panicked after she had texted that she was probably going to stay in Pennsylvania another couple of nights.

*How much longer are you going to be away?*

*You can only run after her for so long, you know.*

*Trudy will be home from her mother's the day after tomorrow.*

*What am I supposed to do if you're not back by then?*

Greg's texts grow increasingly less readable as the afternoon goes on. His narcissism provides a constant shield between his self and his awareness.

Audrey taps angrily on her phone before placing it face down in front of her, the modern equivalent of hanging up angrily—but without any of the intended results.

*Thea is my daughter, too, Greg.*

*If I'm not here for her, who will be?*

She had been away for barely two days so far, and Greg was growing impatient with the demands of caring for himself. No matter that Audrey had finished all of the laundry before she left town, and baked not one, but three dishes that she'd placed in disposable trays with reheating instructions on tiny yellow post-its affixed to each tray.

No matter that he had more vacation time accrued than he'd ever use, or that if Audrey stayed for a few more days, this would be the first time Greg was forced to spend real quality time with his own daughter in years.

None of that mattered.

Greg still viewed every minute Audrey spent on issues that didn't concern him as a personal insult *to* him. He'd been punishing her every minute she'd been gone and she wasn't looking forward to the even colder treatment she would encounter when she went home to Ohio; her heart raced a bit every time she thought those words in her head: *home to Ohio.*

Trudy, the stepdaughter Audrey loved so much, was the only reason standing between her long-term exodus and her imminent return to Ohio. Without a biological tie to Trudy, Audrey was sure she'd be kept from seeing her if she and Greg split up. Some days Audrey felt like she was the only parent Trudy even had in this world. Lately, Trudy was starting to feel like Audrey's only anchor to this world at all.

◆

As she sits in the diner for hours, Audrey can't turn away from the nonstop coverage of Juniper Lane pouring down from the television sets blaring in every corner of the restaurant. They have been mentioning her daughter with that ridiculous cartoon avatar that Audrey hates. She has been calling the rehab almost daily since Thea was moved there from jail. It crushed Audrey that Thea wouldn't see her or talk to her—in jail *or* in rehab. Ever since she learned of Thea's arrest from a quick text—*a text, for God's sakes!*—Audrey had been calling and speaking in a cursory fashion to her lawyer and then to her psychiatrist, both of whom seem to know very little about her. Or at least are revealing very little.

Thea's only communication had come the day of her arrest:

*Mom, I'm going to be MIA for a little bit—dealing with some legal issues—nothing to worry about—I'll keep you updated. Stay in Ohio, whatever you do. That will just make things easier for me, believe me.*

"Will Cann—that's her counselor, Mrs. Brown," Dr. Barrett has said on several occasions. "That's who you'll want to talk to eventually. But HIPPA rules and state law prevent me from saying much more than that."

Audrey has started to hate Will Cann. He won't take her calls. Won't return her calls. He just keeps sending her to Dr. Barrett, who seems fairly arrogant, although Audrey has to concede some gratitude to her for saving Thea from a longer stay in jail, a feat Dr. Barrett takes every opportunity to brag about whenever Audrey does manage to corner her on the phone for any length of time.

After a generous slice of lemon meringue pie, Audrey looks up at the television in time to see yet another segment about Juniper Lane, this one about a flamboyant pop musician who is being released along with his zen coach after a shortened stay for "fatigue and over exhaustion."

The pop star has called a press conference outside the very gates of Juniper Lane, and is thanking the staff, and his fellow patients, and especially, Will Cann, for helping him through a really tough few weeks.

*Ugh. I'm so sick of you, Will Cann.* Audrey would have turned the television off right then and there if she had had any access to the remote.

"Freaking, Will Cann," she mumbles under her breath.

"You look like you're hiding from someone, Miss," the sweet diminutive waitress says as she pours yet another cup of coffee. Audrey has let herself believe—possibly incorrectly, as it turns out—that the sweet waitress who is pouring coffee in a near empty building does not have a warm and fuzzy home life that would interrupt a potential chain of empathy between the two women.

"I am. Hiding from a terribly cruel husband."

"Oh honey. Do you need me to call someone for you? Are you in danger?"

"No. The cruelty—it's—subtle."

"So he doesn't hit you?

"No, he ... it's different than that. But it *feels* like abuse."

"Honey, he sounds like he's just a man. Just a man. They ain't none of them perfect. And you've got one with a job and no parole officer, right?"

Audrey nodded, surprised at the waitress's response.

"Right. Same here. And he loves your baby, right?"

"Well one of them at least, but yes." Audrey didn't bother getting into the distinction between Trudy and Thea in Greg's mind.

"Right. Same here. So even though my Marcus drives me absolutely nuts, forgetting to bring home the groceries I ask him to grab, and spending too much money on those stupid comic books he collects and even though he leaves his dirty underwear on the rug next to the bed every single morning—every *single* morning—I'm not going to be so stupid myself as to kick him to the curb and think there's something better out there. Someone who's going to love me and my kid better. You get it?"

Audrey finds herself nodding. And then stops herself.

*But wait, that's not what I'm dealing with.* The words were strangled in her throat.

"The stuff most people call abuse—it's really just trouble getting along, you know what I mean? My sister, Jenny, now *she's* married to a drug addict. He goes on long benders and disappears for days taking their rent money and the baby's food money and then he shows up again, beats her bloody and apologizes, crying with promises of staying sober which he does for about 2-3 days before it happens all over again. That there is abuse, honey. Maybe you just got a man you can't get along with. Not the same at all."

"I was married to a drug addict once," Audrey confesses.

"So you know, then. You know what real abuse is." The waitress says real with two syllables, elevating its meaning.

Audrey nods solemnly.

"And you left?"

Audrey shakes off the shock. "Left? What makes you think I left?"

"Well, abusers don't leave and you moved on to a new husband, so you left, right?"

The waitress looks like her patience with Audrey is running thin.

"I didn't leave. He left. He—died."

"Ah, yeah, that's the only other way to get rid of them, sweetie." She starts wiping down the table next to Audrey as she says, "But as I say, you only wish that on the real abusers— not the ones like your husband—the ones hard to get along with."

On the still-blaring television screen, the news has obtained a photo of the heroic Will Cann and they are posting it on the screen next to a picture of the pop star who just thanked him profusely.

Audrey stares at the screen with silent tears streaming

down her face. She had wondered over the years if she would recognize him. If he ever came back, would she know him?

But she sees that time and sobriety have not made him unrecognizable as she often feared. The man she left behind 23 years ago– now he was unrecognizable. But the man on the television screen?

All too familiar.

*John. It's him. He's been at Juniper Lane with Thea all along.*

The waitress refills Audrey's coffee cup one more time, wrongly assessing the reason for her tears, as she advises: "You just stay with the one you're with and wait it out—the alternative is much worse, sweetie."

Audrey quickly finishes up her bottomless cup of coffee, leaves a $20 bill on the table, and heads to Juniper Lane to find out if the waitress's words are true or not.

On her way to Juniper Lane, Audrey stops in a small chapel, and asks if there is a priest available, and could she make a confession?

It has been years since Audrey has set foot in a church, or even admitted to being Catholic, and she realizes as she sits face to face with the gray-haired priest that maybe she is stalling, or maybe she really is ready. To confess to someone what she has done. She's ready to confess to someone other than Greg.

"I'm not a very religious person. Not the best start, right?"

The priest nods and says "Keep trying," and so Audrey keeps going: "I *am* spiritual and do believe in an overarching cosmic karmic force in the universe. I can't help but think that's why everything's happening now. You see, I did some-thing a long time ago. I stole someone's identity."

The priest's expression is arranged in careful non-judg-ment. "Were you prosecuted for your identity theft?"

"No—you see I didn't actually steal someone's life. I stole

their death." Audrey notices the first change in the priest's expression since they sat down. It is disconcerting to think she could actually surprise this man who is used to hearing people's worst sins. She shudders.

"How—" He stops himself, and then: "Do you want to tell me how?"

She tells him about the idea coming to her. Suddenly, like an epiphany, as John lay in bed, half-dead, but still devoted to the life that was killing him. "When I got to the hospital later that night, I felt as if John really *had* died. I had no illusions about how this would all play out. I knew I was doing something so immoral, so terrible, I'd probably be cursed the rest of my life for doing it. I rubbed my taut belly as I crossed the threshold through the hospital's automatic doors.

"I thought: *No turning back now.* I reached the morgue and a small staff was assembled, hunched over their notes and schedules. One of the morgue workers, Bill, had a sandwich from the hospital cafeteria. I was always sickened by the way he'd bring food so close to the bodies, but that night the smell of the salami and the knowledge about what I was about to do made me gag. I made it to a trashcan in the corner just in time to retch violently.

"Bill yelled and jumped out of his seat as if I had just vomited in his lap. 'You got pregnancy pukes? At night?' I wiped my mouth and nodded as I walked past him.

"I asked, 'Has anyone checked the body?'

"Bill said, 'The police did. They didn't spend a lot of time with him. Just said no one's reported him, and he didn't have any id on him. They told us to take some photographs, do the autopsy, and label him as county.'"

"A 'county' label meant he'd sit on ice for a few more days before being commissioned for a taxpayer funded cremation. His ashes would be labeled and categorized among volumes of other homeless and mentally ill and drug-addicted bodies that had come in over the years, never to be heard from again, and never to be sought by anyone living.

"I used to think about how many people were moving in this world without a connection to any other living person. But that night I realized how wrong I was. Everyone has a connection to some other living person. Everyone. I walked over to the gurney and I wasn't acting when I put my hand over my mouth to gasp.

"Because he actually *looked* like John.

"He was bloated and pockmarked with the scabs and bruises of an addict. He had unkempt thick dark hair swirling around his bony shoulders. He was wearing baggy, filthy clothes that smelled of giving up.

"He *looked* like my John.

"'It's him.' I whispered through tears. They looked over at me, and I pretended to pull the id I was palming in my hand out of his dirty jean pocket. 'It's John.'

"The staff looked at me worriedly. Bill didn't come too close as if he was afraid I'd throw up again.

"And he said, 'Right—Audrey—it's a John Doe. You ok?'

"And I said, 'No. You don't understand. It's John. My husband.'

"And then I probably fainted. Because I don't remember much else, except waking up in another part of the hospital altogether, with a concerned doctor leaning over me, saying he was trying to give me something to stop my labor. Premature labor he kept saying over and over again.

"I drifted in and out of consciousness and in my few moments of lucidity. I remembered that it was Leap Day, an uncomfortable day for a baby's birthday. Would we celebrate her birthday in February or March from here on out? I alternated between pain and thoughts about how this baby was going to come into the world in a fury of confusion, which might not bode too well for the future. She'd be arriving with a dead father. And a dark secret hanging over her mother's head at the exact moment she arrived."

"Did you ever try to track down the real John Doe's family?" The priest breaks his silence.

"No. I never thought about the real John Doe's family. I have sat with that absence for many years wondering why."

Audrey looks up into the priest's eyes directly for the first time.

"A heroin addict who was not unlike John and who met his last fate on the side of a dumpster in a shopping center parking lot deserves a burial just as surely as I do. I'm not disgusting enough to believe otherwise. But the truth is, I have always conveniently assumed he had no one but me. That someone would have come forward immediately if there had actually been any family.

"I told myself that I had done him a favor."

The priest's left eyebrow shot up crookedly.

"I know, I know. Very patronizing," Audrey sighed.

"Years later, in a busy playground, my eyes found a woman who resembled me in the same loose way the John Doe resembled my John. I noticed that hollow-eyed woman held tightly to a dark-haired girl who wanted to run and play but instead remained attached to her mother involuntarily by the grip of someone who might well have lost someone. The little girl resembled Thea in the same way sisters might, or rather cousins, and it was the first time I allowed the possibility that maybe the John Doe from long ago had a wife and daughter who looked just like that. The connection and reference was tenuous, of course, since it couldn't very well be *that* dark-haired daughter or hollow-eyed woman that was a relative of the John Doe. By that time, I'd moved Thea and me across state lines to Ohio. So it's not likely they were anything more than random people on the playground. But still, they got me thinking.

"And much like you cannot be a little bit pregnant, once I acknowledged that possibility, I couldn't be a little naïve anymore. I couldn't stay in the dark anymore. I had to own that somewhere there just might be an orphan child who was mourning a father just the same way my Thea was, and that both of them were linked by my doing. By a situation of my creation.

"Let me tell you something, Father. Such knowledge? It can kill you. Quickly, like a noose of coarse rope that you tie around your own neck. Or slowly, like a series of decisions designed only to undo all you have done, even if that means depriving yourself of a single moment of happiness the rest of your life and living with a mean and abusive sex addict."

After her confession, Audrey sits in the small chapel for a little while longer and then leaves. As she walks to her car, she sees the priest she'd just confessed to, head from the chapel across the street to the bus stop. "Do you need a ride somewhere, Father?" She calls out to him.

"No, thank you, I'll just grab the bus." He pats the bus schedule for reinforcement in his rejection.

Audrey feels it that way: rejection. Even though he is a man of the cloth, and all she was offering him, truly, was a ride home that he really didn't want. Still she feels rejected.

"You sure?"

"Yes, I'm sure."

Audrey tries to tell herself that maybe he thinks it will look bad: a priest getting into the car with an unknown woman. Audrey tries to cheer herself up with rationalization. She looks into the rearview mirror and catches a glimpse of her dark eyes above lines and hollow circles. Nevertheless, she tells herself that he finds her attractive and doesn't trust himself to ride alone with her.

But as he walks away from her open car door Audrey realizes his previously careful expression has rearranged itself into a mix of pity and recognition. It isn't that he doesn't trust himself. It's that he doesn't trust *her*.

Audrey slumps with that realization. She's also panic-stricken at the idea of coming face to face with John after all these years. She is worried and angry and sad about Thea too. She's mad about Greg's continuing texts and worried about Trudy eating junk food at her mom's house while Audrey is away.

All of these emotions join together and distract her as Audrey pulls into the gas station parking lot. She doesn't notice the red pickup truck weaving over the median as it pulls into the gas station behind her. She doesn't pay attention to the smell of booze on the pickup driver's breath as he buys cigarettes next to her in line. She doesn't see his drunken excitement as he grabs the purse she absent-mindedly leaves on the counter while heading to the pump. And she definitely doesn't see him peel out of his parking space as she's running back across the lot to retrieve her forgotten purse.

Not until it's too late.

# Chapter 24

My mother is coming today. She called back after I called her, and got permission from the powers that be to see me and while Dr. Barrett is quite confused, I say simply, "Yes. It's time. I'm ready. I *want* to see her."

I sit in the common area waiting for my mother to arrive, and notice Margot a few tables away. She has a woman with her. A thinner, younger, much less pretty and much more haunted version of Margot, with eyes that are sunk deep within her face.

I stare at them both for a while.

And then Margot whispers something to the girl and they walk over to me together.

"Thea. I want to introduce you to someone," she says. "This is my sister, Nia Hamilton."

But if that isn't surprising enough, she follows with: "She's checking in today to Juniper Lane."

And then Will comes over to me with a very somber police officer, and so Margot and Nia excuse themselves.

*Audrey Brown has died.*

This is what Will and the police officer have come here to tell me. She was hit by a drunk driver on her way to Juniper Lane yesterday. She was here in Pennsylvania to see me. At least that's what her husband Greg told the police officers when they tracked him down yesterday. Right after he said "What in the hell am I supposed to do with my daughter, Trudy, now?" Apparently, tracking Greg down took a while, which is why it took the police even longer to come tell me.

Audrey had set out on her promised road trip from Ohio to Juniper Lane, and she had been 3.4 miles away from me yesterday when a drunk driver plowed her down in the parking lot of a gas station nearby. He is currently drying out in county jail. He will be moved to a higher security prison later today to face charges of reckless manslaughter.

I stare blankly at Will and the police officer, until Will finally excuses him. "Thank you, Officer Ben. Thea has received a lot of tragic information just now. As her treating counselor, I'm going to have to ask you to allow us to help her process it now. My assistant will help you out through that exit right that way."

Officer Ben looks happy to leave and walks quickly toward the exit that Will has pointed out to him.

I'm left alone in the common room with Will, who is now sitting across from me, and he puts his hands on my shoulders, misunderstanding my blank expression as he says: "Thea. Do you understand what we're telling you? I know this is very difficult information to wrap your head around. Thea, your mother is dead."

I grab hold of his words and stand up so that I am high above him; high atop my mountain built on everything I have done and said and let others believe about me before that moment; I don't bother letting his words roll around in my brain long enough to understand all I'll be giving up if I confess. I can't let this go on one minute longer. I spit out the words more harshly than I intended.

"Will. Audrey Brown is *not* my mother."

And then because I cannot take back those words, I tumble from the cliff I have built of lies and wrongs and misdeeds. And one look at Will's expression tells me something I did not expect to see.

I am pulling him straight down along with me.

◆

I first became obsessed with finding Audrey in high school. Over a decade ago.

My mother had never been angry enough. I was angry enough for the both of us.

My mother had let my father destroy her life when he was alive and then let Audrey prevent us from rebuilding after. I was only three when my father died. Young enough that I could have forgotten the whole thing. My mother could have reinvented us as a young widow and her sweet, pretty daughter. But instead, we were the family whose deadbeat dad and husband deserted them.

Freaking Kevin Murphy. I didn't even know what people said about us behind our backs until he said it to my face.

Everyone thought my druggie dad had run off. We knew differently. We knew he was dead. But we had no body, no funeral, and all of that added up to no dignity. People treated us like pariahs. And my mother let them. We stayed in our rundown house. My mother stayed in her deadend job as a motel housekeeper. We stayed who we were when my dad died. And I hated us for that.

My mom said she knew it was my dad. What she didn't know was why that other lady was so hell bent on claiming him for her own. My dad's druggie friends apparently had come to my mom and told her that they had left him near that dumpster, that they were sure he was dead or they wouldn't have just left him there. Nobility among thieves.

She didn't care. She actually said to me, "I don't care. I don't care why that lady is burying someone she knows is not her husband. She probably has her own reasons. Like I have my own reasons for not wanting to go through the pain of burying the man who was your father." I remember her saying it that night, but then I forgot again. Replaced the memory with some story in my head that he died of cancer. I kept a hold of that story until I was seven years old. That day Kevin Murphy shocked me in the second grade sharing circle, I suddenly remembered what had happened. Remembered it all from when I was just three years old. And when I went home and told my mother what Kevin Murphy had said in the sharing circle that day, she said, "We just have to forget all that, Kira. That was a long time ago, and it doesn't matter. Your father is dead. Nothing has changed."

Later, when I tried to tell all of this to Marta, the shrink I saw in high school during the complimentary and yet completely unsatisfactory session that sort of ruined me on counseling, Marta said it was remarkable that I remembered any of this if I was only three at the time.

"This is all true?" she kept repeating.

In hindsight, I realize she didn't believe a word I said. She was just playing along, hoping I'd take her flyer home to my mother for some more billable hours.

But I kept nodding and repeating to Marta, "Yes, yes, it's all true."

It's laughable when you think about it: how many truths there really are, no?

I got my first Facebook account the day it launched in 2004. I was only 13. I used my mother's birthdate and stock photos to set it up, and I used it mostly to stalk celebrities before I remembered I could try to track down Audrey this way.

I was too young to be surprised at how easy it was. Youth assumes success, and so when I set out to find her, I expected to find her. And find her, I did.  She hadn't changed her name at that time. She was still: Audrey Morris. The only things that were public about her were her profile pictures: a rotating selection of close up views of both her and a little dark-haired girl that looked not unlike me, but a few years younger. She listed her hometown and her prior jobs, including at our local hospital, so I knew it was the right Audrey Morris.

I tried to friend request her but she only had about 43 friends and she turned me down, apparently selective with her approval at the time.

But I watched her. Through my teen years, I watched her. When her profile picture showed a wedding gown, and a teenage Thea and another little girl smiling angelically, I memorized every detail. When she added vacation photos and forgot to change the privacy selections, or when others tagged her in charity dinner pictures, I got extra glimpses. I kept track of where she was working and googled the hospital staff page to verify that she was still there. I watched her from afar for years, unfolding the narrative behind the pictures.

She and Thea had moved to Ohio. Audrey had remarried, and Thea had gotten a little stepsister in the deal. They had reinvented themselves. They were happy.

They had not stayed who they were.

It was an otherwise remarkable day when Audrey Morris Brown accepted my friend request.

I had created a brand new profile, a new name and new photos. Less glam shots, more mom jeans.

Google had told me where she went to high school, what year she had graduated, and who was the reunion coordinator.

I managed to add some mutual friends who must have believed we graduated together and who didn't exactly vet their friend requests too carefully. Eventually I had 423 friends—none of whom I had ever met in person—and Audrey Brown and I had 10 mutual friends. I would smile when her beaming profile picture ended up on my newsfeed now and then with an innocent enough caption: "Do you know Audrey Brown? Send her a friend request!"

And then one day, I did. I took a chance. I thought about attaching a small note: "Hi Audrey! Remember me? From high school math? You haven't changed a bit!" But that seemed a little overkill, and so I just sent the friend request, and within seconds she accepted. I imagined her clicking mindlessly on a steady stream of friend requests without thinking of them, as her newsfeed suddenly opened wide to me, an ambrosia of personal information that both delighted and sickened me.

Everything I had dreamed up in my head was exactly right.

They lived in a gorgeous Mcmansion in Ohio. Audrey was married to a doctor now, and Thea was applying to college. Their entire lives were splayed open to me and I could follow Audrey's every move.

I could stumble upon her at the coffee shop where she often stopped in for breaks: *thank you Beth for the latte break today—you're the best!*

I could eavesdrop on them at dinner: *McNally's risotto is to die for!*

I could watch her help Thea try on prom dresses: *where has the time gone? Look at my little girl!*

And I could see that stepsister, Trudy, up close: *#sisters.*

By 2011, I was out of high school, and squirreling away waitressing money, trying to figure out my next moves, still stalking Audrey Brown and her adorable, perfect family only as a hobby, when I saw the news that made me literally laugh out loud.

Thea Brown was coming home. To Allman College. She'd be living down the road from me.

There were lots of dramatic scenes in my head. I'd show up at Thea's dorm room with a loud and angry: *Who do you think you are?* I'd show up at a frat party, offer her a joint and get her expelled. I'd crash one of her classes, pretend I was a student, and accuse her of cheating off my test.

Of course, none of those scenes held a candle to the drama that actually ensued when Thea and I finally met.

# Chapter 25

Kira has finally asked to see me. After she had me kicked out of her hearing. After she rejected my attempt to visit at the jail. After I sat patiently while she was in rehab. This week, she finally called and said, "Mom, come to Juniper Lane."

Her 90 days is almost up. She will be heading far away when she gets out of here. I know that. It's been my fear all along. I'm afraid of losing her, but I'm afraid of holding on too tightly, too. This has been my constant struggle that defines our mother/daughter relationship.

Kira opens up all of the sugars in the table top carousel in the common room at rehab and dumps them into her iced tea. I cluck out loud in spite of myself. "What? I'm feeling feisty, Mom," she says.

When I arrived today, she was sitting with Will Cann. That threw me for a moment. I recovered quickly. He didn't recognize me. I didn't expect him to, but still it hurt that he didn't. He looked shell-shocked by something he and Kira were talking about. That didn't surprise me at all.

Kira didn't introduce us, and Will just excused himself awkwardly.

"Thea. We'll discuss this later. After your visit. We'll get to the bottom of this all, once and for all."

*Ah, so she's still playing Thea,* I thought.

Having visited my dead husband at countless of these places over countless years, I keep wondering how Kira got herself locked away in rehab. When I'm not also wondering how she didn't get herself locked away sooner. She's not addicted to booze or drugs. But of course, I keep wondering why the hell not. Is it that she hasn't had the time? The opportunity?

If she had a little more time on her hands and a good dealer, would she be addicted to heroin the way her father was? Is this false identity obsession really just a stand-in addiction like that courtroom shrink had told the judge?

It was, in a word, unnerving to see my daughter in the courtroom that day.

In the getup they had her in, she didn't look like a young entrepreneur or a budding criminal. She looked like a college coed and the image made me shudder a bit, allowing myself to acknowledge for a moment how far we'd come.

While the attorney spoke to the judge, a lengthy conversation that ended up getting me booted right out of the courtroom so they could carry on their private session, I sat quietly, staring up at the courtroom ceiling. It was an ornately carved recessed tray ceiling painted in soft shades of taupe and beige. Along the top of the walls of the courtroom were five raised bas-relief sculptures of a blindfolded woman.

Others would call her Lady Justice, but that wasn't quite right. I knew her. She was Themis. I stared at her impressions jutting out from the ceiling, wondering if there was any angle at which I could catch a glimpse of her hidden eye.

In various poses, she looked down on me, alternately holding scales and a long sword. The folds of her gown peeled away to reveal her legs and I took offense, not to the various states of undress, but rather to her skinny legs. Too skinny. Much too skinny for that woman. She was strength itself and would have had stocky well defined legs if depicted correctly. Which she wasn't of course, as she had that ridiculous scarf tied around her eyes. Why did sculptors always believe being blind made her better than who she really was?

Love is blind. Not Justice. The thought made me shake my head at a discussion I was only having with myself in that uncomfortable courtroom.

I've always had a thing for Greek mythology. I read every book on Greek mythology I could get my hands on. Themis was the creator of the divine laws, the divine right, the order that governed even the gods themselves. I would have shuddered underneath her but I remembered. Themis was thought to be able to see the future; she was the Oracle of Delphi for a short time even. Until she had a child. Then all bets were off. She loved her kid, Apollo, so much, she gave him the power instead, rendering her just an impotent creator of laws and a delegator of power. I almost wanted to yell out to her hanging above me in arrogant glory.

I whispered her name under my breath as I waited for the expert hearing to begin.

*Themis.*

Not to be confused with the name: *Thea.*

Thea was the nickname of a Greek Goddess, Alethea—the goddess of truth. When she was in high school, Kira had to do a report on a Greek myth. They had to use real books as sources, rather than the internet, and Kira raided my bookshelf for a story about Thea. I was thrilled that she was showing interest in something other than the internet. At the time, it seemed impossible to drag her off that thing, and every time I asked her what she was doing, who she was researching, she just shut everything down. Shut me out, too.

But when she came to me to borrow my Greek mythology books, she was enthusiastic and interested. I tried to steer her toward other myths, other stories that I thought would make much more interesting reports, but there was no talking her out of writing about Thea.

"No. I want to write about Thea," she said. And so she did.

Together, we pored through my Greek mythology books until we found the story of Thea. It seems that Prometheus, an ancient god and great sculptor, set out to sculpt the very form of Truth. He was called away by Zeus, the big daddy of the Greek gods, and put an assistant in charge of his workshop. The assistant, being a rather ambitious young guy, decided to make an exact replica of Truth—but ran out of clay when he got to her feet. So when Prometheus got back and discovered the forgery he was able to tell the difference between Truth, which kept moving forward, and Falsehood, which stayed stuck in its tracks.

*This is a parable,* she wrote, in a report that earned her a rare A that year.

*Truth. It's paramount,* she wrote. *It's what propels everything forward.*

I remembered that A and that report as I was asked to leave the expert hearing before it began. I missed out on the process that ultimately resulted in my daughter being offered up as a sacrificial lamb to Juniper Lane as Thea Brown.

*Another Greek tragedy,* although I tried to feel happy about it. Maybe she'd get the help she needed, now. It was what I wanted for her ultimately.

Kira was three years old when her father, Darren, died. She actually thinks she remembers it although a shrink once told me that was impossible.

I would also have thought it impossible that a man could fake his own death and get away with it.

Darren's dealer, Wolf, had told us exactly where he was. He had overdosed messily, spectacularly, right next to the dumpster outside the discount shoe store on Walnut Street. Wolf had made an anonymous call to 911, and when he called, he told me, "Darren is probably on his way to the city morgue right now."

I felt like someone had hit me in the gut, but I also felt a strange sort of relief. Like I had been waiting for that call for a very long time. I sat down on the edge of my bed and waited for a call from the hospital asking me to come identify my dead husband.

I sat there all night.

The call never came.

At Juniper Lane, I look out the window at the residents in their various stages of living. One is on the porch swing with her foot dangling over a macramé swing. Two are walking down the path with dark circles under their eyes and loose wool blankets over their shoulders in the obvious aftermath of chemical detox.

And here is Kira. Looking like a million bucks. Like always.

I could almost believe she IS here by accident. Like I should be smuggling her some booze and pouring her a nice martini so we could laugh at the normals by ourselves. But we're not, of course. None of us are normal. Not in any real sense. And we can play with the hand we are dealt. Or we can grab an opportunity when we see it. We can stay the same. Or we can reinvent ourselves. It's not a line drawn in the sand. And this is what I try to explain to her, as I tell her finally, what I have known for quite some time.

She needs to know the truth about this Will Cann that she goes on and on about. I decide on the spot, as she is talking, that she needs to know finally what I know.

I've known ever since I tracked him down here—to this very place, shortly after her father died all those years ago. It wasn't that hard. He was an addict just like Darren, running in the same circles, not good at covering up his tracks. Easy to find if you wanted to find him. I watched from afar as he reinvented himself.

And all the while, Kira and I, we stayed who we were.

# Chapter 26

"My mother told me."

Thea's eyes are so red and bloodshot that for a moment Will is convinced she is drunk. But then he realizes that she is something far worse. He has learned in sobriety that desperate sadness is not reserved for drunks. Sober people have it, too.

It looks so gruesome on them; he's never really gotten used to it.

Will is momentarily distracted by her bloodshot eyes and it takes a moment until her words sink all the way in.

"My mother told me."

*But Audrey? She's dead? And anyway, Thea said yesterday that Audrey wasn't even her mother?*

Will had been trying to make sense of all of it since the day before. He had gone over it and over it with Margot last night after she got Nia settled in at Juniper Lane.

Why was a woman who was not Thea's mother trying to claim her? Was she just some deranged woman who was stalking Thea because of her pseudo-pop star status? But no. The pickup accident that had killed Audrey had made the news. They had tracked down a picture of Audrey Brown from her social media accounts. She looked familiar. She looked like *her*.

She was *his* Audrey. And she believed this girl at Juniper

Lane was *her* daughter: *their daughter;* she believed it enough to drive across state lines to see her unannounced. Will had always suspected Thea was his daughter, since the day he heard her name on the news and certainly on the day she had arrived at Juniper Lane. Now Audrey's journey to see her had confirmed everything he suspected.

But in an instant all that Will thought he knew had changed.

Either Thea was lying about Audrey not being her mother.

Or Thea was lying about *everything.*

*"You knew him."*

She looks at Will with those terribly bloodshot eyes, and he tries to think of who she could be talking about.

"Who?"

"My father—you knew him. My mother told me. You did drugs with him? Before he died?"

Will is trying desperately to catch up. He's trying to decide if this is a trick. Maybe Audrey's not dead at all, and she and Thea are conspiring to trick him into lying again?

He thinks about revealing everything from "Audrey made me do it" to "Thea, I think I'm ready to be your father, now" and "I'm so sorry, Thea."

Instead he says: "Thea, I don't understand."

"Don't lie to me!" Those bloodshot eyes are pooling over. "Don't lie to me anymore! I know everything now. The reason you're so invested in me, in *her* ... it's because you're *him.* And you actually knew him. Did drugs right next to him. But still you stole everything. Our dignity. Our lives. I always swore if I ever found the man who prevented my father from a proper burial, prevented us from actually moving forward in our lives, I swore that if that man was actually still alive, I'd kill him with my own hands."

"Oh, Thea." Will reaches out and grabs both of her hands as she is reaching up to slap him.

"Will you stop it already? How many times do I have to tell you? I'm NOT THEA!"

She lowers her hands from his grip, and slaps him with her words instead.

"You want to know the truth about Thea, Will? *Thea. Is. Dead.*"

And then she tells him the whole truth.

And when she leaves, Will remains behind to wonder what in the hell has just happened and why he feels like he has just lost his daughter all over again.

# Chapter 27

I'm scheduled to leave in 5 days.

I've been blowing off everything and avoiding Will since yesterday, ever since we both learned what we learned.

Will sends a note to my room telling me to come to group at least. He says he doesn't know if he can—in good conscience—sign off on my leaving papers. I tell him I'm leaving with or without his permission. And I mean it. There's money. I told him that, too. I tell my mother to come see me this week with a bank check made out to "Cash." I want all of the money we deposited two years earlier after Thea Brown died. I haven't been sleeping. I have been going over everything again and again. And I finally know how I'm going to use that blood money after all.

By the time Thea started at Allman, she and I were "friends" too, although not via the same profile I used to be friends with Audrey Brown. I had set up a new Facebook account that had me as a student at Allman, and by the time I had racked up 327 new Allman friends, I reached out to Thea and she promptly accepted without knowing who the hell I was. She was relentless with her sharing. I knew where she was every minute of the day. I watched her change boyfriends, hairstyles, and get a nose ring. I watched her mother chime in on some of her less appropriate posts, and watched her promptly delete her mother's comments instead of the posts.

I went to some of the same parties where she was. I drank from the same kegs, danced to the same music. I'm pretty sure I even made out with a few of the same drunken frat boys that she did. But I didn't approach her. It was one thing to stalk her online, quite another to get the nerve to walk up to her in the real world. I watched her from afar. Online and in person. I watched her always from afar.

And I would have kept on doing so ... if she hadn't walked right up to me at that party on High Street, and said, "Hey. Katy, right?"

She recognized me. Well, the fake me at the time, at least.

When Thea came up to me, I wasn't using my real name, so her aggressive hello threw me for a minute, but only for a minute.

By then, I was using some real photos. I had shots of myself at Allman parties and on campus, so I used them to make my fake profile of Katy P seem more legit.

Shut up. Yes, after Katy Perry.

"Yeah. Hey, Thea."

I stared back down at my cup, willing her to just walk away. I wasn't so comfortable with her so close to me. Without a computer screen separating us. All the things I thought I'd say to her if we ever met, all the accusations I thought I'd make and the punishments I thought I'd exact, they all seemed sort of—mean—by that point.

I glanced back up from my solo cup and she was still there. Smiling at me. She had three dimples when she smiled. I know. Who even knew people could have three dimples?

I hated her. But I also kind of liked her.

So I said yes, when she said, "Come on. You want to go smoke?"

We grabbed beer bottles from out of a garbage can filled with ice nearby and headed upstairs. I learned later it was a stranger's room. They didn't know Thea. Not too many people at the party that night actually knew Thea or were sober enough to know the difference.

Which is how I got away with it.

# Chapter 28

I go to group, but I don't say much. Will doesn't give me up, and I don't give him up either.

Something in me is grateful. Grateful for the freedom I now have, and begrudgingly, I credit Will for part of that.

When the rest of group files out for lunch, I linger, and I hand an envelope to Will.

"This is for you. You're her only living blood relative now. It's your money. Do something noble with it. Make them name a wing after you or something."

"Kira," he says sadly, but takes the envelope I am shoving in his direction.

I walk out quickly and start packing my room. I'm leaving in just a few days, and I can't help it. I gave him the money because it's his, but I can't ignore another truth.

Will has taught me that.

I also hope that the money prevents him from turning me in, so I can just leave peacefully when my 90 days are up.

# Chapter 29

Margot walks into Will's office and closes the door behind her, violating as she does occasionally, Will's open door policy.

He looks over her shoulder to see the familiar Hamilton quote only visible at this angle with the door closed.

*Who?*

*Who will tell her story? Or Mine?*

He wonders for the thousandth time in just a few days what will become of Kira when she leaves this building. Will she really be able to go on and live a normal life? Can he help her? Should he help her?

"Will, I don't have a lot of time. So I need to be short and sweet and to the point here." Margot is holding papers and as she unravels them on Will's desk, he recognizes them as the blueprints he spied on her desk under a pile of papers at her home, not so long ago.

"I've been keeping something from you. For your own good, mind you. I didn't want anyone to accuse you of being involved if everything went south. But I always hoped I'd have the opportunity to tell you the truth, and here we are."

Will sighs, thinking about the hidden blueprints, and detailed construction figures. He thinks of the piles of retail envelopes and other trash that Margot had asked him to get rid of. The separate trust account into which she'd deposited

Wolf's money, and who knew how many other countless dollars? The nagging thought that he'd been hoping wasn't true could no longer be ignored. She had come to confess.

Lucky for her, she'd come at a time when everything in his heart and mind was unraveling so dramatically. He didn't have the energy to turn her in. She'd come to confess the truth at the perfect time.

"You've been embezzling money from the construction site, haven't you?"

Margot looks at him, relieved.

"Yes," I have. "Do you know why?"

"Does it matter?"

Margot looks offended. "Well, yes it matters, Will. Of course it matters. I've been siphoning some of the development money to Dominica, where we've built—in less than a year—a retreat home for addicts. I've been furnishing it from here. And stocking it with clothes and shoes and other supplies for the new residents. It's money that will never be missed from this place. Let's face it, Will. This has become the posh-est resort in the state. I'm proud of using some of the excess money to build a tranquil home in a place that needs it. And besides, I raised that money. Why shouldn't I have a say in how it gets spent?"

"Dominica needs a new rehab facility?" Will asks dubiously.

"Well it does now. I need it. Well, *we* do. I'm taking Nia there."

"Taking her?"

"Yes. I'm going back there, Will. I'm moving back to Dominica. Not far from the ruins of my family's banana farm, I'm rebuilding my and Nia's life there."

Will looks at her, crestfallen. He is trying to reconcile her dishonesty and crime with his desperation to keep her here. With him.

"Just like that?"

"Well, not exactly. I've been planning this ever since Wolf

died. But like I said, I couldn't bring you into it back then. It was too dangerous. But I can now."

Margot places a check in front of him. For $100,000.

"From Wolf's donation. No one deserves this money more than you, Will. Do you know what $100,000 can buy you?"

"A couple of roundtrip tickets to Dominica, I'm guessing."

Margot shakes her head. "No, no. Don't you remember what we've talked about? You can buy economic citizenship in Dominica. You can buy a passport, and you can live down there. If and when you are ready. To counsel at the new Tranquility Retreat House. To help Nia, and countless other women we will treat there away from any distractions. Away from the internet and social media and the chaos of this place. We need you there, Will. *I* need you there."

Will stares at the check in front of him.

"Don't say anything right now. Think about it. I have to go tomorrow. I have everything lined up for Nia and me, and we have to go right away. Before her parole officer gets wise. Before anyone tries to stop us. So just think about it, ok?"

Margot stands to leave, and although she told Will not to say anything, he does. He says, "Please. Take *her*."

"Who? Thea? But Will, I thought she wasn't even—"

Will shakes his head, and thrusts the check in Margot's direction. "No. She's not. But she needs to get out of here. And she needs more treatment. Please. Take *her*."

# Part III
## A NEW CHAPTER

*Day 180, January 2018*

Dominica is as beautiful as Margot promised.

It took 36 hours to get through customs. Margot and Nia had no problems, but I had some. Will wouldn't use any of the money I tried to give him or any of the money Margot tried to give him to buy his own passage to Dominica, so he's not here yet.

"No, Kira, I have a better idea for that money," he said to me when I pressed him again on my way out the door of Juniper Lane.

After everything he's learned about Audrey and Greg and Trudy, he's using the money from Thea's death to set up a secret trust fund for Trudy. Greg won't know about it. Trudy can use it to get out from under him when the time comes. I support that project 100%. But still, it's too bad that Will's arrival in Dominica is now delayed.

He is selling everything he owns and cashing out all of his savings, working part-time in a BYOB restaurant in town, and any other odd jobs he can find, just to raise his own $100,000. Honestly.

*Leave it to Will.*

He has promised Margot he will be here in time for her birthday. Which is only a few weeks away. I feel a little nervous about whether he will make it in time, but Margot seems cool as a cucumber. She's sure he'll make it in time.

"He'll be here," she says confidently, every time I ask, "But how do you know?"

"She just knows, ok? Be patient." Cassandra keeps trying to shove that patience mantra at me. I'm still resisting, but boy am I happy to hear her say it anyway.

*Cassandra.*

Yes. Margot had enough extra money to bring someone else down here, and we used it to bring Cassandra. It was a last-minute decision to drive to Cassandra's house and grab her, but now that we are here, I could almost believe this was always the plan. Always. Since Day 1.

We arrived at Cassandra's just a few hours before our plane was set to depart. I had only been brought in on Margot's and Nia's plan with hours to spare. I didn't hesitate for a moment. I hoped Cassandra wouldn't either. When we got to her home, she was so round and pregnant and tired, and she just kept saying, "I can't leave. I can't go with you, Thea. I'm so sorry."

But when I hugged her, she winced, like there were fresh bruises hidden under clothes. Probably under her skin.

"Where's your husband, now?"

"He's buying a crib. For the baby. He's been so helpful lately. He's trying. He really is." Cassandra kept rubbing her arms up and down as she said it. Her husband showed up while we were still talking her into leaving.

He walked in, took one look at all of us, and said, "What the hell's going on here? You having a party instead of making dinner?"

I smiled gratefully at his scathing arrival, thinking that would be the final straw, but it wasn't. She fed him and he let out a stream of criticisms and nasty comments about the house and the stack of magazines on the coffee table and a dozen other failings. Then he left the table with his plate half-eaten, with no attempt to clear his plate, or help Cassandra with the dinner dishes, before plopping himself down in a velour lazy boy chair within eye sight of the kitchen like he was Archie Bunker or something.

What? I've seen the reruns.

We stayed to help Cassandra clear the dinner dishes, and clean up the kitchen, while we whispered continually over an assembly line of dried plates: "Go get your passport. We'll get you out of here today. We'll take care of you and the baby. You'll never have to live like this again."

But she just kept repeating rejections. Over and over she said, "I can't come. I'm sorry." And we were about to give up. Time was running out. Our plane was leaving in two hours. We'd barely make it through security at this point.

Just when we were about to give up, Cassandra called out to the other room, "Peter, did you get the crib today?"

He came back into the kitchen and plopped a metal object down on the counter in front of all of us.

"No. I was too busy for that. But I did stop by the grocery store, and pick this up for you. A kitchen timer. So you'll stop burning the food maybe. And get your act together."

Cassandra stared at us and that kitchen timer for a few long minutes. Then she went into the other room, and as we were leaving, she left right along with us, with one small bag that turned out to contain a change of clothes, a toothbrush, and her passport. She walked right past Peter, who kept his head in the paper, and didn't even ask where she was going when she walked out the door. He probably thought she was walking us out.

But just to make sure he didn't bother us or follow after us, I turned back and walked over to his Archie Bunker chair and I hissed, "You ever give Cassandra a moment's grief again—you follow us, or look us up, I'll make sure the congregation knows exactly what you've been doing. And with whom."

I left him there with his mouth dropped open and Margot, who'd heard my hissed threat as she shooed Cassandra quickly out the door, said to me later when we got to the airport, "How'd you manage to get any dirt on Peter in the few hours you've been out of rehab?"

"Oh, I've got nothing specific on that dirtbag. Just a hunch based on a long history of dealing with people I'd love to forget."

She squeezed my hand, and said, "Clever, Thea." And I winced and she said, "Sorry, it's habit, still. I'll get used to calling you Kira by the time we get down there. I promise."

As we boarded the plane, I saw Cassandra holding the kitchen timer she'd grabbed on the way out the door. I tried to take it angrily from her hands, but she pulled it away quickly, and hid it behind her back, away from me.

"Oh Cassandra. Please. When we get to Dominica, are you going to destroy that ugly thing?"

"No," Cassandra replied peacefully, with a beauty in her eyes, I hadn't even known was there. "No way. I'm keeping this forever. I never want to forget the exact moment that strength became my truth." And then she started to cry a little. "Thank you. You came to rescue me. Like I'd always hoped. Like I needed. You came for me. I didn't know who would be the one. But it doesn't surprise me that it's you. You are a *healer*. It was always *you*."

We've been here at the Tranquility Retreat House for over three months. There was lots to do at first, cleaning up from new construction, putting furniture together and unpacking the clothes and shoes, and linens that arrived down here before us. All of it was arranged carefully by Margot from her perch back in the States, while she was also supervising the expansion and new wing of Juniper Lane. We've heard there was a ribbon-cutting this month, and the newly expanded Juniper Lane is housing lots of new clients, and a few familiar ones as well. We get some news from Will via Margot, and so I've learned that the major celeb is back with a patient new zen master with a ponytail and a Russian accent. I smile warmly at that news.

Here in Dominica we've been asked to start each day with a Truth. I've been resisting until today. Today I wake up and decide to finally tell the group the truth about that night.

The same one I had confessed to Will finally after Audrey died.

The whole truth.

"I'm so wasted." Thea held the joint between her pointer and middle finger and for a moment it looked like she was flipping me off, until I realized she was just handing it to me.

"I broke up with my jerk boyfriend last night and I just needed a change of scene tonight, you know?" I refrained from saying: *I know you broke up with Chase. He's actually making out with Monica Thompson right now across the way, so don't spend too long mourning that relationship.*

I bit my tongue to keep from telling her how very much I knew about her, and how little she knew about me.

"We could be sisters, you know that?" She giggled. And I choked on my reluctant inhale. I was petrified of doing any drugs harder than alcohol, even then, but still I gave in that night. For Thea, I gave in that one time.

"I always think that when I see you on Facebook. We could be sisters. I knew I remembered seeing you around. I just couldn't place you. And then when I saw you tonight, I was like—ohhhh, she hangs out *here*. We can hang out together now!"

We were both sitting in the huge stone windowsill in a stranger's room, with the screen popped out and leaning against the wall below us. We had our legs draped carelessly—one in and one out. The buzz and the cool April wind were playing tricks on my mind. I was starting to think Thea and

I were actual friends.

*Maybe we* will *start hanging out,* I thought to myself.

*Maybe this is how I finally reinvent myself. I get over what happened. I befriend this girl. I move on. I never tell her what happened. Or maybe I do tell her—but by that time we're best friends, bridesmaids at each other's weddings, godmothers to each other's daughters, and she throws her arms around me when I tell her who I am and says—I knew it! I knew were we were connected cosmically, karmically. We were meant to find each other.*

My phone lit up, and I hit decline on my mother's number.

"Ugh. Just my mom. She's a pest, lately. Follows my every move, it feels like." I apologized for the disruption.

"I think it would be wonderful to have a mom who is focused on your every move. Mine is utterly distracted. She's so wrapped up in my little sister, Trudy, she barely has time to call me back, let alone actually focus on what I'm saying."

She used air quotes when she said the word "sister" and that made me feel badly for this Trudy whom I had never met but had seen many, many pictures of, during my years of cyber-stalking.

"Well you know what they say—the grass is always greener, right? Sometimes I wish my mom had just a little less interest in me. And sometimes I wish she had a little more..." I looked off to the side of the quad where a few straggling drunks were making their way back from the bar. The yard was otherwise desolate and empty.

Where was everyone? Where were all our friends? Our connections? Between us, Thea and I had 1,734 friends by that point: 83 of them mutual, but only online. I felt so utterly alone. Even sitting there with Thea, I felt alone. I waved off the joint, and took a menthol cigarette out of my pocket instead.

"You really need to start vaping you know," Thea said as she watched me light my cigarette, while she was taking a drag from her joint. "That shit will kill you."

I shrugged with one eyebrow to the black sky. "Well, something's gotta, right?"

"Hey. What are you doing after graduation?" Thea asked between drags.

"Not exactly sure yet. How about you?"

"I'm looking for psychologist jobs here in Pennsylvania. I really don't want to go back home to Ohio. I can't deal with all the drama back there."

"Drama with your mom?" How could there be any unwanted drama? Her life looked absolutely perfect back in Ohio.

"No, not so much drama with my mom. Mostly my step-dad. He's a creepster."

I winced, and thought about all the stunning pictures of Audrey's new doctor husband that she posted weekly. What a sham. Did Audrey really replace Thea's living dad with a molester?

She must have seen me wince, because she said quickly, "No, not like he'd do anything like *that* to me. But he's just really mean to my mom and me. She was kind of desperate when she met him. For lots of reasons."

We sat quietly for a few moments in the windowsill, and I thought about how my mother used to take me to the zoo every June. They had half-price admission on the first Wednesday of the summer, and that was our signal each year that the summer had officially begun. For some reason my mother thought I looked forward to it all year, even though I actually dreaded it. Half-price admission day attracted huge crowds of families with moms and dads and strollers and our little family always felt so conspicuous in that setting. But, she didn't seem to notice and so I kept my mouth shut and just went along with her so as not to disappoint her.

But the last year we went to the zoo, I was 11. And it was a particularly gorgeous day in Pennsylvania. The drive into the zoo had been beautiful and colorful with the trees in full bloom, a warm June welcome. We wandered along, with the droves of other bargain shoppers, through the meandering pathways that separated the animal enclosures. I remember I was just walking into the reptile house when I turned and realized I'd lost my mother.

I had no idea where she was and figured she was probably frantically looking for me, so I retraced our steps calling her: "Mom, Mom!" When too many mothers starting turning in response, I called her first name out loud: "Carol! Carol!"

I wandered like that for what seemed like an hour, but in hindsight it could only have been about 10 minutes or so. There was no response to my Carol refrain except from some parents who gripped their own kids harder and asked without meaning it, "Are you ok?" I just kept nodding. None of them offered to help me, so their questions didn't seem sincere enough to warrant more politeness.

I saw a sign for "Lost Children" up ahead next to the first aid station. I was just about to turn myself in, even though I didn't feel lost; I felt like my mother was the one who was lost, but I knew she'd see it differently if I ever found her—*when I found her*, I allowed myself one more hopeful thought before desperately turning toward the lost child station.

Which was when I spotted her.

Up ahead on the trail, in a place we hadn't yet stopped together, she'd become stuck in her tracks on our way to the reptile house, at the bear enclosure.

She had her head cocked to the side and she was seemingly locked in on a cub just beyond the safety moat within the enclosure. I didn't call out. I just approached her from behind and watched her as I did. As I got closer I realized she wasn't focused on the cub at all, but on the mother bear who had been hidden behind a tree, not visible to me until I had only gotten this close to my mother. As I got closer, I could smell her familiarly cheap perfume on the wind with an undernote of perspiration that her perfume was meant to cover, but didn't. I watched my mother's profile and then

I started to volley back and forth between her and the mama grizzly off to the periphery. They seemed locked in a stand off; the grizzly and my mother stared at each other in an almost hypnotic trance. I was afraid to startle my mother. She was standing so perfectly still, she almost looked unreal. If not for the perfumey, sweat-filled wind I could even taste at this distance, I would be questioning my own judgment that this was in fact my mother and not a doppelganger.

A word I knew back then because my mother used it to describe John Morris.

*You father's doppelganger. His clone. An evil twin of sorts.*

But this wasn't a clone of my mother. It was her, unblinking and unmoving, stone-like, staring down a mama bear who stood her ground beyond the woodsy replica, for what reason, I couldn't fathom. The cub seemed likewise confused, glancing back and forth between my mother and his own mama bear as if some secret challenge had been made between the two females that neither of their offspring would dare challenge, notwithstanding that they couldn't understand it. I reached my arm out to my mother, about to touch the sleeve of blouse, carefully, as afraid to startle her as I would be to wake a sleepwalker. But just as my hand was about to make contact with her, she blinked and shook her head, coming back to me and glancing down with no acknowledgment that we had been separated briefly but powerfully, with only a, "Ok, honey, where to next?" I suggested the reptile house and we picked up where we had seemingly left off, but for reasons I never quite understood, the next year we went out for ice cream instead of the zoo on the first Wednesday of June. After that, every June, we kicked off the summer with an ice cream field trip.

I didn't realize, sitting there with Thea, that I'd actually be giving up the ice cream ritual after that night as well. I didn't realize how much I'd be giving up after that night.

"Truth or dare?" Thea asked me.

"Hunh?" I was still picking out our bridesmaid dresses and thinking about the zoo in my mind when Thea startled me.

I was feeling fuzzy from the few hits I had taken from the joint, supplemented by menthol.

"Sure."

"You go first," she said before inhaling.

"No you go." I shook my head, trying to shake off my buzz in case she said "truth": I was afraid of what I might tell her. It was too soon. We needed to become best friends first.

I don't remember saying Truth. But she told me, so I must have.

"My dad faked his own death," she said.

"You have got to be kidding me." I couldn't believe she was telling me this, and we didn't even have to take a blood oath or get matching BFF necklaces first. I was annoyed, realizing she probably got drunk and told her story to everyone. I was so angry, realizing that she kept wasting her story on people probably too drunk and/or high to remember it the next day. To honor it.

I waved away the joint again and stubbed out my cigarette. I was suddenly feeling very sober.

"Hand to god." She put her right arm up like I had asked her to swear out an oath or something. "He was a heroin addict, and my mom helped him disappear right before I was born so I would never have to suffer the indignity of being a heroin addict's daughter." She pinched the end of the roach and then swigged from the beer bottle that had been waiting next to her on the windowsill, and I watched her burp up a little droplet. Even her burps were adorable. I was so annoyed with how this was all going.

I took a drink of my own beer and waded in.

"So how did he do it? Fake his death?"

"My mom. She's a pathologist. She gave his identity to a John Doe—another heroin addict who came into the hospital one night after my dad had been out on a bender. She let him disappear. Just disappear. From our lives. And he never came back. Not once to find me."

"Wow. When did she admit all of this to you?"

"Never. My jerk of a stepdad is the one who told me. My mom always just let me believe my dad was dead. But my stepdad told me before I left for school years ago. He told me the whole story. He said, 'You better appreciate all I've done for you, because I'm the one who stuck around. Not your deadbeat addict dad. He never even came to look for you.'"

"That's horrible!"

"I don't know. Much as I can't stand my stepdad, he had a point." She swigged more lager.

"I always thought my mom and I had a great life before my stepdad arrived on the scene. Turns out it was all just a big lie. I guess I'm hoping my dad really IS dead by now. It would serve him right. Ok. Your turn."

"What?" I looked over my shoulder distractedly. I felt a little woozy and I gripped the stone window pane underneath me.

For a minute I thought I wouldn't. But then I had to. I told her.

"My dad was a heroin addict, too. He disappeared when I was three, and we never found him. My mom tried to identify a John Doe who disappeared the same night he did. She showed up at the hospital the next day, but when she arrived, the workers at the city morgue shooed her away and told her that the John Doe had already been identified. It all went down in a hospital not too far from here as a matter of fact."

Thea looked at me carefully. But she wasn't clear eyed.

"Is this a joke? What are you saying?"

She dropped the beer bottle out of her hand and it went crashing to the yard below—three stories. We hardly heard the crash. Thea leaned over to watch the bottle's gravity pull it down, letting go of the stone windowsill as she did.

"Thea, no!" I leaned toward her. I only leaned toward her to grab her—I swear—but she backed away from me like I was diseased. She backed away from me like every other person had ever backed away from me in my life when they learned my truth. And then all I heard was silence after Thea fell.

I jumped off the windowsill and ran down the three flights of steps I had walked up with Thea a short time earlier, certain there would be a crowd when I arrived. But there wasn't. There wasn't anyone there. I burst through a crowd of drunk and high college coeds gathered in the building and in the doorway into the air outside. I was alone with her crumpled body directly below the windowsill above. I could hear the music and the laughter inside. I could hear the buzz of a hundred people telling lies and secrets and truths to one another that would never be remembered in the morning. A stumbling couple walked by and groaned, "Oh, is she ok? Is she sick? You need help getting her home?"

I waved them off, and they assumed she was just a drunk girl, passed out outside a frat party, being helped by her caring friend. It was starting to rain harder, and they didn't notice the blood seeping into the mud. Or that her face was gone from the fall. Appearances are never what they seem. I reached inside her jeans pockets, and found her ID and cell phone. I replaced them with mine.

Even though I made such a definitive decision at the scene, I was filled with doubt and regret in the hours and days after Thea's death.

Emergency personnel showed up quickly at the scene: a horrible sight a few stories below the window ledge where we'd been sharing secrets and pot just a few moments earlier. Gawking bystanders were shooed away and I was whisked into a small room in the college administrative building for an interview.

The deceased was identified as Kira Matthews. The only witness at the scene was recorded as Thea Brown.

I kept thinking someone else would come forward. Would say they saw me standing over the body. That it wasn't Kira Matthews who was dead at all. But no one did. Hours went by and no one came forward to say they had seen Kira Matthews alive. Perhaps all the witnesses were too drunk to weigh in; also true: no one knew Kira Matthews. People knew Thea Brown, though. Her phone that was stuck in my pocket as the emergency personnel questioned me had no password lock and was blowing up like crazy.

I silenced it and deleted the messages as they came in.

*Did you hear about that girl who fell out of the window?*

*Did you know her?*

*Did you see it happen?*

*Are you ok?*

*Holy Shit, Thea! Where are you?*

But, the college administrators? They didn't know me or Thea. They were the great equalizers. They had a file on me, I mean on Thea, but it had no picture affixed to it, so they just kept clucking over my many accomplishments and accolades, and I could tell they were confused as to whether they should treat me as a potential suspect or not. I kept answering their questions demurely, and the administrators looked at each other back and forth. *Is there someone you'd like us to call for you, Miss Brown?*

"No, I just want to get home. To my real home. I need to get home for a little while." They looked confused again. They weren't sure what to do with me, I could tell.

I wasn't a minor. They couldn't call my parents without my consent, which I wasn't giving them.

I played on their confusion. I kept asking if I had to stay.

They had summoned an attorney in right away, and he looked even more confused.

They had also tracked down my mother, Carol, to tell

her that her daughter, Kira Matthews, had been in an accident. But not before I had called her from the bathroom from Thea's phone.

"Mom, something crazy has happened."

That's how I felt about it at that point. Not terrible or sad or tragic. Just crazy and karmic.

"A girl named Thea Brown died, Mom. I'll explain later. I was there, and they think it was me. They think I'm the one who's dead. And they think I'm Thea Brown. Just come and get me out of here, and I'll explain everything. But remember that I'm Thea, for now."

And my mother, who had stared down a mama bear at the zoo, but yet stood by meekly when another woman stole my father's identity at his death, continued to surprise me by asking zero questions before she said, "Ok. I'll see you soon. Everything will be ok. I'll be right there."

When she arrived, she played the stunned mother of a dead girl pretty well. She didn't try to overdo it, with wailing and rending of garments. She just sat stoically, patting her eyes, and gasping in between breaths, saying, "This is all very overwhelming. I've spoken with Thea's mom, and promised to bring her home with me for a short vacation. Is that all right?"

More confused looks back and forth.

I left with my mother as Thea Brown, and I was never anyone else again.

Of course, I wasn't Thea Brown out in the open. I hid out, starting up my underground business and secret clients. None of Thea's 632 Facebook friends came to find her in the secret Alibis office. They just went on with their lives. I was glad she wasn't alive to know that little piece of disappointing news.

I texted Audrey from Thea's contacts some short and sweet texts:

*Mom, there was an accident at the school. A girl I know died and I was there. The college is letting me take a break from classes and finals. I'm going to stay here and get some counseling. I'm feeling really stressed right now.*

And then a week later: *Thea! Where are you? I called your roommate and she says you haven't been back for while. Where are you staying? I need to know you are safe!*

I tried to keep her staved off with some generic texts over the next few days and weeks. And then I learned from Audrey a few weeks later that the college had sent a pretty bland letter home confirming the leave of absence and advising that no charges were going to be pressed and that Thea Brown was welcome to resume her studies and her impressive career at Allman College in the future.

*THEA! I NEED TO TALK TO YOU! WHAT IS GOING ON? I JUST RECEIVED THIS!*

Attached to the text was a photo of the bland college letter.

Audrey was adorable with her all caps.

*Mom, I'm not ready to talk about all this. I'm leaving college for now and I need some time to be on my own. Please respect me in this, Mom. I really just need some alone time now.*

*I'M HERE IF YOU NEED ME.*

Her shouting caps appeared less reassuring than she intended, I'm sure. I remembered that Thea had mentioned a little half-sibling that demanded most of her mother's time and attention these days. I hoped that little kid would be enough of a distraction to keep Audrey away until I could figure out what to do next.

Some days I wanted to go to the police and tell them what had happened. But when I thought about them unraveling my stalking of Thea and Audrey, I was certain I knew how it would all look. I worried that no one would believe me. That I'd be arrested and I'd end up in jail for something that was not my fault.

From my point of view, it was all Audrey's fault. And for once, my mom did not disagree on that point. I confessed the years of stalking Audrey and Thea via social media. When

I brought my mom up to speed on all I knew about them, she said, "She brought this all on herself. She'll have to accept that some day. I'm sorry her daughter is dead, but it's just not our fault. It's not your fault, Kira. You have to move on. It's time now to move on from all of this. All of it. They all got to reinvent themselves. Now you do, too."

They released Thea's body to my mom, and she went through the motions of planning a quiet burial. She didn't expand the charade to our extended family or neighbors or anyone else. We just quietly buried Thea in the same church cemetery where my dad was buried. My mom signed a waiver not to sue the school which resulted in a $200,000 settlement. We put it all in the bank, other than a little bit that we used to bury Thea near the gravestone that contained her father's name but not his body. My mother and I giggled at the irony—it kept us from becoming too morose.

I vowed not to use the rest of the money. To get it to Audrey eventually. Anonymously. After I got my secret underground company, Alibis, up and running and could use it to make Thea Brown disappear once and for all.

In the meantime, I became better and better at avoiding Audrey. One day when I had a bad cold, I actually picked up the phone when she called.

"Thea? You sound terrible!"

"I am. I'm sick. Mom, I'm sorry. I know you'd like me to come home and behave like nothing has happened. But I can't. Don't worry about me. I'm a grown up. I can take care of myself."

"But where are you living? How are you paying your bills?"

"I actually got a job at this up and coming tech company."

"Tech company? You're a psychology major. Since when do you know anything about that stuff?"

"Mom, what are you talking about? I know LOTS about that stuff." But of course, Thea didn't. Kira did. I was indignant anyway.

"Listen, Mom, here's my PO address. I'm staying with a friend right now in Lancaster, and I've lined up a new apartment. I'll shoot you that address when everything's confirmed."

"Ok, Thea, I miss you. I love you. Trudy—" her voice got soft and low as the phone drifted away from her mouth and she yelled something indiscernible to the someone in the background.

*Damn, Thea was right: she was so distracted, this was going to be easier than I thought.*

"Tell Greg I said hello."

"What? Sure, I will. Take care of yourself, honey. Come home soon."

"And those were Audrey's last spoken words to the woman she believed was her daughter. We spoke only in texts and missed calls from that time forward. I would have developed a heroic narrative for Thea's death for Audrey before I made her disappear for good. And I would have gotten that money to her. It was hers, after all. And maybe she could have gotten out from under that jerk of a husband of hers. I was working on that. But then Carmen Fierro went and got herself blown up. And I got arrested. And everything got derailed.

"I feel badly that Audrey's dead, but also, I can't help but think it's kind of good that she doesn't know about her daughter. That she never learned the truth about Thea, after all."

Cassandra is wiping tears from her eyes. I feel badly for making her cry. She's seemed so healed in her short time here. Hardly any tears fall from her eyes down here in Dominica.

"You were so afraid of what they'd think about you that you actually pretended it was *you* who died?" Cassandra asks.

"It wasn't that I was trying to get away with something. It wasn't. This is my real truth: As I called 911 from Thea's phone that night, I actually told myself I was doing a good thing. Thea had a great life. At least before that horrible stepdad ruined it for her. And Kira Matthews—aka Katy P— aka me—had a shitty one. Therefore, Thea deserved to live out that life more than I did, right? So I was just making sure that happened."

"No." Margot is the first one to speak and she looks at me coldly. "That's where you made a mistake. You both deserved to live. It's sad what happened to Thea. But Kira Matthews deserves a real life now. You focus on being *you* down here or everything else? It was all in vain."

She looks hard at Nia as she says this, and Nia nods back at Margot. They share a secret, those two. I'm sure of it. Maybe eventually it will come out down here. Who knows? I'm not focused on other people's stories any more. I'm focused only on my own these days.

*Tell me the story you want me to know.*

Cassandra walks over to me. "Was Leap Day your birthday or Thea Brown's?"

Our identities had effectively merged in so many ways, the day Cassandra had tried reading my numbers at Juniper Lane, I had just given Cassandra Thea's Leap Year birthday instead of my own. I was still protecting myself then.

"Hers."

"Here. Give me your hand. What's your birthday? Your real birthday?"

"September 9." It had come and gone while I was in Juniper Lane, pretending to be Thea Brown.

Cassandra draws numbers on both of my hands, and makes sharpie points on my palms and whispers—"Nines. Just like I thought. You can still be a healer. To a great many, Kira. Including me."

I daydream about bringing others down here one day, too. Like pretty Ali with the stringy hair. Maybe that poor

Trudy. Maybe even my mom.

*My mom, Carol.*

She understood why I had to leave. After all those years of keeping us stuck like the footless replica of truth in her Greek tales, she was happy to see me moving forward. I'm in treatment down here, but I feel there is some other future for me, too, at Tranquility Retreat House. Some calling. A profession eventually, although I haven't quite decided what it will be yet. Margot and Will and I will discuss it when the time is right, I'm sure of it.

I wrote all of that in a letter to my mother recently.

I write her letters every day. It's true that the internet is crappy down here. So I write letters instead and work on myself.

"Yes, Kira, there is power in written words. Real and authentic ones, at least." Elizabeth Barrett smiles at me from her own seat across the room at Tranquility Retreat House. Her hair is no longer a dull mousy brown color. Since the Daubert Hearing, she's let it grow out around her shoulders and it's acquired an interesting reddish tint. Much more fitting to her personality than the mouse brown she acquired to impress the judge at my arson and conspiracy trial.

It's always been hard for me to accept her new name, knowing her for so long as I did under her previous name. But I honored her wish and called her by her preferred new name—and usually Dr. Barrett just to be funny—from the moment of my initial arrest.

*Yes, Carmen Fierro no longer exists. Not since the fire that we were both accused of setting.*

*Carmen Fierro no longer exists, because she is now Elizabeth Barrett.*

That was my last surprising revelation to Will and to Margot before we left the U.S.

Margot was sure that she herself had orchestrated Will and me meeting. That after Will had revealed his past to her, after Wolf, in his final moments, had helped her connect the dots about who Thea Brown might be, she had arranged for Dr. Barrett to provide the expert report at my trial. Margot truly believed that she had been responsible for my arrival at Juniper Lane when in fact, that was the plan all along.

Carmen had said to me, "If anything goes awry, Kira, I will come in as Dr. Barrett. I will get you out of any legal mess you are in. Trust me." And I had. We had bonded, Carmen Fierro and I, over the many months we had worked together to scrub out Carmen Fierro completely.

She'd told me about her abusive mobster husband that she was trying to get out from under to pursue the life she'd created secretly and on the side. She had become Dr. Elizabeth Barrett. Using her middle name and maiden name, she'd pursued a psychology degree on the side and had developed a very impressive résumé, all of it true. And now she needed to escape Duke Fierro. Carmen Fierro needed to disappear, and she would do so in a factory explosion that would harm no one but her husband—financially speaking that is.

In return for helping her, she and I spent long days talking, she counseling me, sessions that continued when I got to Juniper Lane. She helped me come to terms with Thea's death. With the aftermath. She spent hours and hours with me. But never charged me a cent. I was not a hooker's john to her. We were friends.

And now, in an unplanned turn of events, Margot and I have brought Elizabeth Barrett to Dominica, where she can finally live out her authentic life: counseling young women who have detoured due to addiction or bad choices. She will help Nia; I have no doubt. That is what I told Margot when I convinced her to use more of the extra funds to bring Elizabeth Barrett aka Carmen Fierro, aka my best friend in the entire world, to help Margot run Tranquility Retreat House in Dominica.

◆

This morning, we all stand on the porch after breakfast, listening to nothing but the wind. I offer Cassandra the most comfortable chair, but she insists on standing instead in her bare feet, her belly round and full, her legs no longer stiff, looking prettier than I've ever seen her.

I make a mental note to nag her about getting back to her long-abandoned art after the baby arrives. She can be a healer too, I am sure of it. And maybe she can finally work on infusing that healing into her art just as that shaman advised her all those years ago. I honestly cannot wait to see what it is Cassandra will create down here.

Over the wind, I ask no one in particular: "Do you really think we can do it? Reinvent ourselves down here?"

Margot shakes her head and answers first.

"We're all who we are. We've done what we've done. Those truths don't change, Kira."

My shoulders relax. I've finally gotten her to stop calling me Thea.

Nia only sighs in response. She is still tentative, but Elizabeth is drawing her out a little more each day.

Elizabeth chimes in then. "It's what people *think* we are that changes constantly. Our story—that's what changes. Down here, we'll work on a better story. And maybe that will have to be enough. Maybe we'll never really understand what our single truth is." Cassandra nods, her eyes closed, her face turned toward the wind.

Margot nods in agreement as well, and I nod along with all of them, even though I'm not sure that I do agree.

I've been many people in my life. I've lived so many lies and helped others live so many lies as well.

And right now, here in this place, surrounded by this group and all of their layers, all of their selves ...

I feel the most ... *me.*

The End

# ACKNOWLEDGEMENTS

It's been three years since an award-winning indie publisher with over fifteen years in the business took a chance on a manuscript from an unknown writer that landed on her desk called *Lemongrass Hope*. I feel immeasurable gratitude to Nancy Cleary and Wyatt-MacKenzie Publishing, for taking yet another risk with this book, adding it to a two-book deal when it was still little more than a concept, early chapters, and a synopsis. When Nancy dropped everything to read the finished manuscript in just two days, and reached out immediately with a giant thumbs up, I was reminded just how lucky I am to have this amazing publisher in my corner. Every author should be so lucky.

Thank you to my agent, Bob Diforio, for keeping me humble, and working zealously on my behalf.

Thank you to my parents for their unconditional support and love. I'm so grateful for your example.

Thank you to my sisters, Megan and Katie, for their beta read-throughs and comments. And to Caroline Leavitt, editor extraordinaire. I've gotten in the habit of never submitting a book that Caroline hasn't read through first. Not sure I'll ever be able to break that habit.

To my Tall Poppy Writers—never could I have imagined I'd find a group of women so devoted to supporting each other. That you all are amazing and talented writers who inspire and mentor me? #priceless.

Thank you also to the Bloom community for helping me and the other Tall Poppy Writers realize our mission of creating a bookish community that does good *and* reads good books.

Thank you to the readers, libraries, and many, many book club groups (both online and live) who have embraced my novels with such enthusiasm over the last three years, with a special shout-out to the Moselem Springs Golf Club Book Club for the amazing book-inspired menus you have created at each of our Book Club discussions. In turn, you inspired me to make sure there was some delicious food mentioned by name in this book, just in case you happen to invite me again!

This story, along with the tales of the Juniper Lane residents, is of course, pure fiction. But I have—like so many of you, I suspect—been touched in my life by souls worn thin by abuse, addiction, depression, and/or loneliness. It is with the utmost respect and admiration that I pulled apart and re-drew those stories to create the fabric that is this story. It is with the deepest gratitude that I reflect on the stories of those who have crossed my path along this journey.

To my family and friends, an enormous thank you for the support and pride you have always granted to me. Writing sustains me. Your support makes it possible for me to keep doing the thing that sustains me. The enormity of that cannot be overstated.

To my husband, Paul, who started me on this whole journey with a single sentence in response to the premise of *Lemongrass Hope,* my first novel. He said, "You know, that's actually *not* a bad idea."

And finally, to my children, Paul, Luke, and Grace, my love and devotion for you is my greatest truth.